Chapter 1

My strapless bra dug into my ribs. Not for the first time, I cursed gravity on land. In my ocean home, bras hadn't been necessary.

Not home, I reminded myself. Land was home now. There was nothing under the waves for me anymore.

I straightened my shoulders, took a deep breath, then slid a tray off the bar counter. The bartender nodded at me but didn't say anything. Although his skin was dark, I knew he dyed his naturally white hair to blend in. He was another half-human like me, cast upon the shores to find a new life away from oppression below. I was neither the first nor the last to crawl ashore, spat out from undersea politics like a fishbone and hoping for a more fruitful life. Too bad dry land wasn't much of an improvement.

I sashayed across the busy club floor in my despicable silver heels. I'd practiced enough in the past year to walk with confidence in a pair of stilettos, but that didn't mean I liked the torture devices strapped to my feet. I preferred barefoot, but when that wasn't practical, I had comfortable boots that did the trick.

My silver gown embroidered with lacey filigree and sparkling crystals drew the attention of the women I passed, and my swaying hips and deeply cut neckline caught the attention of the men. Although all the servers were dressed like me—the club's theme tonight was "Siren Seduction"—I wore it best since my locks were naturally white and my eyes didn't need contacts to

1

achieve the palest gray. The club was very exclusive and could afford to go above and beyond with the details. I ignored everyone. I had one mission tonight, then I was out of here.

My destination was a corner booth reserved for the owner of the club. Branc ruled the half-humans under his "care" with the weight of an anchor. When he said dive, we asked how deep, or suffered the consequences.

Branc nodded when he saw me. His black eyes were intense in his pale face, but they matched the inky darkness of his slicked-back hair. I suppressed a shudder and yearned for the day when I would be free of his baleful influence. It would be a long time coming.

"A special order for the gentlemen here?" I said in a low, seductive voice that made me want to curl my lip in distaste. I hated the role Branc made me play. But if I didn't earn my keep, I would never pay back the debts I owed him.

"Hello, gorgeous." The skinny man in a tailored suit sitting with Branc grinned at me with a leer. He shuffled over to make room on the bench. "Come sit, beautiful."

I pasted on a fake smile and slid gracefully next to him. I offered the drink and looked at him through my eyelashes. It was too easy to seduce a man. I almost didn't need to use my special talents.

"Enjoy."

The man tipped back his scotch and smacked his lips. I ran my fingers over his shoulder, and he looked at me with hungry eyes.

I'd had enough of this. Chewing on rotten seaweed was more pleasant. Time to speed things along.

I glanced at Branc. He'd been watching a server pass by—her white tresses and silvery dress a mirror of my own look, although a wig covered her human hair—but his eyes snapped to mine. He nodded with a slight tilt of his head.

I ran a fingernail along the man's neck.

"Tell me," I purred with the special cadence that loosened tongues. "What are you hiding?"

"I can't spill my secrets to you," he chortled. "No matter how pretty you are."

Whatever he was hiding must be valuable if he could resist my initial push. I hummed deep in my torso while I spoke and pressed my chest against his arm. The sound was too low to properly hear, especially in the noisy club, but the man would feel it. And, with that encouragement, he would do whatever I asked him to.

"Sure you can."

I leaned forward and ran the tip of my nose against his jawline. He shivered, and his mouth opened as words poured out.

"The coast guard confiscated a whole crate of weird stuff. They have no idea what it is. Now they're making discreet inquiries and sending anonymized samples to labs. Word is, the crate's being held in a warehouse in West Van until they figure out what to do with it. We think it's a new type of drug from Asia, but I need my guys to test it first."

I glanced again at Branc. He nodded, then jerked his head to indicate that I should leave. I stood quickly, eager to follow his instructions. I didn't want to be here any longer than I had to be.

The man stared at me with glassy eyes, but I ignored him. I turned on my ridiculously pointed heel and strode to a door beside the bar that led to the back rooms. I wanted to ditch this slinky dress, these terrible shoes, and the taint of Branc's business.

The work tonight would help pay down my debt, though, and I was begrudgingly grateful for that. I slammed into the manager's cluttered office where I'd left my street clothes and unzipped my dress with a sigh.

My relief was short-lived. Before I'd put my shirt on, Branc entered the room.

"Good," he said. "You got it out of him."

I scowled at Branc and slipped my shirt over my head. "Of course I did."

I wasn't fussed about changing in front of Branc—siren culture wasn't as prudish as human society—but annoyance coursed through me at the suggestion that I might have been unsuccessful.

He shrugged. "You'll fail one day. But, until then, you're useful." Branc looked me over with a critical eye. "You're one of my best assets, actually. When you don't get squeamish. For tonight's work, I'll waive half your rent next month as payment."

My mouth dropped. "That's it?" At Branc's dangerous look, I backtracked. "I mean, thanks. Let me know if I can work off my debt with anything else."

"Oh, I will," he said with a satisfied smile. "I'll be in touch, Lune."

The hermit crab might have pincers, but it was soft and defenseless without its shell. I knew the feeling.

"Come on, little guy," I crooned through the glass.

A young boy with wild curls peered at me curiously as he toddled by, but I ignored him. My regular shift at the aquarium was almost over—thankfully, no stupid heels or dress required—and if I wanted to watch the sea creatures for five minutes instead of cleaning their tanks, then I would. It wasn't as if this job was taking me places.

The hermit crab was tiny, no longer than the first joint of my thumb, although it had clearly outgrown its old home and was on the hunt for new real estate. Moving day was a dangerous time for a hermit crab, even in the confines of a tank. The little crab scuttled, its mottled brown pincers waving and its antennae scouring the currents for danger.

A new home—a topsnail shell I'd dropped in earlier today as an enticement for growing crabs—made the hermit's antennae twitch furiously. It grabbed the edge of the shell and prepared to shove itself inside.

A larger claw darted out of nowhere and deftly flicked the smaller crab aside like an unwanted crumb. I could almost hear smug clicks of success as the larger hermit crab settled into the empty topsnail shell with a wriggle of satisfaction. It ambled off, its new home wobbling above it, and the first crab scuttled under a nearby rock to recover its dignity.

"I feel for you, little buddy," I whispered to the smaller hermit crab. "Just when you thought you'd made a fresh start, some bigger bully sweeps in and blows ink in your face."

I stood with a sigh. What was the human expression? Out of the frying pan, into the fire? The turn of phrase was too graphic for my taste—the foreign heat of fire gave me the shudders—but it fit my situation perfectly. I had arrived on these shores last year as a dripping wet, clueless twenty-four-year-old, running from my old life only to find new perils topside. After only a year on land, I was still learning many figures of speech. English was full of oddities, unlike the clear-cut language of my people.

My former people. I wanted nothing to do with them anymore. I scowled and strode to the staff room, squirt bottle and cloth in hand. The glass was clean enough, even with the sticky fingers of children pressing their curious faces against one side all day and algae trying their best to grow on the other side. My shift wasn't over for another half-hour—although I didn't wear a watch, I knew the time from the pull of the moon's gravity on my body—but I had things to do. With some mild encouragement, my boss wouldn't mind letting me go early. I could be very persuasive.

I blinked rapidly to moisten my contacts. They were horribly irritating, especially in the dry air of land, but I'd learned quickly that my pale gray eyes attracted too much attention. I didn't mind looking good, but looking strange brought the wrong sort of interest. When I'd discovered colored contacts existed, I'd bought myself a pair.

They were urchin green today, but I liked to subtly switch the color depending on my mood. Colleagues at the Vancouver Aquarium noticed a difference, but they didn't understand what they noticed. I usually got asked if I'd cut my hair recently.

I pushed the swinging door to the staff room open with a flourish. It banged against the wall and flew back into my face, but I caught it in time to give it a firm glare. The first time I'd opened it, the result hadn't been so graceful.

The room contained a kitchen area with a sink and microwave, and a long lunch table strewn with expired magazines from the gift shop. Other staff members loved to thumb through glossy pages of scuba diving photos filled with colorful fish shell-shocked by the flash bulb, and anemones forever caught in a frozen ripple of movement. I never looked at the pages. They prodded the knot in my gut that threatened to unfurl into grasping, tentacled arms that pulled me into the depths of homesickness.

Two glass-fronted offices lined the windowed side of the room, filtering the only natural light through multiple panes of glass. One door was partially open, and through the frosted window, a seated figure was silhouetted. I slid around the doorframe.

"Hi, Darryl," I said in my low voice. "Working hard, or hardly working?"

My boss turned with a smile. His eyes crinkled at the corners over baggy skin that pooled underneath them. It was hard to get used to human wrinkles. Gravity really did a number on skin. It was not something my people ever worried about.

Not my people anymore. I ground my teeth, then

7

smiled sweetly back.

"Hello, Lune," Darryl said. "Did you get all those mucky fingerprints off?"

"I'm sure they've miraculously returned already, but I did my daily pass, yes."

I didn't like manipulating Darryl because he'd been nothing but kind, but I was done with this day. The glass was clean, and it was Saturday, the start of my weekend. Letting me leave half an hour early was nothing to him. Anyway, I had to meet Mark the Shark.

"Would you mind if I left early? I have an urgent appointment I can't miss. I tried to reschedule, but..." I allowed my voice to trail off and gazed imploringly at him with wide, innocent eyes. My shoulder dipped, and I looked at him over it with my chin dropped and a sweet smile of hope on my face. When I could, I relied on my other attributes and avoided sirening others. Sirening stank of control and the tasks Branc forced me to do. I wanted to leave that part of me behind as soon as I could.

Predictably, Darryl nodded. "Of course. If it's important. Off you go."

"Thanks, Darryl." I grinned and blew him a kiss. "See you on Tuesday."

My smile fell off my face after I turned, and I strode deliberately to the lockers at the other end of the lunchroom. My persuasion ability would have removed the uncertainty of Darryl's answer, but sirening was almost too easy on land with unsuspecting, susceptible humans, so I resisted unless coerced otherwise. I had standards. Usually.

I breezed into the staff locker room. Unfortunately, I

was not alone, and I sighed my frustration quietly. I didn't want any more obstacles between me and my weekend freedom.

Mireille, one of the aquarists for the tropical section, nodded at me. Her long brown hair was neatly pulled into a French braid, and her kelp-brown eyes glanced at my face then at my hair. She was friendly to me—friendly to everyone—and often tried to get me out for drinks with the other aquarium workers. This day was no exception.

"Lune," she said. "I'm glad I caught you. I'm meeting Sophie and a few others at Juanita's Tapas tonight. Want to come along? It's two-for-one margaritas on Saturdays."

"Thanks for the invite," I said with an attempt at a regretful tone. "But I have an appointment tonight that I can't put off."

My meeting wouldn't take more than ten minutes, but I didn't tell Mireille that. Beneath Mireille's cheerful exterior, who knew what motivations lurked? Why did she try so hard to get me out? There must have been something she wanted, and the last thing I needed was to give another person a slice of me.

"Oh well," she said with mild disappointment and turned to her locker. "Maybe next time."

I silently sighed, opened my locker, and traded the uniform pants for my jean skirt. I hated constrictive pants with a passion and only wore them at work because I had to.

Shoes were next, and I kicked off my work shoes and pulled on my sturdy, army-style boots, with laces from toe to ankle and solid, flat heels that could stomp through anything. I liked the protection they gave me. Even after a year on land, my feet were still more tender than most, not to mention the translucent membranes that clung between my toes. Thank Ramu that I'd inherited my human father's smaller foot size, although I couldn't count the number of times I'd cursed their useless dimensions in my old home. Who had known there would come a time when I would be thankful for their dainty length?

After extracting my specially reinforced backpack from the locker, I slammed it shut.

Mireille looked up and frowned. "Lune, did you get your hair done recently?"

"No." I glanced in the mirror at the end of the locker room and prodded my new wig. I could dye my white hair, but something always stopped me. One day I might take the plunge, but until then, wigs gave me the freedom to choose. "I got a new wig."

"Oh." Mireille put her hand to her mouth. "I'm sorry for prying."

I hid my smile. Mireille, like most other humans in this city, was so worried about giving offense. It was sweet, really. My people were far blunter.

Former people.

"It's fine. Nothing to worry about. Just a fashion statement." I grinned at her. "Have a good weekend."

Now I was running late, and that was never good. Mark the Shark demanded punctuality.

I jogged through the aquarium, my backpack thumping against my side. Around a dim corner behind a large shark tank where dogfish circled in never-ending loops, I opened a "Staff Only" door and slipped inside. Gurgling sounds echoed through a narrow hallway, and colored pipes covered the entire side wall.

I sidled my way to a corner and stepped onto a foot ledge to peer over the edge of the short wall. Open water glowed a bubbling, garish turquoise that I'd never seen in real waters. I looked up and down the hallway. When I was satisfied with my solitude, I pressed my face into the water and let out a clicking call.

Before I had fully wiped my face dry, an octopus the size of my two fists together emerged to twist sinuously on the surface. His textured skin changed from mottled brown to pale gray and then to patchy orange. I grinned with the first happiness I'd felt since my encounter with Branc last night.

"Hi, Squirter," I whispered. "Time to go."

I took out the insert of my backpack, unscrewed the top, and lowered it into the water. Squirter climbed in, and when all eight squishy arms were safely tucked into the container, I screwed the lid on and hauled it out of the water and into my backpack. The familiar weight rested on my shoulders, and I directed my feet to the exit.

I'd met Squirter a year ago. He'd been so curious and playful that I'd immediately fallen in love with him. With my abilities, I could understand his emotions and the direction of his thoughts, such as they were, and I gathered that his sense of adventure was more finely honed than the other octopuses he knew. I was different and interesting, and he loved to join me wherever I swam.

He'd followed me around, as frisky as the puppies at the dog park near my work. Before long, we were firm friends. He'd wanted to see my dry-land world, so I'd cut out a milk jug and hauled him home to my bath. He asked to visit often, and he made the dingy apartment feel like a home instead of the holding pen it was.

I hummed soothing thoughts of the ocean to Squirter as I walked. He could feel the vibrations through his container since my back was pressed against it. We were due for a swim after my meeting, and Squirter's happy hum echoed my own.

Every day I worked, I took Squirter along and popped him in a safe tank at the aquarium. It was our version of doggie daycare, and Squirter loved exploring the different environments. We avoided the shark tank, but otherwise, Squirter was wily enough to survive any new fish he encountered.

Once outside, I strode along a wide sidewalk through Stanley Park, where the aquarium was located. Children's shouts and the whisk of bicycle tires on pavement filled the summery Saturday afternoon. Large, leafy trees overhead swayed in the warm breeze like kelp in the waves. My eyes closed when the smell of salt wafted past me on the ocean breeze. I must have hummed my longing because an answering vibration from my backpack tickled my spine.

I couldn't swim yet, though. Mark was waiting.

CHAPTER 2

A man sat at ease on a park bench overlooking the harbor. Walkers, joggers, and bicycles flowed past him on the path that circumnavigated Stanley Park, but he was a still point in the current of humanity. A ballcap was clamped over black hair pulled into a messy ponytail at the nape of his bronze neck, and the familiar sight made my lip curl.

I hated meeting Mark.

I came around to the front of the bench and glowered down at him from my considerable height, enjoying the brief feeling of superiority. That vanished as soon as he tilted his sunglasses to the end of his nose and pierced me with pale eyes that were accompanied by a smug grin.

"Moongleam Seafields," he said, drawing out my full name with relish.

"For vents' sake. It's Lune, and you know it."

Moongleam Seafields was the literal translation of my birth name, but it hadn't taken me long on land to realize that Moongleam was the most ridiculous, attention-seeking name I could come up with. It sounded better in my mother tongue. "Lune" was an acceptable human name with a nod to my given name's true meaning.

Mark laughed and patted the bench. "But I love riling you up. Come, sit with Uncle Mark."

A sticky shiver ran through me at the name. Mark Tempest was only a few years older than me, but he loved to rub my nose into his position of authority whenever he could. He was half-human, like me.

13

though he'd come to land years before I had, he'd spent enough time in our former home under the waves to languish under the unjust system there. It was such a novelty for him to be in a position of control that he took full advantage of the chance. And that I was female to boot? Double bonus.

I flopped beside him as far away on the bench as I could get and crossed my arms. Mark reached into a pocket and drew out four small, waxed envelopes. My eyes flickered to them involuntarily, although I fixed my gaze at a kayak in the distance after my first guilty glance. Mark worked for Branc, and he distributed monthly allotments of Grace to half-sirens like me in a perfect circular economy that benefited only Branc. He wiggled the envelopes to make a crinkling sound.

"Let's get down to business," Mark said. "If you're not interested in playing catch-up. How much Grace do you want for yourself this month, and how much will I keep to pay off your debt to Branc?"

I bit my lip until my teeth threatened to break skin. Inside the wax envelopes was Grace, slices of a certain sea anemone that only grew in my former home. It contained a substance that enhanced our abilities and made us who we were. With enough Grace, I could breathe underwater, swim to great depths, and manipulate anyone to my bidding. With Grace, I was fully myself.

Without Grace, the ocean was not as friendly. Sure, I could hold my breath for a while and communicate with sea creatures, but it wasn't nearly as welcoming. I was a sad echo of what I could be. And without access to

Grace for long enough, I would succumb to the Curse of Land and die.

Mark shook the envelopes again, and I scowled.

"I'm thinking, I'm thinking," I said. "Give me a minute to decide."

"I don't have all day, Moongleam." Mark waited until a jogger passed our bench before speaking again. "There are plenty of other pale folk to distribute Grace to. Don't think for a second that you're anything special."

That was true enough. I had never been anything special to anyone. There were many reasons I wanted to pay off my debt, and chief among them was to be free of my shackles. I ached for the liberty to choose a solitary path and visit Mark the Shark only long enough to buy my Grace with no strings attached.

Well, not an entirely solitary path. Squirter was always welcome to swim with me.

"Just one envelope," I said with decision. "That will do. Use the rest to pay my debt." I rustled in the front pouch of my backpack for my wallet. It was stuffed with bills from this morning's withdrawal. I handed over too much of my month's paycheck to Mark's grasping hand. He nodded and shoved it into his pocket, then withdrew a small notebook and jotted down numbers on a page with my name on it. With a brisk motion, he snapped the notebook cover shut and tucked it into his pocket again. A child cried in the distance, and I wanted to wail along with it at the loss of the other three envelopes of Grace.

"That's the regular business settled." Mark slouched into the bench and gazed out to sea. "There's a chance for more, if you want it."

My spine stiffened. I was always interested in learning about new opportunities to pay off my debt. When I'd first come ashore, dripping and lost, wandering the bewildering labyrinth of human roads and buildings, I'd followed the only signs I understood. The nautilus shell of the Seamount, the underwater city of my former home, was painted like graffiti on walls and glowed in the night on bus stop advertisements. Below the beacon of the shell were the scratch-like runes from the Seamount which read:

At the sea's edge, on the sunside of the great river, help is waiting.

It had been a ray of hope at a dark time, and I'd gratefully turned my wobbly legs to an oceanside warehouse on the Fraser River's southern shore. The nautilus shell was easy to spot painted on the side of the windowless warehouse, and the welcoming office lit with a bluish glow in the night had drawn my battered heart onward like a shrimp to an anglerfish's lure. I didn't realize how apt that comparison had been until it was too late.

"What's the assignment this time?" I asked.

"The Seamount is in an uproar right now," Mark said carelessly, clearly uninterested about the cause of the turmoil. "Politics, who knows. You're lucky I had any Grace to give you. Our supply lines are totally disrupted. But, silver lining, we have a steady stream of newcomers. Bess, the woman on the night desk, is going on holiday." The word "holiday" dripped with disdain, showing exactly what Mark thought of employees taking vacation time. "She has a daughter down south, apparently. Wants to visit. Anyway, we need to fill the night shift."

"To greet newcomers?"

The woman at the front desk of Branc's warehouse on the Fraser River had welcomed me with literal open arms, given me warm clothes, food, Grace, and a place to sleep. Next had been lessons in English, fake identification from a contact in the government, an apartment to live in, and a job. I'd been overwhelmed with gratitude until I'd understood how deep a hole I was digging for myself.

"And other desk work. It's not like new pale folk come every day. But we need someone available just in case."

My stomach curled into a tight ball of apprehension. I tried my best to stay under the radar and away from other sirens. Greeting every new half-siren that washed on shore was the exact opposite of that. It was too risky. I couldn't be recognized if no one saw me. "No way. Not interested."

Mark shrugged. His eyes followed two women in bottom-hugging shorts as they strolled by.

"Your loss. The boss was going to shell out for the job. He's also looking for a niche escort for a client of his." He looked me up and down with his eyes lingering on my chest. I shifted my crossed arms higher up. "You're pretty enough. You'd probably clean up okay. Get rid of those ridiculous green contacts, lose the wig."

"Thanks for the endorsement," I snapped. The pay would be mouthwateringly good, but I had standards. I wasn't that desperate—yet. "I'll give it a pass. Find some other desperate bimbo for that gig."

"You'll never pay off your debt with that attitude," Mark said. "Just as well. I would miss our delightful little talks."

"Someone has to deflate your massive ego, so it matches your other small parts," I said automatically, but Mark's words bit right to my core. When I refused these assignments, I was only stretching out my indentured servitude for longer. Everything I had went toward payment of my debt. The interest—a new concept for me—was exorbitant, but who was I supposed to complain to? The government, with my false ID? How long would I be under Branc's thumb? How long before I could be in control of my own destiny for the first time in my life?

"You wound me," Mark said. "But it's cute, like a guppy trying to nibble a shark."

"Is there anything else?" I said, trying to keep the desperation out of my voice. "Other jobs?"

"You didn't accept the front-desk gig, and Branc doesn't take rejection well. Maybe next time." Mark stood and put his hands in the pockets of his worn leather jacket. "See you next month, Moongleam."

"Bite me," I replied, but he only laughed and sauntered away.

I fumed for a few minutes, the familiar tension of my monthly meeting with Mark crawling under my skin, but stewing in the injustices that plagued me never helped anything.

"Come on, Squirter," I said to my backpack with an accompanying hum. "Let's go for a swim."

"Hey, Lune!"

The shout of a familiar voice made me turn around with a smile, and my shoulders eased slightly. Hades Sweetcurrent, the twin brother of my best friend Byssa and one of the few people I trusted, jogged toward my bench. His hair was striped black and white like a zebra fish and carefully styled despite a full day on the job. I stood to greet him and attempted to smooth my brown wig into place. It was a lost cause.

"Hi, Hades. Are you done work already?"

Hades also worked at the Vancouver Aquarium, but as a veterinarian-in-training for the rescue unit, taking care of marine mammals until they could be released back to the wild. Like me, he and Byssa were half-human, half-siren, although they had lived on land with their human aunt since they were five years old. Hades, like the rest of the pale folk, had a knack for communicating with sea creatures. The humans he worked with called him the Whale Whisperer.

"Yep." He eyed my backpack. "Are you and Squirter going for a swim? Want some company?"

"Yes, and yes."

"Come on. My bike's over here. I hate diving into the harbor. Too many onlookers and boat traffic."

"The water tastes like diesel," I agreed. "But a vehicle is definitely not in my budget. Lead the way."

We hopped on Hades's sport motorbike, and I strapped on his spare helmet before we roared down the road to the North Shore. Car exhaust fumes almost drowned out the scent of the sea, but my sensitive nose could still smell its intoxicating aroma. West Vancouver had plenty of beachfronts, as befitted the expensive part of this coastal city, and currents swept along the shore to bring fresh, cool water close to land. I closed my eyes and let the warm summer breeze sweep past Hades's leather jacket and over my face. By the time Hades pulled into a busy parking lot at a beach access and turned off the engine, Squirter was vibrating with excitement in my backpack.

"Over here." Hades waved me forward. "There's a private spot."

He didn't bother to lower his voice, and the mothers of a few families picnicking on the sand frowned disapprovingly in our direction. I gave them a wave with fluttering fingers and a cheeky smile, then sauntered casually after Hades. They could think what they liked. If they assumed Hades and I were getting frisky among the rocks, then they would keep their inquisitive children away from us.

Hades was great, but he was too busy pursuing Rachel, the head aquarist, to even think about dating his sister's friend. That worked fine for me, because I had no interest in letting myself get romantically close to anyone. My mother had been involved with someone, and look where it'd got her: a daughter she was ashamed of and a stigma that followed her even after she abandoned me to be raised by other half-sirens. No, thank you. I didn't need any more entanglement, and I already felt like a fish in a net.

Hades's wiry body was stripped to his boxer briefs when I hopped over the rocks. He rummaged in his pants pocket and extracted a wax envelope.

"Sucks that there's so little Grace to buy," he said. "I

just want to take a full dose one day, you know?"

A stab of jealousy lanced through my gut. Even if the supply of Grace on land allowed it, I couldn't afford to buy as much as I chose. I wanted so badly to be like Hades and Byssa, free of constraints, free to spend my paycheck however I chose. Everything Hades earned was his, and I envied him that.

"That's the dream," I said and opened my own envelope. This had to last me a whole month, so I carefully pinched one sliver of dried anemone and placed it on my tongue.

The flavor exploded in my mouth. It was so strong that my other senses got in on the act. Phantom whale calls rang in my ears, my fingertips tingled as if they had fallen asleep, and bursts of color flashed behind my closed eyelids. It was the sweetest squid eggs I had ever tasted and the scent of a stormy sea all wrapped in one delectable slice. Beside me, Hades groaned.

"Damn, that's good." He chewed with his eyes closed, then swallowed with a look of regret. "And just like that, it's gone. Come on, let's not waste it."

Hades ran over the sand, splashed into gentle waves, and dived confidently out of sight.

I swallowed with a pang of grief for the lost sensation, but my body tingled with the substance coursing through it. The Grace of Ramu, we called it. In our religion, the goddess Ramu stole leftover Grace from the creation of all living things to transform a group of humans into her people of the waves. It was this Grace that kept us alive and helped us to live how we did.

With a pang of homesickness, I unscrewed the

container in my backpack and tipped Squirter into the water. He jetted away, following Hades, while I stripped off my outer clothes.

For ease, my one splurge was underwear that was comfortable yet durable and colorful enough to act as a bathing suit. Changing into another outfit was way too much work. This day's underwear was lime green with metal studs along the edge of the bra and panties. Although I admired dainty bras, I wasn't a lace girl. The need for a bra was new—gravity, in general, was new— but I'd come around with the colorful options. With enough toweling afterward, as well as a lounge on the beach, my clothes would stay dry.

I dived in after Hades and Squirter, and the cool water surrounded me like the comforting embrace of Ramu. My eyes adjusted after a moment in the different refractive quality of the water. The ocean was murky this time of year, with algae blooming rapidly in the summer's heat, so I dived deeper, following the ripples of current on my skin that told me where Hades and Squirter were.

When I was below the thermocline, where the visibility cleared and the dim coolness stretched into darkness further away, I exhaled all the breath from my body. With a slow inhale, water poured into my lungs.

It was uncomfortable in the extreme as salty water filled my chest. My lungs seized, then expanded. When a signal from my brain had brought my lungs up to speed, they unfurled the extra membranes in each alveolus that allowed me to extract more oxygen from the water. It took a few painful seconds, then I gulped slow breaths of water with a grin on my face.

Squirter jetted toward me and landed on my arm, then crawled over my torso with a ticklish motion that had me chortling.

Hades floated past with a contented smile on his face. *Where do you want to go?* he said. He didn't use English—we had no air for words, and I couldn't have heard them even if he did—but instead spoke in the pale folk language of clicks, hums, calls, and body motions. It must have been complex to learn as a second language, not that anyone ever did, but it was natural to me.

I don't care, as long as the current is in my hair and I'm not cleaning glass, I replied.

Squirter groaned quietly and wiggled his tentacles in a motion that made his desires clear to both of us.

Squirter has spoken, Hades said with a grin. *Deeper it is.*

We followed the tiny octopus into the darkness of the depths. The lack of light didn't bother me since I rarely relied on sight. Instead, I closed my eyes and sensed the currents that flowed over my skin with a gentle caress. It was as close to romance as I wanted to get. The thought made me smile grimly. Without easy access to Grace, my persuasion talents were limited, and I didn't trust human men. It was too easy to let intimacy turn into submission.

A vision of the seascape filtered into my mind from the motion of the water around me. Plumose anemones covered rocky boulders, brittle stars waved their arms above the muck of a silty slope, and bryozoans encrusted the treads of an old tire. Calm drifted over my body and mind like marine snow falling from surface waters. Being underwater, swimming like I'd done for the first twenty-four years of my life, was necessary in a way that I didn't often admit to myself. A sharp pang of regret stabbed me at the thought of the three other envelopes of Grace that I'd given up today, and panic ate at the edges of my calm at the tiny amount of Grace that would have to sustain me for the next month. I wanted this, I needed this...

Then I remembered that every piece of Grace I denied myself meant less time under Branc's control, and my resolution hardened. I would be free of my debts soon, then I would only contact him for Grace the way Hades did. I could wait longer before my next swim.

It was so easy to say when I was currently in the water.

A push of current alerted me to the approach of Squirter, and I reached out my hand to touch the octopus's squishy body. Squirter hummed his contentment, and I hummed back. Squirter had needed a swim. We both had.

CHAPTER 3

Sunday mornings were a mixed blessing. I didn't have to wipe any glass, wake up early, or wear pants. The downside was that I had little to fill my day.

"You're a little goof, you know that?" I said to Squirter.

He ignored me and focused on his toy puzzle. It was a kid's bath toy Byssa had bought for him, and he loved the plastic pieces that slotted into holes in a hollow ball. The rainbow colors were garish to my eyes after a lifetime of blues and greens, but Squirter lapped it up. His favorite was the hot pink star shape, and he waved it at me before sliding it neatly into the corresponding hole.

I pulled out my phone and flipped through job listings for part-time work. I'd already asked my manager at the aquarium for more hours, but no opportunities had come up yet. Maybe the restaurant Byssa worked at needed a dishwasher. I texted her on impulse, eager to find something to earn me extra cash.

A drip from the ceiling made me crane my neck upward. The water stain above the tub was worse today. Had the little boy who lived above me with his single mother left the tap on again? I chucked the toilet brush at the ceiling, where it bounced off harmlessly.

"Turn off the water!" I yelled, then slumped over the edge of the tub. Did it matter if the water dripped? My eyes traced the cracked tile grout, the yellowed linoleum on the floor, and the doorjamb's peeling paint. I hated this apartment with all my considerable force, but it was the only rental unit I could afford in pricy Vancouver, largely thanks to the landlord, Branc.

"When I pay off my debt," I said to Squirter as he curled a tentacle around my finger, "we're going to get a really nice place. I'll buy you a big tank for when you're on land, with plants and toys and a castle. Would you like that?"

Squirter couldn't understand me, of course. Even had I been underwater with him, his comprehension wasn't enough to understand the details. He enjoyed the suction cup tickles, though, and poked my fingers for more. I grinned and obliged.

I closed my eyes and checked the time by the pull of the moon's gravity deep inside me. Slowly, another realization dawned. In a few weeks, the Seamount would celebrate Grace-Harvest. Grace was collected all year round, of course, but it was best at the height of summer when certain sea anemones grew in abundance and the waters were warm yet still productive. Grace-Harvest was the highlight of our calendar. Last year I'd been running for my life and had hardly noticed missing Grace-Harvest, but this year I would truly be on my own.

Good riddance. I sniffed away the memories and swirled water around Squirter until he chased my fingers. The Seamount had done nothing but screw me over my whole life, and it didn't deserve my tears. If I only ever saw pale folk to buy Grace from again, I would be happy.

Well, Byssa and Hades didn't count. They were practically human after all their years on land. The rest of them could go beach themselves, for all I cared.

Finally, noon rolled around, and with it, my lunch date with Byssa and Hades. I said goodbye to Squirter with a new toy and a few fresh mussels for him to crack open. We planned to meet at the Crispy Prawn, the restaurant where Byssa worked as a sushi chef-in-training. She came by it honestly—all three of us preferred our fish raw.

A tone beeped when I pushed open the door, and a stylized cat waved at me endlessly from its perch on the windowsill. Byssa looked up from her work at the sushi counter and smiled at me.

"Hades is in the back. I'll be there soon."

I nodded, and Byssa bent her head to her work. With her hair dyed black and her dainty features, she could almost pass for the daughter of the restaurant's owner if she kept her head down. But when she looked up, her startling green eyes gave her away. Byssa used foundation and bronzer to tone down the luminescent white of her skin, but it was a tough sell. I had it easier since I'd inherited a warmer skin tone from my unknown human father.

I walked casually along the corridor that led to a back room in the narrow restaurant. Here, tables were separated by rice paper screens with illustrations of bamboo painted in black. Cup-shaped frosted glass lights dangled from the ceiling to illuminate each table, although a bank of windows into the back alley was enough to light up the room during the day. Most of the tables were full for the lunch rush, but Hades lounged in the back-corner booth we preferred. His black-and-white striped hair was easy to spot.

"Hi, stranger," he said cheerfully. He was usually in a good mood. Even bad news didn't ruffle him for long. "Still coming down from your Grace high?"

"That wore off hours ago." I sipped at a glass of water on the table. The hollow sensation after my body used up its Grace took a while to get used to. I gave myself a sharp mental slap and filled my mind with a vision of my crumbling apartment to stop the pity party of one. "Now, I need some sweet sushi to fill me up."

"Coming, coming." Byssa slid a huge platter of sushi, sashimi, and nigiri onto our table and heaved a breath. "That was heavy. I hope you're hungry." She dropped onto the bench next to her twin brother and bumped his hip with hers to shuffle him along.

Hades bit into a tuna sashimi and groaned with satisfaction. "So good. I was starving. Why don't we do this twice a week instead of once?"

"You're the best, Byssa," I said with my mouth full.

Byssa waved me away. "I know how much you two love it. Auntie could never get behind our sushi fascination, even if she understood where it came from. She's great, although she doesn't know anything about the Seamount." Byssa snapped her chopsticks in preparation for eating. "I'm glad you found us last year, Lune. It's almost Grace-Harvest down there, isn't it? Can you tell me more about it?"

I shrugged, feeling surly. Not at Byssa, whose wide-eyed enthusiasm was sweet on her fine-featured face. She didn't know about my animosity toward our homeland.

She and Hades had only been small children when they'd left the Seamount.

I followed a curl of seaweed on my plate with my chopstick while I considered our very different upbringings. The three of us had lived in the half-human ghetto together for the first few years of our lives, but, unlike me, their mother had actually cared for them. When Byssa had developed land lung—she could hardly breathe at times—their mother had taken them to the surface to find their human relations. Neither of them knew why I had left the Seamount years later and what had spurred me to do so. I wanted to keep it that way.

"There's not much to know," I said. "Everyone gathers, they say some words and do some dances, they pass out fresh Grace, and that's it." I didn't mention the days of preparation and ritual that culminated in a huge celebration that involved everyone, even lowly half-humans like us.

"Did you really expect her to tell us more?" Hades poured more soy sauce into his dish. "Lune never talks about her past. I have theories on that, by the way." He grinned roguishly. "You're the secret daughter of the Seamount Protector and Canada's Prime Minister."

"Ha, ha," I said without enthusiasm. If only that were the reason for my reluctance to tell them my past. A flash of black blood crossed my mind's eye, a vision of the crime I'd committed. "I wish. Unfortunately, my mother was entirely typical, and who knows who my father was? I doubt my mother even knew his name."

"Stop bugging her," Byssa said in a protective voice. "It's obviously painful, whatever it is. She'll tell us when she's ready, not before. Honestly."

Byssa was a gem. I didn't look at either of them, but my heart warmed at Byssa's words.

"Lune knows we don't care about her secrets." He raised his water glass in a toast to me and smiled warmly. "We're here, no matter what."

Okay, Hades was pretty great too. I don't know how I'd been so lucky to find these two.

"I'm doing something for Grace-Harvest, actually," Byssa continued. Her voice trembled with suppressed excitement. "Placida and Eris, those half-human girls I met at the pool, they invited me to a small celebration at their house. Nothing fancy, but we'll do something, at least. It will be my first Grace-Harvest ever."

"The Moonpull dance is hard with only three." I dipped a sashimi into my soy sauce. "More is better to form the moon shapes." I looked up to catch Hades and Byssa glancing at each other and backpedaled. "But I'm sure it will be fine."

"They don't remember much from the Seamount, either," Byssa said. "Would you like to come? You could show us what to do properly."

I shook my head before she even finished speaking. "Thanks, but I'd rather not. I'm over the Seamount life. Embrace my human side, you know? Honestly, you're better off without all that."

Byssa slowly prodded her sushi with her chopsticks, and I almost felt bad for saying no. But taking part in a mockery of Grace-Harvest sounded worse than nothing at all. And it would bring back too many memories of years of hunger and ridicule and loathing, and I wasn't ready to face those.

"There's an apartment for rent in the building next to mine." Hades changed the subject, and I looked at him with relief. "You should apply, Lune. The building is old, and it's not exactly Yaletown quality, but it's way better than your current place. Rent's not bad, considering this city's prices."

My gut clenched. If only I could apply. *One day*, I promised myself fiercely. One day, the person with the freedom to change apartments on a whim would be me. My friends didn't know about my debt to Branc, and I had no plans on enlightening them. They would be the first to offer help, I had no doubt, but I didn't want to transfer my debt to someone else, no matter how kind they were.

"My lease isn't up yet." My finger traced my plate's edge. "I wish I could. I'll have to survive the hole of doom for a while longer."

"How much would it cost to break the lease? It might be worthwhile if you can swing it. Oh." Hades reached into the pocket of his jeans and pulled out a folded piece of paper. "I forgot about this. Maybe you can make enough to break the lease with this opportunity."

Hades spread the paper on the table. Byssa and I leaned closer to read the words.

CHAPTER 4

At the top of the paper Hades passed to me, a logo of a house outline was superimposed on the familiar spiral of a nautilus shell.

Byssa looked at Hades with surprise over her plate of sushi. "Is this from the Lodge?"

My eyes continued to scan words written in the familiar script of the Seamount as I absorbed their meaning.

"It's an advertisement," I said. "Listen. 'Temporary help wanted. Three-week guide and housekeeping positions to service our underwater guests. If qualified, please bring this advertisement to the Lodge before August fifteenth to apply. Upon acceptance, positions will start immediately. Successful applicants will be paid in cash and Grace.'" The number below made me splutter. Would they really pay that much? If I gave all my earnings to Branc, my debt would almost be paid off.

Hades smiled. "I'm glad you're around, Lune. I had to get my buddy to translate for me when he gave me the ad. I'm terrible at reading those chicken scratches."

"Wow." Byssa ran her finger over the script, mouthing soundlessly as she translated to herself. "That's amazing. Wait. If we go for August fifteenth, that means we'll be at the Lodge for Grace-Harvest." Her eyes almost bugged out of her face. "I bet they do it right."

"What is the Lodge?" I asked. It sounded familiar, but I couldn't place it.

"It's a resort," Byssa said. "For pale folk who want to escape the Seamount for a while. Some use it like a high-end vacation spot, others use it to visit family on land. Humans stay there too, so the pale folk have to blend in."

"There are special underwater rooms, I've heard," Hades said.

"And the restaurant is supposed to be divine." Byssa gripped a piece of sushi between her chopsticks and brought it unseen to her mouth, her eyes lost in daydreams. "Fresh seafood all the time."

Well, that was an easy answer. A resort filled with pale folk straight from the Seamount? Vents, no. I was trying to get away from them, not submerse myself in a hotel full of elite, upper-crust sirens who had the means to leave the Seamount whenever they wanted. What if someone recognized me? I'd escaped for a reason.

My gut clenched as a memory of black blood in an opulent cave washed over me. My heartrate quickened, and I tightened my fingers on my chopsticks.

"Yeah, no," I said, attempting to sound casual. "You two have fun. I hate cleaning at the best of times, and I would be terrible in customer service."

"Lune's right, she would be terrible in customer service," said Hades to Byssa. "I think it's her gentle charm and winning charisma."

"Don't be mean," Byssa said absentmindedly as she skimmed the advertisement again. "You're doing it, Hades, right?"

"That much Grace? I'd be a fool to say no. And I'd like to think no one has ever mistaken me for a fool. I have some holiday time to use up, and the aquarium doesn't mind me taking unpaid leave occasionally." He grinned at me. "Come on, think of how good it would feel to hold that much Grace at once. You could swim properly every day for a month with that amount."

I squeezed my lips tightly together and gazed at the logo on the ad. I wouldn't swim every day for a month, but I would be free, and that would be better than swimming.

I couldn't do it, though. It was way too risky. If I were recognized…

"Nah," I said. "You go clean toilets and tell me all about it. I'll stick to the aquarium tanks."

After I said goodbye to Byssa and Hades—Byssa taught swimming lessons in the afternoon and Hades planned to ride his motorbike to meet a friend—I didn't feel like going back to my crappy apartment and wallowing. Squirter often took a nap at this time, so I wouldn't even have him to play with.

I climbed on a bus heading south and rode it for a while, staring out the window at the human constructs whizzing by—bridges, car dealerships, fields of blueberries—and letting my thoughts stray to previous Grace-Harvests celebrated with my friends at the Seamount. Despite our fringe status as half-humans, we were allowed at the celebrations, and it was the best taste of Grace all year.

Even Eelway, the man I regarded as a father figure, grew animated and cheerful on that day. Memories of my friends Pelagia and Cetus dashed through my mind, and I swallowed through my thickening throat. I missed Pelagia's unquenchable cheer, Cetus's soothing calm, and Eelway's steadfast presence with a dull ache that pushed painfully against the organs in my chest.

I took another bus seaward and got off at a tiny oceanside community called Steveston. I meandered along busy streets filled with families and sightseers. When I passed a parking lot, the doors of a nearby church opened and a crowd of people in their Sunday best streamed out to their cars like a flowing tide. I wondered what these humans believed, with their wooden churches and clanging bells. Ramu had always been my goddess, one of a pantheon of deities. She oversaw the Folk of the Sea, all the races, and we worshiped her with quiet adoration.

I was far from Ramu's oversight and the connection of others who loved her. Our stories hardly ever spoke of the other deities, except as they related to Ramu. Now, I wondered if any humans worshiped them.

A shop caught my eye as I wandered past. Some of the books in the glass-fronted window had the words "spirituality" written on them. With my current ponderings, I impulsively opened the painted teal door.

Windchimes accompanied the door's movement with a musical rattle. A burning smell scented the shop, which almost made me turn around right then and there. I wasn't a fan of smells at the best of times—the foreign sensation rasped at my nose and lungs—and burning set

35

my teeth on edge. I promised myself that the instant I saw flames, I'd be out of there.

"Good afternoon," said a calm voice from behind the counter. An older woman with long gray hair in a braid smiled pleasantly at me. I didn't want to open my mouth to allow more incense in, so I nodded tightly and continued to peruse.

There were books, boxes of cards with strange illustrations for reading the future, figurines of placid-looking women, and plenty of gemstones. I appreciated the objective beauty of their glittering colors, but nothing compared to the iridescence of an abalone shell. A few pearls in a bowl reminded me of the Seamount cave's opulence where my journey to land had begun.

I turned away from the pearls. My eyes lit on a bowl on the counter with a sign that read, "Mermaid's Tears". Inside lay pieces of smoothed glass.

I suppressed a snort. I was sure that mer folk never cried. They made others cry instead. And how would someone even collect mer tears underwater? They would mingle with the ocean instantly.

"You look lost, my dear," the woman said from her counter. I jumped and looked up in surprise. She gazed at me with a warm smile. "Would you like me to read your tarot cards? They can be enlightening."

She held up a fan of cards with strange illustrations on them. I was irresistibly reminded of the fortune-telling of my people, using certain blessed shells and rocks.

I shook my head. "Thanks, but I should be going."

The woman nodded, and I fled the store. Being surrounded by someone else's beliefs only cemented how alone and how far away from home I was. A wave of grief threatened to crash over me, but I squared my shoulders and lifted my chin.

No one looked down at me here. I might not be part of something larger than myself, but at least I wasn't a reviled part.

A few days later, I opened my closet, intent on finding my tiny stash of old metal coins used as currency back at the Seamount. The coins were salvaged from drowned ships—we had no way of crafting metal ourselves—and were a useful commodity for trade. Mark the Shark's job offers ate at me. I wanted to pay my debt, but the cost of some gigs was so high. I needed something more to offer Branc.

My closet was nearly empty. A year of land-living hadn't amounted to much, possession-wise. The shelves contained a stack of beach towels for swimming, a set of sheets, and a pair of shoes that I'd never worn. I nearly closed the door again when the box I was looking for caught my eye.

It was an old shoebox that my boots had come in, back when I'd spent Branc's money with abandon, not understanding the true value of the cash he'd given me. Its orange lid was dull with dust. I slid it out from the back of the shelf and stared at it. Did I really want to open it?

With a sigh, I lifted the cardboard lid. Inside rattled a

handful of tarnished coins and the folded fabric of a greenish-brown dress crafted from prepared kelp blades. My heart squeezed, and I put the box on the shelf to hold the fabric in both hands. It was stiff, but I carefully worked the creases out with warmth from my hands until it lay supple over my arm.

This was the dress I'd worn upon arriving on land. It had been my only clothing and the only possession I'd taken from the Seamount beside the coins in a pouch around my waist. Truthfully, it had been only one of two that I'd owned. Living on the fringes of society hadn't come with a swim-in closet.

I sighed and carefully folded the dress back into the box. I was tempted to wear it on my next swim because nothing flowed around the body like a Seamount-made dress, but I couldn't bear the thought of ripping it. The mends where my friend Pelagia had artfully sewn delicate strands of mussel-made byssal threads were visible along the hem. Looking at the dress reminded me too much of the life I'd left behind. I'd hated it, had wished to escape again and again, but now that I had, it was hard to let my past go.

"The Seamount is full of elitist hagfish," I said out loud to bolster my resolution. I swirled the coins with my finger, their number only enough to buy me an envelope of Grace. I couldn't work up the nerve to let go of the last vestiges of my former home, especially to pay off such a paltry portion of my debt.

If I took the job at the Lodge, I could keep the coins. Was it worth the risk of being recognized by the elite who supposedly swarmed the Lodge? I swallowed audibly and my lips tightened. Eelway would have been ashamed of my cowardice. Surely, I could avoid being recognized.

If I wanted to be free, I had to take the risk.

The hairdresser gave me a mirror to hold while I looked at the back of my hair. I gave it a cursory glance before handing her the mirror. It was trim and tidy, short enough to fit under my wig easily but long enough to sway around my shoulders underwater.

"Looks good," I said.

The hairdresser nodded. "The layers give you nice volume if I do say so myself. Your hair is very dry, though. Do you swim a lot?"

I suppressed a chuckle. "Yeah, a bit."

"I'd recommend this conditioner." She swiped a purple bottle off the shelf behind her. "It's a deep moisturizer, perfect for dry hair."

"How much is it?"

When the hairdresser said a number, my eyes widened. Living on the poverty line had given me a crash course in finances. I touched my locks and wrinkled my nose at the crispy ends. I could use that conditioner.

I started a deep hum in my chest, lower than a human could hear. It vibrated through my arm when I touched the hairdresser's elbow, and when she sensed it, her eyes grew distant.

"I'd love to try a small bottle as a sample," I crooned

softly, careful to not let others nearby hear. I didn't have a lot of ability now that the Grace had passed through my system, but I had enough for this small persuasion of one. "If I like it, I'll come buy more. That's reasonable, isn't it?"

It took a moment for the hairdresser to answer, and I waited in anticipation for her reaction. My conscience squirmed. I shouldn't use it on unsuspecting humans. It hardly made me any better than the upper echelons of the Seamount that I reviled.

The woman opened her mouth, but I stopped her.

"Never mind, I'll get a bottle next time," I said. "Thanks for the cut."

My fingers brushed my crispy ends when I pulled a floppy sunhat over my head and tucked my white hair into the cap to avoid notice. My heart was lighter, though. Distancing myself from my past always brought satisfaction.

I strode down the sidewalk after paying, keen to put some distance between myself and the salon in case the hairdresser wondered what she'd felt during my brief compulsion. When I deemed myself far enough away, I slowed to an amble.

My phone rang, and the screen showed an incoming call from "The Blobfish". My heart sank.

"Hi, Branc."

"Lune." Branc's gravelly voice snaked into my ear. "You've heard about the Lodge hiring."

I didn't know how he knew everything, but I'd long since given up wondering.

"Yes."

"You're going," he stated, as if I had no say in the matter. If I'd decided against it, I might have fought back, but I was going.

"Yes."

"There's someone I need information from. I'll send you the identification of the target. It's the eccentric uncle of a high-ranking Seamount elite—I'll give you the details later—so you won't need much Grace to make him pliant."

Males were far more susceptible to pale folk abilities, even within our race. There was a reason we were a matriarchal society.

"I'll be waiting with bated breath," I said tonelessly.

"No need for cheek," Branc said. "Do it and it'll pay your rent for the next two months."

He hung up, and I sighed heavily. It was a distasteful assignment—persuading unwitting people to part with their secrets was never fun—but it could have been far worse.

And now I had double the reason to work at the Lodge. I hoped it was the answer to my problems. Suddenly, a lot was riding on this job. I calculated a few numbers in my head, then my jaw dropped as the truth hit me: with the rent paid for two and a half months, my upcoming paycheck from the aquarium, and the money and Grace the Lodge promised, I could pay off my debt in full. I couldn't afford to miss this opportunity.

As soon as Byssa pulled into the Lodge's parking lot a week later, I wanted her to turn around and drive away. This was a terrible idea. There was no way I wouldn't get caught. I pulled down the sun visor of the passenger's seat and checked my reflection in the mirror. My least startling brown contacts, check. Properly attached auburn wig, check. Enough bronzer to give my already pinkish skin a healthy human tan, check.

"I never took you for the vain type," Hades teased from the backseat.

I stuck my tongue out at his reflection. "There's a difference between being vain and having a fish bone stuck in your teeth. I have some standards."

Hades chuckled as he unfolded himself from the back and stretched beside the car.

Byssa joined him, her body quivering. "I can't believe we're here. I'm so excited for Grace-Harvest. I hope they'll let us watch."

"That's the whole point of Grace-Harvest," I said when I joined them outside. "Everyone needs Grace, so everyone gets it. For one day, at least. If they're being authentic, then the pale folk staff will be involved in the celebrations as much as the guests."

"Good," Byssa said. "I'm sure they must be planning something special with so many pale folk here."

"There will be something. Remind me to look up the local pubs. I'll be skipping out and will need somewhere to amuse myself."

"You're not really going to miss it?" Byssa stared at me. "I thought you were joking. I was looking forward to celebrating a real Grace-Harvest with you."

"It's not that exciting," I lied. "Trust me, you'd probably have more fun at the pub with me."

Byssa pursed her lips but didn't answer. The three of us gazed for a quiet moment at the Lodge nestled in a grove of Douglas fir trees. It was less imposing than I had pictured in my mind. Cedar shakes were layered on the walls in a rustic, coastal style that continued onto the roof. A wrap-around porch contained wicker chairs with comfortable cushions and even a wooden swing that hung from sturdy chains. Forest-green double doors were wide open in the August warmth, inviting us into the large main building. It was three stories high, with balconies overlooking the view of the sea and forested islands beyond. Another similarly styled building was tucked into the trees to our right.

It was idyllic in the extreme, although I couldn't imagine pale folk appreciating the elevated rooms.

"Where do the underwater guests stay?" I asked.

Byssa pointed. "Look out there."

I shifted to the side. A long floating building jutted into the water, anchored by thick pilings. The cedar shake theme continued along the residences and the next-door dock, which contained three tiny outbuildings and a few kayaks.

"They've got it all, don't they?" I muttered. "Come on, let's get this over with."

I squared my shoulders and strode with falsely confident steps to the main door, feeling like I was confronting a school of sharks, not entering a twee resort filled with rustic charm. Byssa hurried after me, and Hades chuckled as he followed.

The lobby's counter ran along the left side and a seating area to my right was filled with overstuffed armchairs surrounding a cold fireplace. I shuddered. This was clearly the human entrance. No self-respecting pale folk would have a fireplace. I couldn't imagine anything more ridiculous than lighting a fire in a wooden house. Why were humans so insane?

"Good afternoon," a bright voice said from behind the counter. It belonged to a woman in her late forties with honey-colored skin and brown eyes but with a full head of pure white hair. She was likely half-siren. Her nametag announced her as Sandy. "Welcome to the Lodge. How can I help you today?"

Hades stepped forward. "We came about the advertisement." He took the folded ad out of his pocket and laid it on the counter.

The woman unfolded the paper, scanned the contents, then nodded. "Excellent. We're still in need of help. Wait here, please, and I'll get Levi."

The woman bustled to a door behind the counter.

I turned to the others. "Are you ready to wow Levi with your tour guide skills? This is an interview, after all." I flicked my wrist in a circular motion. "There, I'm limbered up for my toilet-cleaning evaluation."

Byssa twisted her hands in apprehension, but Hades laughed.

"From what I heard, they won't be choosy," he said. "With all the turmoil down below, pale folk are flocking away from the Seamount, and the Lodge is busier than ever."

"Can't argue with that," said a smooth voice behind

me.

I jumped and twisted around to see the newcomer.

CHAPTER 5

Before me stood a man in his mid-twenties with wavy dark hair and height enough to look down on me. The logo on his tee-shirt matched the one on Sandy's, but the similarities ended there. Hints of toned muscle peeked out from the sleeves, and his skin was a delicious warm tan that reminded me of a caramel apple that Byssa had bought me once. It had been almost unbearably sweet and delicious on the outside, but crisp and firm in the center.

I know Byssa would say he was hot, but I had never understood that human phrasing. Hot wasn't something I ever wanted. What Levi reminded me of was the blissfully cool feeling of sliding into the ocean after weeks of parched land with the delicious taste of salt on my tongue. I bet his kiss would taste like a mouthful of Grace.

With a mental shake, I pushed down the flare of interest and tried to look competent and worthy of cleaning toilets. I would be glad when these three weeks were over, and I could escape with my money and Grace. Maybe I should have bought a human calendar just for the satisfaction of crossing off the days as they came.

"I'm Levi Storm," the man continued and reached out his hand for me to shake. The motion exposed a strange discoloration of skin that ran from his hairline down the side of his neck and into his shirt. It was mottled, and a strange silvery gray in patchy patterns. Was it a birthmark? I brought my eyes back to his face as he continued to speak. "Manager-in-training of the Lodge. And you are…"

"Lune Seafields," I said with a squeeze of his warm hand. I'd never gotten the hang of shaking hands, no matter how much Hades had coached me on it. I tried to shake with Levi, but I lost the rhythm and quickly extracted my fingers. His mouth twitched like he was trying not to grin, and I hid a scowl.

"I like your shirt," he said with a wave at my torso.

I looked down. This day's shirt showed a sad-looking fish crooning into a microphone, with the caption, "Blues in the key of sea".

"I didn't think applying for a housekeeping job needed formalwear," I said with mild trepidation. I really wanted this job. "But if it does, please overlook my clothes this once. I promise I clean up okay."

Levi chuckled. "I believe you." He turned to the others. "And you're also applicants? Great." Hades and Byssa introduced themselves, and Levi shook their hands with the same firm grip he had with me. "I'm glad you're here. There aren't as many pale folk interested in working at the Lodge as we need right now. With the political upheaval down below, plenty of sirens are flocking through the barrier to vacation here. We're almost completely booked, with more arriving." He ran a hand through his hair, and I tried not to think of how silky it looked. "I'll tell you right now, you're hired for the next three weeks if you want it."

Byssa and I looked at each other with surprise. Her dismay over my choice of clothing—graphic tee, black jean skirt, and my usual boots—had been an unnecessary

47

waste of breath during the entire ferry and car ride.

Hades beamed. "Sign us up."

"I'll take you on a tour. But first, the rules. No mention of underwater lifestyles or anything related unless you're with staff only, okay? We have lots of human guests here."

"Understood," Byssa said. "We can be discreet."

Before I followed Levi out of the lobby, I took one last look at the empty fireplace and shuddered. Levi caught my expression and tilted his head at me.

"I hate fire," I explained. "Don't understand the human fascination with it. Horrible stuff. Luckily it's summer and that thing doesn't need tending."

Levi's mouth twitched. "It's a gas fireplace. No tending needed. Don't worry, we usually leave it off until October."

Levi led us through the interior of the main building and pointed at a wide, central staircase. Shells were artfully displayed in sconces up the wall. My shoulders relaxed a fraction. Levi hadn't reacted with shock and horror at the sight of my face, so either he wasn't clued into Seamount news, or my disguise was working better than expected. Maybe this trip wouldn't be as catastrophic as I'd feared. I didn't want Seamount-style justice enacted on me for my past crimes.

"Rooms for our land visitors are upstairs. We often get requests for the dockside rooms from them, but unfortunately, they're always booked up." He grinned at us. "We have enough staff for those rooms, but we'll need help with the dockside suites. Were you interested in the tour guide position or housekeeping?"

48

"Housekeeping for me," I blurted. "The other two want to be tour guides."

"Lune is a professional scrubber," Hades said with a wink at me. "She's a genius with a sponge."

I glared at Hades, who grinned back, unrepentant. Levi eyed me but didn't comment.

"On your left is the restaurant for guests," he said.

Byssa sighed sadly beside me at the sight of the large dining room. It was light and breezy from picture windows that overlooked the bay, and tables were covered in elegant cloths and silverware.

Levi must have heard her sigh, because he chuckled. "Don't worry, there's a dining hall for staff which serves the same food. Since the Lodge is remote, most of the staff stay here during their working days, and we provide room and board."

Byssa's eyes sparkled. "I've heard great things about the food here. I'm training to be a chef."

"In that case, don't forget to try the cedar-plank salmon. It's my favorite."

"How long have you worked here?" I asked. His lack of visible pale folk features intrigued me, and I wanted to know more. It was purely professional interest, I reminded myself as I tore my eyes away from his silky hair. If he'd been blond, I might have been tempted to try out men again and see if kissing his mouth would taste as good as he looked. Oddly, his eyes were the flattest, dullest blue I had ever seen.

"How long? Since I was old enough to fold napkins and tie ropes. I didn't get paid until later, of course." At my curious look, he said, "My parents own the Lodge.

They're training me to take over when they retire."

"Is that imminent?" Hades asked.

Levi shrugged. "Pretty soon, I think. They don't have the energy anymore. I do most of the day-to-day managing now."

He held the door open for us, and we funneled down wide steps to a woodchip-covered path that led to the docks. The summer warmth pushed against me like a presence, but it was tempered by a cool ocean breeze that I breathed in eagerly. An older man with graying hair stomped on a pitchfork and turned the earth over in a flowerbed. Levi called out a greeting, and the man pierced us with eyes as pale gray as my own. He was clearly half-siren.

"New recruits?" the man said in a voice hoarse with age. "Welcome to the Lodge. Best place in the world. On land, that is." He wheezed a chuckle and returned to his dirt-flipping activities.

"That was William," Levi said to us after we had walked by. "He's been here since my parents started the Lodge, well before I arrived. He's known me since I was a toddler."

It was odd phrasing. Wouldn't William have known Levi from babyhood if his parents had started the place? I wanted to ask, but Byssa would have glared at my rudeness, so I refrained for her sake. What intrigued me more were the attitudes of the half-sirens we had met so far. Sandy at the front desk, William, and Levi all seemed happy with their work at the Lodge.

I didn't understand how. The Lodge catered to the Seamount elite, who had enough Grace and ability to escape for a visit of pleasure. Surely, the half-humans here were treated with the same disdain as at the Seamount. I couldn't understand why they were so enthusiastic about being treated like scum for a career.

"The dockside rooms are on the right dock." Levi pointed in their direction. "And the left dock has supply rooms and kayaks as well as the Grace-house at the end."

"There's a whole building to store Grace?" My mouth watered, and I exchanged a greedy look with Hades.

Levi smiled wryly.

"We're a distributor for the region. And it needs to be stored properly, so it doesn't lose its effectiveness." Levi checked his watch, then said with a hint of apology, "Do you mind starting right away? We're running behind schedule. There are a few groups that have been waiting for a private tour for two days, and some rooms that were recently vacated haven't been cleaned yet."

"Of course," Byssa said quickly. "Just tell us what to do."

"We'll get your uniforms first, then I'll show you the bunkhouses so you can settle in."

Levi led us to a building in the trees that I hadn't noticed from the parking lot—this place was far bigger than I'd first supposed—where he opened an exterior door to reveal a storeroom filled with clothes.

"There are shirts in all sizes," Levi said. "Here, Hades, the men's clothes are on this side. Byssa, Lune, help yourself to this side. You can wear pants or a skirt, it's up to you. Lune, if you need a swimsuit for cleaning the underwater rooms, you can grab a spare over there."

I quickly grabbed a plain black skirt in my size—no

51

pants here, thank you—and a shirt. Both were lined with two layers—one absorbent next to the skin and the other water-resistant—and I marveled at the innovation. My wet swimsuit would never leak through my clothes with these layers added.

I was never without swimming attire, thanks to my underwear choices, so I skipped the swimsuit section. We followed Levi back outside, where he pointed to another door in the dappled shade.

"Grab yourselves a bunk each, whichever isn't occupied. When you're changed, Byssa and Hades, come back to the front desk. Lune, head over to the dockside rooms. Sheila will be there cleaning, and she can show you the ropes." He checked his watch. "I have to fly, but I'll get you papers to sign tonight. Thanks for coming."

He strode off, leaving us blinking at his sudden exit.

Hades held up his polo shirt with the Lodge logo embroidered on the chest. "I'm starting to think the universe doesn't trust my fashion sense," he said. "I'm forever getting jobs with uniforms."

"I certainly don't trust your hairstyle choices," I said. "I'm on the universe's side on this one."

Hades touched his striped hair with mock outrage. "No one insults this masterpiece and lives to tell the tale."

"Come on, you two," Byssa said with a roll of her eyes. "We have jobs to do. If you need motivation, think of all the Grace we'll get at the end of this."

The bunkhouse was spare but clean. Interior white paint and a cluster of creamy white oyster shells artistically piled in a large vase on the windowsill lightened the outside's cedar shake theme. Three rooms with two bunkbeds each allowed for plenty of staff, and this was only the women's side.

"This is a way bigger operation than I expected," I said to Byssa. "I had no idea how many snobby elites took joyrides to the coast."

"I think it's humans a lot of the time," Byssa replied. "This number of pale folk is unusual. Shotgun the top bunk."

Byssa threw her suitcase over the railing of a neatly made bed without any personal belongings and climbed up the ladder. She flopped onto the mattress with a contented sigh, then rummaged in her bag and extracted a camera enclosed in a waterproof housing.

"Looking for more specimens to add to your photo collection?" I asked. Byssa had made it her mission to photograph an example of every living creature in our local waters. Because she spent so much time in the sea, she'd amassed a huge number of exquisite images.

"Of course." She tucked the camera on a shelf above her pillow. "But I'm always up for more pictures of Squirter if I can't find anything new."

I tossed my new uniform on the bottom bunk and shimmied out of my jean skirt. The new skirt was a modest length, but it fit better than I expected for a uniform.

A young woman, barely out of her teens, bustled into our room and stopped with a jolt. Her dyed-purple ponytail swung with the rapid motion.

"Oh! You must be new," she said in a bright voice. "I'm Kim. A waitress for the restaurant."

"Lune and Byssa," I said, reluctantly giving our names when she looked at us expectantly.

A faint frown crossed her features when she studied mine.

"Do I know you from somewhere?" she asked uncertainly.

My cheeks flushed—a trait inherited from my human father that I'd often been mocked for down below—and I turned my head to fuss with my clothes on the bed. This was it, the moment I had dreaded. It would only take one person to recognize me for what I was, and my whole fragile, land-based world would come crashing down.

"I don't think so. I wouldn't have forgotten your hair."

Kim laughed, and my heart slowed with relief. "I change it all the time. That's the great thing about white hair. It soaks up the color so well. It's the only pale folk trait I managed to inherit. Sirening might have been more useful, but I'll take what I can get." She grabbed a hairband from her bunk and moved to the door. "Nice to meet you."

I took a few deep breaths to calm myself when Kim left. The dry air scratched my throat from my forceful inhalations, and I longed for a swim. It didn't take much to plunge unwilling into memories: walls of a Seamount cave pressing against me, escape from my crime necessary and almost impossible, blood drifting past outstretched fingers. My palms grew sweaty, and I banished my thoughts with difficulty.

"I should go," Byssa said once she'd wriggled into her

uniform and turned around in front of the mirror a few times. "Levi is probably waiting with a tour group. Oh." She whirled around and looked at me with a mischievous expression. "He was pretty hot. Like, scorching."

I'd known she would say that, and I shuddered at the comparison. Byssa mistook my motion for dislike of Levi.

"You can't deny he is gorgeous," she said in disbelief.

"Meh, I prefer blonds," I said.

I was lying, of course—not that I didn't prefer blond men, but Levi almost qualified for gorgeous even with his hair color—but Byssa was a terrifying and persistent matchmaker. She had tried to set me up with friends of Hades, culinary school students, other sushi chefs, and lifeguards at the pool where she taught swimming lessons. I wasn't interested, but she wouldn't take no for an answer. She was mild-mannered in every other way, but in this, she was relentless.

"Channel your match-making energy toward yourself," I said. "Why don't you make a move on Levi, if you think he's so gorgeous?"

Predictably, Byssa looked horrified at the thought, as if she were a star-struck teenager.

"No, that's okay," she babbled. "He probably has a girlfriend. And he's our boss. It wouldn't be right."

"And yet you tried to pawn him off on me a moment ago," I teased.

Byssa sighed with a huff. "I'll see you at dinner. Good luck cleaning your toilets."

Byssa skipped off to the main lodge, eager to start her tour, so I smoothed my skirt and trudged to the dockside building. I still wore my boots, because Levi hadn't offered me uniform shoes and I hadn't brought any others. I was only the cleaning lady. No one would see me. And if they did? I didn't care. I was here to do my work, get my Grace, and get the vents out of here.

The doorknob to the seaside building was a spiral nautilus shell cast from some silvery metal. I still couldn't identify metals very well because I'd rarely encountered them before I came to land. We were a little short on forges in the Seamount. The knob was a nice touch, and I bet the visiting elite cooed over the little detail.

When I opened the door, the hallway inside was dim and cool. I immediately breathed easier. A humidifier must have been running in the ceiling because the air was moist and wonderful in my lungs. Although I was used to dry air on land, that didn't mean that this cool moistness wasn't a welcome balm.

The hall was covered in plaster ridges and whorls to look like a rounded tunnel, and it was painted soothing greens and blues. Or was it paint? The colors subtly shifted in an ebb and flow that relaxed me to my core. I peered around until I saw a small white projector above the door lintel.

Dense carpeting muffled my footsteps down the corridor. Doors tucked into the swirling patterns were covered in plaster whorls themselves. The numbers on the doors were in Seamount-script.

I shivered. This was a little too much like home. Not home, I chastised myself. It was too much like the place where I grew up. The shifting colors, the textures, the script—I was intensely curious to see the inside of these rooms.

A door was open halfway down the hall, and I strode inside. As soon as I stepped in, I hoped it was the cleaning lady Sheila who was in here and not a guest. Aside from the awkwardness of barging into a guest's room, my main goal at the Lodge—besides earning Grace—was to escape unnoticed by vacationing pale folk.

Luck was with me because a middle-aged woman with short brown hair, pale skin, and a Lodge uniform looked up and smiled.

"Are you a new employee? I'm Sheila, head of housekeeping. What's your name, dear?"

"I'm Lune." My eyes wandered around the room. "Levi said you could show me the ropes."

It was a comforting place, at least from my half-siren perspective. The dry part of the room was again plastered to look like a rocky cave but painted in muted gray. A sage green duvet covered a soft bed. Two couches sat at right angles to each other before a heavily tinted window overlooking the coastline, and an unobtrusive door led to a bathroom beyond. It was sparse but luxurious, without many features, but those present were done with consideration of the clientele. Even the lights, illuminated while Sheila was cleaning, were a dim cool blue. Human clothes filled an open closet, with a shelf of wigs at the top and shoes on the floor.

"Not quite a human hotel room," I said. "But not as different as I'd expected, either."

Sheila laughed. "That's because you haven't seen the rest of the suite."

I looked around for a sign of what Sheila was talking about, but when nothing presented itself, I settled for an expression of polite curiosity. Sheila pressed a button on the wall.

A smooth, mechanical sound vibrated my feet. I jumped back when a floor panel dropped from beside the sitting area and slid out of sight. My eyes blinked at the shifting water below.

"It's underwater?"

Sheila nodded with an amused glint in her eye. "Plenty of pale folk have trouble sleeping on land. Some want to try it, and that's why we have human beds as well." She waved at the bed. "Underwater is quite a different sensation, I've heard."

"Are you—" I didn't know how to ask. Was it a delicate question? "Aren't you half-siren yourself?"

"A few generations back." She grimaced and waved at her face. "Grandmother gave me her easily sunburned skin and not much else."

I nodded and looked in the hole. It was dark down there, but when I entered the water, my eyes would adjust.

"How do we clean down there?" I asked.

"Did Levi give you a spare swimsuit? Get that on, along with this weight belt, then take a scrub brush and give everything a good once-over. The water does most of the work for us, but we need to fight the good fight against algae. It gets everywhere as soon as you turn your back. Grab the cleaner fish while you're there—we don't like leaving them in the dark for longer than a day. When you finish scrubbing, come back up and I'll show you the finishing touches."

Scrubbing algae. It sounded suspiciously like what I did every day at the aquarium, but I smiled brightly at Sheila. This was only for three weeks. I could handle anything for three weeks, especially if it meant that I would make enough Grace and money to pay off my debt.

"I already have my swimsuit on."

I stripped down and took the offered brush. Sheila pressed another button, and the square of dark water glowed a ghostly green. I unpinned my wig—maybe I would start wearing a hat instead of a wig during working hours—dangled my feet off the edge into the cool water, then slipped in.

CHAPTER 6

My eyes adjusted immediately, and I looked around, curious to see where the elite slept away from the Seamount. The water was crystal clear—maybe they filtered it for guests because it certainly wasn't clear outside this room—and the walls were encrusted with tiny glowing lights behind translucent shells that dotted the enclosure. The space was achingly familiar in style but far more opulent than I'd ever encountered. Instead of a human bed, wide kelp fronds were neatly rolled against one wall, meant to anchor sleeping bodies to stop them floating away in the current. No currents tugged at my body in this space, but guests would undoubtedly feel more comfortable in trappings like home.

Large windows covered one wall, garnished with gauzy curtains that drifted in the water's motion, although both the tops and bottoms were contained by rails. A gathering area typical of a Seamount home was in front of the largest window, recognizable by a wide stone table. The table's sloping edges had five long, shallow grooves carved out to support bodies lying on their stomachs. Embedded in the table's ridges were shells and pearls, giving the piece of furniture a luxurious look.

I set aside my wonder and homesickness and started scrubbing. The water grew murky, but the filters soon cleared away floating algae. A hinged door in the interior wall opened to a smaller, unlit room. One wall was lined with toiletries including combs, sponges, and a jar of three striped cleaner fish no longer than my finger. I scrubbed the walls then peeked into a narrow door with handholds on the wall beside it.

The current was strong here—a pump must force water to flow between rooms—and I quickly shut the door. Hades could make fun of me for cleaning toilets, but at least the underwater version took care of itself.

When no slimy scum remained on any surface, I grabbed the jar of cleaner fish and kicked to the trapdoor.

"Good," Sheila said when my head emerged from the placid water. She held out a new jar of cleaner fish, two small packages, and three glowing jars of bioluminescent algae with a mechanical agitator on the bottom. "Now, take these envelopes of Grace and tuck them into the sleeping straps, then lock these candles into place on the pillar."

"Free Grace with a night's stay?" I was tempted to come, although I knew I couldn't afford it in a million years.

"Like a chocolate on the pillow of a fancy hotel. Guests rave about the little touches." Sheila placed the envelopes and jars on the floor. "When you're done here, head to the next room along. I'll leave it open for you."

Sheila popped her head into my final suite before I slid through the trapdoor to scrub the underwater room.

"Once you're finished, just drop your supplies in the

storeroom on the next dock," she instructed. "The door with the sea star on it. You did well today. A real asset to this great institution."

I waved a tired farewell as she left, then slipped into the water with my brush once more, puzzling over her words. Was she another devotee to the Lodge? I was still highly skeptical that it was all great all the time. Maybe they slipped something into the food that Byssa was so excited about. I snorted, and bubbles shot out of my nose.

This room hadn't been rented yet, but with pale folk arriving daily, Sheila said that it was only a matter of time. Algae were thick on the walls from underuse, and my aching arms grumbled at me from my scrubbing motions.

One more room, I thought to myself. I was holding my breath, since cleaning these shallow rooms didn't take long and the trapdoor was nearby. Switching to water breathing was worth it for a long swim, but for only a few minutes, the sensation was uncomfortable, and expelling the water from my lungs unpleasant. I could hold my breath for at least ten minutes without a problem, after all.

It took three breaths to fully clean the room and prepare it for guests, but I finally hauled myself onto the floor and dripped on the edge in a haze of tiredness. Sheila had dropped off a fresh towel for me, so I dried off, donned my uniform and wig once more, and trudged out of the suite.

In the hall, a pair of pale folk was exiting their room. The female touched her brown wig with a self-conscious pat, and the male held her hand to his chest to better communicate by humming. I dropped my head so they couldn't see my face, which gave me a view of their elongated feet in plain black shoes, clearly borrowed from the Lodge. My heart pounded at their proximity—if they recognized me as a criminal on the run, I was done for—but they ignored my presence.

I shuffled past and hurried out of the building, unwilling to bump into any more elite. My pulse thrummed until I was on the other dock and behind the floating storeroom building. I leaned against it, fully drained from my busy day and my fright.

It took me a minute to remember what building was at the end of the dock. I turned my head to examine it more closely. That was the Grace-house, the storage room that contained the Lodge's supply of Grace. It must be carefully sealed to maintain the needed humidity and temperature to store Grace long-term, and the padlock on the door dissuaded me from trying to pilfer their stores.

I wasn't above stealing—that's how I'd survived for years in the Seamount, after all—but I wasn't greedy or stupid. The Lodge promised to pay me plenty at the end of three weeks if I worked for them, which was a fantastic deal. I wasn't dumb enough to steal and draw the ire of another group hunting me. Being hunted was a form of control, and Ramu knew I was done with being controlled.

No, I vowed to keep my nose clean and do my time at the Lodge, hopefully avoiding curious glances from the elite along the way. At the end, I would collect my

Grace, pay Branc, and walk away from all controlling pale folk, free to do whatever I wanted without asking anyone for permission.

I pushed aside thoughts of Grace and focused instead on the clinking of cutlery that drifted on the wind from the restaurant and peals of laughter that rang out from the staff dining hall. My stomach growled in anticipation.

I wanted food, a chat with Byssa and Hades, and a pre-bed swim with Squirter, if he'd swum this far north yet. Feeling pleased with my plan, I opened the storeroom to drop off my cleaning supplies, then quietly shut the door behind me.

A motion caught my eye against the setting sun. I squinted, cursing the brightness of land-living. No guests should be on this dock, since there was a "Staff Only" sign written in both English and Seamount-script. It must be another worker.

I squinted harder. Was that the sun glinting off something shiny? My stomach clenched when I recognized flickering. Sweat instantly beaded on my forehead, and the horrible land-based sensation only fed into my terror.

Fire.

My eyes zeroed in on the male figure hovering above a blaze licking at the dock. He saw the fire, but he didn't care. Wait, was that a red can of gasoline in his hand? Had he set the fire deliberately?

My brain could hardly comprehend that anyone would light an out-of-control fire on purpose. Somebody needed to know what was happening, somebody who could stop the figure. I raised my foot to take a step further down the dock, but I couldn't do it. The fire flickered with hot menace, and cold shudders raced down my spine. I couldn't move.

I screamed instead, loud and shrill.

The figure's head shot up at the sound of my scream. We froze for a long moment, his face shadowed and indistinct in a black hoodie.

With a jolt, the figure pushed something onto the dock with a clatter, grabbed the can of gasoline, then flung his body into the lapping waves in an elegant dive. My breath came faster and faster as the flames licked higher. Fire crept up the side of the building.

Oh, vents! The Grace-house. If the Grace burned, I would have nothing for Branc. I would be stuck under his thumb forever, and I couldn't handle that.

I yanked open the storeroom door and upended the bucket of cleaning supplies I'd dumped inside moments before. With enough water, any wood fire could be managed, right? Would it work if the fire were lit with gasoline? My hands trembled. I knew very little about fire.

While I wavered, strong hands pried the bucket away from me.

"I got this," Levi said. He yelled at the people following him, "Grab a bucket!"

The others brushed past my frozen form and took whatever containers they could find. Levi bent and scooped water into his bucket, then flung seawater onto the towering flames and repeated the motion. Others followed, and with every douse, the fire made hissing, popping sounds like the clicks of a hunting sperm whale. I clutched the wall of the storeroom.

Finally, the last of the flames was extinguished. Levi rocked back on his heels and exhaled sharply.

"Look at this, Levi." Another man held up an old-fashioned oil lantern with a crack in the glass. "This must have started the fire."

"I recognize that," chimed in Sandy from the front desk. "Belinda sells them at the market in town. She blows the glass in her workshop. I bet you anything a guest bought one, brought it down here to try it out, then forgot to take it away."

The others nodded, and Levi frowned.

"We'll have to put up a chain on the end of the dock to stop guests from entering," he said. "I thought the sign would be enough, but apparently not."

"The fire wasn't an accident," I croaked, then cleared my dry throat of residual fear. "It was hard to see—the sun was in my eyes—but I'm sure I saw a man with gasoline light this on purpose. When I screamed, he swam away."

Four pairs of skeptical eyes gazed at me.

"Are you saying this was arson?" Levi said at last. His brow furrowed. "Why?"

I shrugged. How would I know who would want to burn down the Lodge?

Arson. My hands rubbed my arms in thought. Someone wanted to burn the Grace-house, but why? He'd come awfully close to destroying a limited supply of land-based Grace. I needed that Grace to free myself, so I was intensely interested in the answer to that question.

A few short minutes ago, all I'd wanted was to work at the Lodge and get out as quickly as possible with the Grace I'd earned. Now, I had to protect that Grace I needed so badly. Who was the figure? Why did he want to burn the Grace-house? How could I prevent him from trying to burn it again?

"Does the Lodge have any enemies?" I asked.

The others exhaled with scoffing laughter.

"Hardly," the man holding the oil lantern said. "Employees love it, guests love it, even online reviews are overwhelmingly positive."

"Why would you think it's arson?" A young woman with a bucket dangling from one hand squinted at me. "You said yourself the sun made it hard to see. Maybe you were mistaken. Or, maybe it was you who started the fire, and you're trying to throw suspicion off."

"What possible reason would I have to burn down the Grace-house?" I stared at the woman. "What would I get out of it? I just got a job here, and I'm looking forward to my payment of Grace as much as the next employee. Burning Grace would be a disgusting waste."

A crowd had gathered at the end of the dock, no doubt altered by my earlier scream, and Byssa and Hades jogged toward me.

"Are you okay, Lune?" Byssa wrapped her arm around my waist.

"I'm fine, but someone tried to burn down the Grace-house."

"Allegedly," Sandy said. "We're not sure of that. Lune couldn't see the details of what happened."

"I saw someone with a gas can," I said doggedly. Why did no one believe me? "And he jumped in the water after."

"Probably an embarrassed guest trying to escape the

consequences of his mishap," said the man with the lantern, and the other two nodded sagely. Only Levi stared at me with a worried expression.

"Why would someone burn the Grace-house?" said Hades. "Nobody who knows what it is wants to see it burn, and the humans don't understand or care."

Byssa rubbed my shoulder in comforting circles, although her eyes crinkled in worry. "Let's go eat," she said. "The trouble is over. You must be hungry."

Would no one act if they thought it was an accident? What would prevent the arsonist from returning to finish the job? I shivered at the thought of so much precious Grace burning.

If no one believed my story, then it was up to me to find the truth.

CHAPTER 7

An older man and woman strode onto the dock, their faces wreathed in frowns. Both their heads sported white hair, although from the woman's pale skin, I guessed hers wasn't entirely the result of age.

Levi walked up to them, and they conversed in low voices. As Levi spoke, the woman put her hand on her chest.

Were these Levi's parents, the owners of the Lodge? They looked nothing like their son, but I couldn't guess who else they might be.

Byssa tried to tug me forward, but I gently disengaged from her arm.

"I need to make sure they know it was arson," I told her. "Since no one else saw the gas can."

Byssa bit her lip and nodded. I walked toward the others, anxious to make the truth known. If the Gracehouse were in danger, so too were my hopes.

"Hi," I said when I was close enough. The others glanced at me in surprise. "I'm Lune Seafields."

"She's a new employee," Levi cut in. "Lune, this is Seafoam and Kane, my parents and the owners of the Lodge."

"I saw someone light that fire," I continued. "A hooded man with a red container of gasoline."

Seafoam narrowed her pale eyes at me. "You'll forgive me if I'm skeptical. We have never yet had a disgruntled employee or a guest we haven't won over. Why would anyone do that?"

My jaw clenched. All I saw was the same disdain I'd seen every day at the Seamount. The same looking-down-their-noses that full sirens did at my freckled skin and small feet. I knew the Lodge had been too good to be true.

"I don't know," I forced out. "Everyone has enemies somewhere. If you give me the key to the Grace-house, I can look for clues. Burning it down was obviously his goal."

Seafoam drew back, and Kane stared at me.

"That won't be necessary." Kane rubbed his chest. His forehead glistened with sweat despite a cool breeze from the water. "We can look ourselves. Thank you for telling us what you think you saw."

Levi threw me an apologetic glance, but he let himself be drawn down the dock by his mother, Kane following close behind. My breathing came fast and uneven, and my fingers twitched.

Byssa snuck her hand into the crook of my arm.

"Let's go eat," she said. "You can tell me more about it there."

I took a deep breath and tried to release my frustration. Then my jaw set. An arsonist had targeted the Grace-house. If I were the only person who believed that, then I was the only one who would investigate. Without that Grace, Branc and I would be acquaintances for far longer than I wanted.

Fear traveled down my back like a drip from an iceberg. Snooping around for clues of the arsonist's identity might expose me to the visiting pale folk more than was safe. If any one of them knew where I'd been on the night I'd left the Seamount—how I'd hurt one of their own—I'd be done for.

Grace, I reminded myself sternly. Freedom. No risk, no reward.

And maybe, if I discovered who the arsonist really was, the Lodge would be so grateful that they would reward me with even more Grace. I could leave early, pay off my debt, and be free of Branc and all he represented. My frustration melted away and left a focused purpose.

"Come on." Byssa tugged my motionless form. "I'm starving. And the burned wood smells terrible."

Byssa's comment made me sniff the air. She was right—the scent of charred wood, even as saturated with salt as the old dock was, grated on the delicate membranes in my nostrils. Burning was such a *wrong* smell.

My feet followed Byssa's gentle insistence, but Levi's voice stopped me again.

"Lune, wait." He strode up to us on the swaying dock, his forehead furrowed. "Can we talk for a minute?"

Byssa squeezed my arm. "I'll meet you at dinner."

She and Hades left, Hades throwing us a curious glance as Byssa dragged him to the grassy lawn of the main building. I turned to Levi and crossed my arms.

"Yes?" I uncrossed my arms and schooled my face into an expression of concern instead of belligerence. Levi was my boss, after all. I might be peeved at his mother, but I still wanted to keep my job.

"I just want to get my facts straight." He gestured at the dock. "You came down here to put away your cleaning supplies, right? Then what happened?"

"I put them in the supply shed." I nodded at the floating building. "When I closed the door, movement at the end of the dock caught my eye. A man in a hoodie was fiddling with a small red gas can, then he splashed gasoline on the side of the Grace-house and lit it." I shuddered involuntarily at the memory of the licking flames crawling too fast up the building like a dreadful parody of disturbed sea snakes. "When he noticed me, he grabbed the gas can and dived into the water. He must have worked hard to stay under with that container."

"Either the gas can was still mostly full, or he was at least part pale folk." Levi stared across the shore, his gaze turned inward. "A regular human wouldn't have the strength to stay under with a buoyant container like that."

"He looked pretty comfortable in the water. And he splashed a ton of gasoline on the wall." My arms crossed again of their own accord. "Do you believe me or not?"

Levi's gaze snapped back to me, and I looked into his searching blue eyes.

"Yes," he said slowly. "I don't know why someone would burn down the Grace-house, but I also don't know why you would bother lying about this. It's worth investigating, anyway." His expression turned sheepish. "Sorry about my parents. They can't imagine that anyone would not love the Lodge. I get it—it's a great place— but I'm also realistic, and I don't want to sweep evidence under the rug just because it suits me."

I was on the fence about the Lodge being such a great place, but I could get behind Levi's realism.

"I'll look into it," I offered. "Since I saw the guy, his

build and all that. It would be such a waste if he destroyed the Grace-house."

"Thanks." Levi stared at me. If he knew of my deal with Branc, he wouldn't wonder at my zeal. "I appreciate that. But we'll have to tread carefully. The lower-profile we can make this for the guests' sake, the better."

"And your parents wouldn't approve," I guessed.

Levi shifted his feet. "They're getting ready to retire, and they don't have the energy for a scandal. But if there really is a would-be arsonist, I need to figure out who it is and why. I don't want to start my stint as head manager under a cloud of Grace-smoke."

I shivered at the hideous image his description conjured and considered my position. I didn't need to help Levi—it sounded like he was willing to believe me and do something about it—but I didn't trust that he could solve the mystery without help. Seafoam's words hung over me like a miasma of vent outpourings, tainting Levi by proxy, but I tried to shake them off. The more of us working together, the faster we could uncover the arsonist and protect the Grace-house. My mouth watered at the phantom memory of Grace on my tongue.

"I'll look around," I said. "Carefully. And tell you what I find."

I left Levi on the dock to oversee clean-up of the fire mess and trudged my way up a green slope to the waiting Lodge. Laughter and chatter spilled out of open windows. The upper floor, level with the ground beyond the Lodge, boasted full glass walls that allowed guests to enjoy sweeping vistas of the coast. Below this level, smaller windows lined a more cramped dining area. Hades's striped hair winked at me from the far window, and I hastened my steps to join my friends.

Seafoam and Kane climbed the slope toward the parking lot, Sandy in front of them. A seagull watched the trio with interest from its perch on the lodge roof. Kane's steps were labored, and Seafoam held his arm in a tight grip. Kane stumbled to his knees then clutched the shirt over his chest, his eyes frantic and his breath fast.

"Kane." Seafoam kneeled in front of her husband. Her gaze raked his features. "It's your heart again, isn't it? Sandy, can you help me take him to our suite?"

"It looks pretty serious," Sandy said with a twisted mouth and furrowed brow. She tucked her hand under Kane's arm and helped Seafoam haul him to his feet. "Do you want me to call an ambulance?"

"It's nothing we don't already know about," Seafoam said. "Chronic condition, I'm afraid. Age takes down the best of us. Rest and medication will solve it for now."

Sandy nodded, and the two women supported a laboring Kane into the Lodge's front doors.

I slunk into the dining hall, unwilling to intrude on the emergency without being able to offer more help. Had the stress of the Grace-house's close call triggered Kane's condition? I rubbed my arms against a shiver that raised the hairs on my skin. Did the arsonist understand the consequences of what he'd done tonight?

Inside the dining hall, floor fans blasted air across the hot space. Loud chatter assaulted my ears from staff eating their dinners at long tables. Along the back, a casual buffet filled a counter. I grabbed a plate, suddenly ravenous after my afternoon scrubbing walls clean of algae.

The table groaned with shrimp tacos, halibut enchiladas, seafood jambalaya, and fish and chips, along with an assortment of sides. Masquerading as garnishes were bites of Seamount flavors like squid eggs and anglerfish liver. I took a little of everything. Then, with a plate heavy enough to need two hands, I picked my way between sprawling chairs to Byssa and Hades in the corner. Kim from our dorm was also there, along with a lean man in his mid-twenties with floppy brown hair and a quiet-looking guy with a scar on his cheek that drew his mouth down on one side.

"Hi," Kim said brightly, her purple ponytail swinging as she looked our way. "It's Lune, right? This is Darren, my boyfriend." Darren nodded, and his hair flopped over his forehead. "We're working here for the summer. And that's Otto. He works in the kitchen, but even cooks have to eat sometime, right?"

"It's my day off." He smiled shyly at me, the scar on his cheek making his expression lopsided.

"Otto and I have been exchanging recipes," Byssa said. "Apparently, I haven't explored the full powers of sage."

I nodded at everyone and squeezed in beside Byssa.

"What did Levi want?" she whispered. Darren glanced at me with interest.

76

"He believes me about the arsonist," I whispered back. "We're going to ask around for clues."

I took a bite of my taco, noting with pleasure the flakes of dried seaweed that hinted at flavors from the Seamount. I didn't mention Kane's health to anyone—it wasn't my place—and the news would spread quickly enough if it were serious. I might not be able to help Kane's heart, but I could help Levi solve the mystery that had triggered his father's condition.

I looked sharply at the others. "Hey, you three haven't seen anything strange lately, have you? Do you know of anyone with a grudge against the Lodge?"

Kim's laugh tinkled lightly above the voices surrounding us. She shared an amused glance with her boyfriend.

"Everyone loves the Lodge," she said.

"Someone might have given them a bad review at some point." Darren slurped his water. "But I've never heard about it."

"Wait, what about William, the gardener?" Kim pointed a piece of roasted parsnip at Darren. "Wasn't there that rumor floating around? How he and Seafoam got into an argument last month?"

"But no one actually saw it," Otto piped up. "A rumor is just a rumor. Besides, I can't imagine it. William has worked here for years. He's a fixture. But he's an amazing gardener, and he could get a job anywhere else if he wanted to."

"And why would he want to burn down the Grace-house?" Hades asked. "He's half-siren. Doesn't Grace work for him?"

Darren shrugged. "As far as I know. He turned up to Grace-Harvest last year."

"Tell me more about the Grace-Harvest celebration." Byssa sat up straight, her eyes shining. "I'm so excited we can be here for it."

"It's lovely." Kim's eyes grew dreamy, and she put her chin in her hands. "The dancers are so elegant, and the way everyone moves and sings together, it's just magical. And the Grace! Does it ever taste better than fresh, right at the ceremony?"

I stuck my fork into an enchilada with more force than it warranted. I had zero interest in joining Grace-Harvest celebrations at the Lodge. I was here to work, get my money and Grace, and get out. My new goal of uncovering an arsonist only meant I had even less time to consider celebrating.

Soon after, Kim and Darren left, hand-in-hand. Hades hailed a new acquaintance and darted out of the dining hall with Otto to join him. I chewed steadily through my meal and tried to absorb the delicious flavors even through my preoccupation. Byssa glanced at me when we were alone.

"Are you okay?" she said quietly. "It must have been scary. I know you're not great with fire. Remember my birthday cake a few months ago?"

I snorted, although the episode hadn't been as funny at the time. Hades had burst out of Byssa's kitchen with a towering cake full of blazing candles, singing at the top of his lungs. I'd jumped away so hard that both I and my chair had fallen onto the floor with a thud.

"Yeah, I'm okay. Levi came soon enough and got a

bucket brigade going."

"Why are you so convinced that the fire was malicious?" Byssa asked.

"Why else would the man splash the Grace-house with gasoline? I know Levi's parents aren't convinced—Seafoam made it perfectly clear what she thought of me."

"What do you mean?" Byssa frowned. "She seemed nice to me."

"You didn't see it?" I played with my bread, my chest heating at Seafoam's disdain. "She couldn't help looking down her nose at me. Ugh, I hate full-folk so much."

"Wow." Byssa laid her hand on mine. "Seriously, I didn't get any of that. I know you had a rough time at the Seamount, but not everyone hates half-humans. Seafoam lives on land, for goodness' sake. She employs dozens of us." She patted my hand and sat back. "I think this one might be all in your head."

I shrugged. Byssa was good at seeing the best in people. It was helpful when she overlooked my flaws, but her innocence grated on my nerves sometimes. I forced the subject back to the fire.

"Levi found a lantern from the market at the end of the dock. They think a guest was trying out his new purchase, and the fire got out of control."

Byssa raised a hand to her mouth. Her wide eyes blinked over top.

"Oh, no," she whispered. "I think the fire was my fault."

CHAPTER 8

"What are you talking about?" I stared at Byssa in puzzlement from across my almost-empty plate. "You weren't even on the dock when the fire started."

"On my late afternoon guiding trip, I took two pale folk to the market. One of the guys was pretty cute, actually." Byssa cleared her throat when I raised an eyebrow in her direction.

"Did your hand vibrate so sensually when you laid it on his firm chest?" I teased.

Byssa kicked me under the table, but her cheeks colored.

"Shut up," she said. "Anyway, he bought a lantern, Fascinated by the idea of it, I think. I promised him that I'd show him how to use it when we got back to the Lodge, but I totally forgot." She twisted her hands together. "I bet he tried to light it. None of the pale folk knows how to deal with fire."

"Rightfully so." I shuddered. "Nasty stuff. But you can't blame yourself for someone else's actions. If a guest doesn't wait for instruction, it's not your fault." Byssa continued to look guilty, so I continued, "Besides, I don't think the fire was an accident. Your guest wouldn't have a gas can, would he? I thought those lanterns were for candles."

"But did he know that?" Byssa stared at me, guilt crinkling the corners of her eyes. "Maybe he heard about gasoline somewhere."

I didn't believe Byssa's version of the fire, but due

diligence was the responsible course of my investigation.

"Why don't you ask the good-looking guest where he was at the time of the fire? Let's rule him out."

Byssa nodded and jumped up. "Yes, good. I'll do it right now if I can find him."

Byssa raced out of the dining hall, and I slowly picked at the remains of my meal. I could have gone with Byssa to interrogate her handsome guest, but that would mean talking to a full siren from the Seamount. Byssa knew nothing of my real reasons for leaving my former home, and I wanted to keep it that way. That, and I had no intention of facing justice for my so-called crime. Self-defense might work as a justification on land, but harming one of the upper echelons of the Seamount carried dire consequences.

I pushed away my plate, slightly nauseous from eating too much and the direction of my thoughts. I needed to investigate this fire, but I couldn't expose myself to too much attention. I'd let Levi take on the pale folk.

I dipped in for a swim after dinner. Byssa was still hunting down her good-looking guest, so I let her be. Hades had left with two other guys to head into town. He'd yelled at me across the parking lot to join them, but I'd waved his invitation off. Hades wouldn't be back until well past midnight, and I wanted a clear head tomorrow. Not only did I have work, but I had a crime to solve. I could join his chaos once the looming threats of arson and discovery by pale folk were over.

Maybe I'd be free of Branc by then, too. The thought cheered me up immensely. On the fateful day I said goodbye to him forever, I would put Hades's partying to shame.

I caught myself whistling as I strode out of the bunkhouse a few minutes later with my white hair tucked into a ballcap. I'd only learned how to whistle a few weeks ago, after Hades had teased me about it. I wasn't very good yet—the sounds were breathy and out of tune—but practice made perfect.

The sun was setting along the western horizon where the bulk of Vancouver Island distantly lay in the sea like the back of a great sea beast. The water gleamed bronze, reflecting brilliant oranges and reds of the sky.

I stopped to gaze in wonder. Sunsets were new to me, and reds and oranges were one of my favorite discoveries of life on land. Those hues were the first to disappear underwater, and my entire life had been filled with variants of blues and greens. Their vibrancy was almost too much at times, but a good sunset always stopped me in my tracks.

Once the light faded into a pale imitation of its former self, I shook my head and continued to the beach. A swim before bed would calm me. I thought best in water, and when I didn't want to think, I relaxed best there, too. Land was fine, even enjoyable at times, but water was my element.

My feet led me down a path south through the woods. I followed signs until a side trail spat me out at a tiny cove embraced by shallow rocky cliffs under twisted arbutus trees. A piece of peeling bark disengaged from its tree and drifted to the water's surface.

With a contented sigh, I stripped off my outer clothes and stepped gladly into gently lapping waves. I picked my way over slimy rocks and jagged shells to find deeper water. My feet were tougher than they were a year ago, but they still weren't up to tromping on rough surfaces.

When the water was thigh-high, I shook hair out of my face and dived after a final breath of air. Cool darkness enveloped me, and I closed my eyes to better feel my surroundings with the senses of my skin.

The cove was so tiny as to be almost claustrophobic, so I focused on scuttling crabs on the sand and the vast openness before me. I followed the deepening seafloor, and soon enough, my undulations brought me into the strait.

The water was cooler here, and a current pulled me northward. I allowed it, enjoying the drifting sensation. I craved control over other aspects of my life, but I didn't mind the ocean pushing me about, especially when I was powerful enough to escape. The sea had no motives.

I sent out a long, low call. I'd released Squirter a few days before leaving Vancouver to give him a chance to make the journey. It was a long distance, but I knew he would enjoy the trip. He was an adventurous little cephalopod. If he were in the area, he would hear me. I would try tomorrow if he didn't respond tonight.

My body twisted in loops and swirls of half-forgotten motions. The Grace-Harvest dances were on my mind after Byssa's excitement over the upcoming celebrations.

I stopped, annoyed at myself. I didn't need to dwell in

my past. The Seamount was finished for me, along with everything it stood for. I didn't want to participate in its rituals, not anymore. There was no point.

The senses of my skin painted a picture of a long body in the distance. It swam with sinuous elegance, but its head was larger than that of a snake, and no snake was that long. It wasn't vast enough to be a ligan, the enormous sea serpents local to the Seamount that occasionally got loose from the mer folk's careful tending.

I frowned. What sort of creature was it? The current muffled its signal so I couldn't feel a clear picture of the strange animal. I debated swimming closer.

A tiny, eight-armed blob jetted toward my back. The movement barely registered on my skin before the blob landed on my shoulder with a familiar suction.

My closed-mouth grin was wide, and I reached up to give Squirter a rub on his mantle. He hummed with pleasure.

You're here, I hummed and gestured back at him with the simple communication we shared. *Happy.*

Happy, he said. His tentacle played with my ear and his skin rippled with texture. His striated green eye stared into mine. *Play?*

I grinned again and twisted in midwater.

Play.

Sheila worked me hard the next two days, and the

unaccustomed activity sent me to bed early after chill evenings playing cards with the other workers. I kept my eyes and ears open for clues about the arsonist, but nothing emerged. Complacency settled over me like silt on a flatfish as time passed and nothing else suspicious occurred.

A knock on the dormitory door surprised us the next morning. Byssa spat out her toothpaste in the sink, and Kim bounced to the door.

"Everyone decent?" she called out. I hastily buttoned my work blouse and nodded. Kim flung the door open.

Levi stood at the threshold, his dark hair wet. He glanced around the room until his eyes lit on me.

"Morning, ladies," he said. "Lune, could I speak to you for a moment?"

I followed him out the door into the central hall between the men's and women's rooms.

"I know you signed up for cleaning duties," he said, his forehead creasing. "But Darren and Frank are indisposed, and we have a desperate shortage of guides. I have eight groups signed up, and only three guides. Would you please consider taking over for the day?"

My face must have shown my reluctance.

"It's easy," he said quickly. "Just follow the guests, pay for their purchases—all guests run a tab with the Lodge that we tally up at the end—and keep them out of trouble."

"What happened to Darren and Frank?"

"Darren twisted his ankle jumping off a tree branch, and Frank is too hungover to avoid puking on the guests' shoes." Levi's brows contracted. "But we're so busy that

I can't fire him. I never thought I'd look forward to a slow season, but there you are. I'll be happy to see the back of Grace-Harvest, at least."

"Me, too," I said with feeling. Levi quirked an eyebrow at me, but I had no intention of explaining my comment. "I don't know. Guiding isn't my thing."

I didn't want to risk the Seamount inhabitants recognizing me, which was far too likely if I interacted with them as a guide. Who knew if my likeness was scratched over the Seamount to warn others of a criminal on the loose? Levi's face twisted.

"Please?" He glanced around as if searching for inspiration, then his eyes fixed on my face. "A bonus. I'll pay you double-time for today."

My breath hissed involuntarily. Every extra dollar counted.

"And a package of Grace," he said. "Tomorrow evening."

"Fine," I said. I wondered what else he would offer if I held out for longer, but I couldn't bring myself to string him along any further. The poor guy was stressed enough as it was. "I'll do it. But don't expect any guide-of-the-year antics."

Levi's face split in a wide smile like a ray of sunlight piercing the depths.

"You're the best. Grab a guide uniform from the storeroom and meet me at the front desk in twenty minutes. I'll give you a rundown before your first guests arrive."

He turned on his heel and strode away. I wanted to regret agreeing to his request, but his bright smile made up for it. My fingers drummed on my leg before I darted back into the sleeping quarters. I needed a better disguise to meet pale folk.

My new guide uniform was more form-fitting than my cleaning outfit, and I tugged at the waistband of my skirt to adjust it. I'd had to borrow shoes from Byssa after she'd heard what I was doing today. She'd firmly put her foot down over the subject of my boots, so now I minced along in a tight pair of black ballet flats, hating every minute of their squeezing containment.

My wig and contacts were firmly in place, and I had a pair of sunglasses and a hat at the ready. The summer sun was already warm on my head as I strode across the lawn, so my accessories were unremarkable. With luck, I wouldn't be recognizable.

"There you are," Sandy said when I entered the front desk area. She shuffled papers in her hand and fastened them together with a paperclip. I surprised myself by feeling let down that Levi wasn't here like he'd promised. "Levi asked me to give you the rundown on guiding. Tim will drive you to the market and pick you up an hour later. Your main job is to act as interpreter, but your second, equally important job is to keep the guests out of trouble."

"What kind of trouble should I expect?" I'd been new on land before, so I had some inkling. Still, I wanted specifics to watch for.

"We like to keep a low profile at the Lodge." She glanced at me over her glasses, her brown eyes piercing me. "Avoid drawing attention if you can. Guests usually wear wigs or hats—too many white tresses stand out— and they are all equipped with human clothing. You can speak to them by holding their shoulders to feel vibrations. Try not to touch chests even though it's easier to hear. Don't let them siren anyone and keep interactions with humans to a minimum." She smiled brightly. "It will be fine. You'll have fun."

I sincerely doubted that, but the extra money and package of Grace that awaited me tomorrow night kept my mouth shut. I attempted a returning smile.

"Oh, here they are," Sandy said, her sharp gaze on the door. She bustled around the counter and reached out to place her hands on the incomers' shoulders.

I quickly pushed on my sunglasses to obscure my face and patted my auburn wig. Then, I turned and raked my eyes over my charges. A bobbed blond wig topped the woman's petite form. Her makeup was inexpertly applied, and a line at her neck exposed white skin underneath orange-tinted foundation. The man wore a wide-brimmed hat over sunglasses with a garish Hawaiian-print shirt. His hair had been badly colored with brush-in dye.

"I don't know if that shirt is low-profile," I murmured to Sandy.

She fought to keep her face straight and took her hands off the other two.

"Lune," she said loudly to the others with a finger pointed at me. "Your guide today." She turned to me.

"These two want to be called Jill and Bob."

I raised my eyebrow.

Sandy shrugged. "They asked William the gardener for human names. Those were the first ones that came to his head."

"Hello Jill, Bob." I reached out for their hands and placed one of each on my shoulders. My heart hammered in my chest as I waited for them to shriek with recognition, for their hands to grip my shoulders tightly to prevent my escape, for Jill to siren me into submission with her greater power. There was no chance that these two were on a restricted Grace diet.

They looked at me expectantly, and I let my breath out slowly. They had no idea who I was. I raised my own hands and began to hum and click so they could understand me.

*I'm your guide for today. Please don't do anything to draw attention to yourselves. If you want to ask a question of a merchant or buy something, tell me and I'll help. And above all—*I narrowed my eyes at the woman, the most likely of the two to use her abilities—*no sirening.*

Jill pursed her lips but nodded.

"Good," said Sandy. "Off you go. Tim is waiting."

I led the way to a passenger van, and we all piled in. The market wasn't far, and Tim let us out with instructions to be at this point in one hour. I checked my phone with a sigh. I could do this. It was easier knowing that Jill and Bob hadn't recognized my face. I didn't know how notorious I was. Had my image been carved on bone tablets all over the Seamount? My pursuers thought I was dead, but if someone recognized me...

89

CHAPTER 9

At the market, Jill and Bob wandered off immediately, and I trailed after the duo with my heart in my throat. Would the other marketgoers recognize them as outsiders? What would they say?

After five minutes of slowly following the pale folk, my anxiety morphed into boredom. No one gave the odd couple a second glance except to evaluate their interest in a product. The market was busy this morning, and Bob's Hawaiian-print shirt was not the most eye-catching garment in the crowd. Some women wore flowing skirts, a man walked by with suspenders and no top, and a whole stall was dedicated to selling tie-dyed shirts. My shoulders relaxed, and I resigned myself to an hour of amusing myself with people-watching.

Jill pointed at a table of jewelry, and Bob waved me over.

We want the leaf bracelet, he said once I'd placed my hand on his shoulder. *To remember our trip by.*

I nodded, although inwardly I was bemused. When would Jill wear the bracelet? As far as I knew, leaving the Seamount wasn't allowed. Visitors to the Lodge had to sneak out for their clandestine pleasure trips. Although, I wouldn't put it past the upper echelon to have their own rules. They probably wore land souvenirs in their own caves at the top of the Seamount, flashing their bracelets and trinkets at each other, laughing at the scum scraping a living below.

My jaw tightened, but I refrained from speaking my

mind to Bob. Instead, I nodded and stepped forward.

"How much for the silver bracelet with the leaf charms?" I asked the vendor. When she named her price, I smiled sweetly and handed over the Lodge credit card Sandy had given me. I would help Jill and Bob pay for their souvenir, but no one had mentioned bargaining for the best price. These two could afford it.

The rest of the hour was much of the same. My gaze traveled listlessly over the market wares. Without money, looking for purchases for myself was a lesson in dissatisfaction. Not that I wanted any of this tat. Except for the beaded bracelet. And the knife with a carved wooden handle was a thing of beauty...

A table with blown glass lanterns caught my eye. They were artfully displayed on different levels covered with a tablecloth of black velveteen. I wanted to run my hands over the fabric, so unlike anything under the sea. A few lanterns were lit with flames that flickered mysteriously even in the broad sunlight that bothered my eyes without sunglasses.

The lanterns were identical to the one that reputedly started the fire last night. I drew closer. What clues could I discover here?

"Would you like a lantern to light your way?" A willowy woman in ragged overalls and a tie-dyed tee-shirt clearly bought from the neighboring stall addressed me. I started to shake my head automatically, then I looked at her more intently. I wanted to find out who the arsonist was, didn't I? Well, this was my first lead.

"They're lovely," I said. "Have you sold many this week?" I didn't know if the arsonist had bought the lantern recently, but my questioning had to start somewhere.

"A fair few." She nodded at Jill and Bob, who poked at carved wooden birds at the next table. "They're popular with Lodge guests. I've probably shifted ten this week."

I bit my lip. Ten potential suspects were a lot, especially since I didn't know how to tease out more information without making the vendor suspicious.

"I guess guests like them as souvenirs," I said.

"Not just guests. I get the occasional employee buying, too. They're handy for our frequent power outages. We're too far from a city for the electric company to rush to fix downed power lines." She gave a deep chuckle. "Sandy bought one on Tuesday. You'll know Sandy from the front desk, of course."

"Of course." My eyes narrowed. The arsonist had been a man, I was sure, but that didn't mean that he was working alone. I shook off my suspicions and smiled brightly at the woman. "The lanterns are lovely, but I'm not supposed to be buying while I'm on the job."

"Looks like your charges are getting away." The vendor pointed, and my head whipped around. I scanned the crowd until Bob's garish shirt met my eye. A gap appeared in the crowd, and I saw what Jill was bent over for.

She tugged at her ugly black lace-up shoe—big for a human woman her size—to free her foot from its trappings. I'd almost got through this guiding tour without drawing attention. What was Jill trying to do?

I pushed through the crowd until I stood beside Bob.

With a hand on his shoulder, I spoke with hums and gestures.

What is she doing?

Bob put his hand on my shoulder in return. *Her shoes are too tight. She needs to take them off.*

I refrained from rolling my eyes with difficulty. My finger poked Jill to gain her attention, then I pointed toward the pick-up location.

You're drawing attention to yourselves, I said. *Most people don't walk around barefoot.* The suspender man chose at that moment to walk by us, his bare feet flapping on the pavement. I inwardly sighed. *Besides, your feet are too tender. You won't last three steps. Trust me.*

Bob searched my face. Had I said too much? Was he looking for signs of familiarity? Brusquely, I jerked my head to get them moving.

Jill had removed both of her shoes at this point, and she was gathering curious glances at her elongated white feet, the webbing between her toes nearly visible. I put a hand on the small of her back to propel her forward. She winced as pieces of gravel dug into her feet, and I held back from saying *I told you so* with difficulty.

A thread of sympathy wormed its way through my mind—I remembered my first few weeks in shoes, and how desperately uncomfortable I'd been—but I hardened my heart against Jill's discomfort. She had chosen to come here for a vacation. Our situations couldn't have been more different.

Suddenly, I longed to be scrubbing algae off walls. Anything was better than leading these entitled upper echelon-types around a human market.

It was with huge relief that I waved goodbye to Jill and Bob in the parking lot of the Lodge. They wandered toward the dockside rooms, and I entered the main Lodge to hand back the credit card and receipts for the guests' purchases.

Sandy greeted me with a smile, and I reminded myself of my investigation. Sandy was in possession of a lantern, and I intended to question her about it.

"How did it go?" she asked.

I placed the credit card on the counter and sighed. "Fine, I guess. Cleaning toilets is a lot less work."

"Like toddlers sometimes, aren't they?" Sandy chuckled and tucked a paperclip over files in her hand. "Well done. One of our groups canceled this morning, so you're off the hook for the afternoon guiding shift. Sheila will want to see you after lunch, though. Those toilets don't clean themselves."

"But they don't take off their shoes in public, either," I said. Sandy shook her head in sympathy, and I waved my comment away with a laugh. "Never mind. It was fine. Hey, I saw some pretty lanterns at the market. I wonder how well they're made. I don't have a lot of extra cash, so I try to buy things that last."

I failed to mention that there was no venting way I would ever buy something to deliberately light on fire. It was a ridiculous notion.

Sandy brightened. "Yes, I have one. Just bought it last

week. It's a gorgeous piece. I love the colors flickering on the wall once it's lit. It's great quality. Belinda, the maker, does a splendid job." She frowned. "Don't take the broken one on the dock the other day as an indication of poor workmanship. Whoever broke that one must have really given it a wallop."

"Good to know." Sandy certainly wasn't hiding her purchase. Surely, she would have downplayed her ownership if Levi currently had possession of the lantern. Still, I had to check every lead. "I'm curious about the long-term employees of the Lodge. This is the first time I've been here, you know. Do you live here all year round? What does your family do?"

"It's just me," she said comfortably. "I split from my no-good husband years ago. Our daughter's grown. She visits often, and to tell you the truth, I imagine she wouldn't come half as often if I didn't live in such a nice locale. Seafoam and Kane are very generous about letting us use the boats and beach, as long as we're respectful of guests. Do you know how much rooms go for? My daughter loves the chance to get out here. One day, I hope she'll bring me some grandkiddies too, but she can't settle on a man, so who knows when that day will be."

I firmly drew a line through Sandy's name in my head. As far as I could tell, she had no close family connection to anyone who might resemble the arsonist's build. I tried one more time.

"You must have a good rapport with the other employees, then. Lots of friends among them."

"Oh, for sure." She sat back and put her hands in her

lap. "Bridge night is every Tuesday with Mary, Priya, and Rosa, and William is always good for a cup of tea. He's busy this week showing his grandson the works. The boy thinks he'd like to garden here, too, but William doesn't suffer fools. The boy will have to work hard to keep up with William's standards. Seafoam made noises about William retiring soon, but he doesn't think much of the idea. Doesn't like to think he's getting old, even if the gardening is getting too much for him." Sandy shrugged, and her mouth twisted sideways. "Nobody likes to have their age pointed out to them. Seafoam was probably out of place."

I said goodbye to Sandy a few minutes later, but my head whirled with this new information. William had a young man working with him currently, and he was sore about Seafoam trying to force him to retire. It seemed far-fetched that William's disgruntlement over his pending retirement might transform into vengeance, but I didn't know the man. People had killed for less. If I wanted to express my rage, I would hit the Lodge where it hurt. Burning the Grace-house would send a strong message.

I left the front desk with more questions than before. I had a half-hour before eating lunch and resuming my cleaning duties, so I wandered down to the water and struck out on a northward path along the shoreline. Was this all Lodge property? Whoever had bought the place years ago must have been loaded. Maybe it hadn't cost much back then, when it had been even more remote than it was now.

The root-strewn trail turned a corner around thick salal bushes and opened to another beach. This bay was larger than the main one, and a small marina filled the close end. Above the hightide line, a large patio area filled the space between trees and sand. Gardens surrounded tranquil tables and benches, and a few Lodge guests lounged with drinks in hand from a tiny stand that offered refreshments. A young woman in uniform wiped the counter while she waited for customers.

My heart jolted. On the far edge of the patio, William wielded a pair of garden shears on a potted shrub. Next to him, with a look of concentration, a teen boy with short, sandy-brown hair and a lanky body not yet filled out shoveled compost on a row of spiky plants.

I kept my advance to a casual saunter. One or two of the guests glanced at me, but at the sight of my uniform, they quickly grew disinterested. Fine by me. Under the radar was where I liked to stay with potential pale folk. I pushed my sunglasses more firmly on my face and hitched on a smile.

"Hello," I said when I was close enough.

William looked up, and his face crinkled. "I recognize you. You're one of the new ones."

"My name's Lune." I nodded at the teen nearby. "I see you have an apprentice these days. Must be a relief to have a strong pair of hands to help you out."

William glanced at the boy critically.

"Finn has a lot to learn," he said. The boy colored but

kept his eyes firmly on his shovel as he worked. William sighed. "But I can't deny I like him doing the grunt work. As much as I hate to admit it, I'm getting old. Maybe it's time to shift into a supervisory role."

I blinked. Those were not the words of a man disgruntled with his employer to the point of arson. Could I scratch William off my suspect list?

"Someone needs to keep an eye on everything," I said.

William laughed. "That's the truth. Finn might get there one day, but he won't be ready to take over for a long while yet." He eyed me. "You're not in maintenance, are you?"

"Housekeeping," I said. "But Levi wanted me to ask around about the night of the Grace-house fire. Did you see anything that night? We're trying to figure out how it started."

William shook his head. "I was eating dinner in my room, didn't see a thing. Finn," he called out to the boy. "What were you up to last night? See anything down by the docks?"

"It was jambalaya night in the dining hall," he replied. "I didn't see anything, too busy eating. Martin from the kitchens was supposed to meet me there—it was his day off—but he never showed."

"Well, if you think of anything else, let Levi know," I said.

My mouth pressed into a firm line as I walked away from William and Finn. While they could still be suspects, it seemed less likely now. William's motive had disintegrated, and Finn hadn't truly been a suspect to start with. Finn's hint about Martin's disappearing act was a lead worth pursuing, although it was a tenuous clue. Investigating a crime wasn't as simple as I'd hoped.

I stood at the edge of the beach and stared out at the marina. It was only small—just boats for the Lodge and visitors, I'd been told—but there were enough to fill the three connected docks. Lines clinked on masts and flags flapped in a light breeze off the water.

I narrowed my eyes. Why did it look like the marina was expanding? I couldn't see anyone steering the boats away from the dock. I blinked and looked closer.

Almost every boat was drifting away from its mooring, untethered by ropes or chains. If left unchecked, the Lodge might be liable for thousands of dollars of damages.

CHAPTER 10

"William!" I shouted to the gardener near the marina. "The boats are untied."

I didn't wait for his answer. Instead, I pounded down the shifting dock, past pilings encrusted with barnacles and mussels, until I reached the nearest boat. It hadn't drifted far, and I leaped aboard easily and grabbed the painter. With another quick leap back to the dock, I wrapped it around a cleat and raced to the next boat.

Thundering footsteps alerted me to the arrival of Finn. Without speaking, he leaped aboard the next boat to grab the rope, and I followed suit.

We managed to tie up ten boats in this way. At the end of the dock, I stopped and gazed in dismay at three other boats. They had drifted too far away to jump to.

"Now what?" Finn stood beside me, panting.

I glanced at him. "Can you swim?"

He looked at me through gray eyes and gave a wry smile. "Better than most."

I nodded, kicked off my shoes, and dived.

My body cut through the green water like a shark fin through a wave, although my clothes restricted my movements with irritating flaps. My eyes adjusted, and I struck out for the nearest hull. A sloshing sound told me that Finn had followed me in, and I twisted my head to look at him. He grinned and undulated faster to catch up.

We surfaced on the far side of the vessel. My wig pulled at my scalp, and I regretted not removing it before diving in. I pursed my lips.

"Do we climb on and steer it to dock?" I stared at Finn. "I don't know how to drive a boat."

"I doubt the keys are in the ignition." His eyes searched the hull. "It's not that windy out, and the current is light. Could we push it back?"

In answer, I swam to the hull and placed my hands on the painted wood. Finn swam beside me, and together we kicked as hard as we could.

For the first minute, nothing happened. Then, as we gained momentum, the boat slid through the water.

"Got it," a familiar voice yelled. The boat rocked, then Levi's head leaned over the side. "Grab the closer boat if you can. I'll get the motorboat and push the far one back to dock."

I nodded, and Finn and I submerged to swim to the next boat.

It took a solid ten minutes, but we managed to push the drifting sailboat back to dock. I hauled myself out of the ocean and squeezed water out of my wig. Finn climbed out and shook his head like a dog, and I laughed.

Levi tied up his motorboat and jumped onto the dock. He walked toward us and ran his hands through his own hair. It stood on end in an adorable, unkempt way that mimicked hair in the ocean in a pleasing fashion.

"You two were amazing," he said. "Not a scratch on any boat."

Finn murmured something, then ambled toward his grandfather. I crossed my arms but couldn't stop my mouth from smiling.

"Guess I earned that double-time pay today."

"Did you ever." Levi glanced at the marina, and his

brow furrowed. "What happened, anyway? William rushed to the Lodge, shouting that the boats were loose. How did they get that way?"

I shrugged, considering for the first time the events that led to the uproar.

"I didn't see anything, but almost every boat had been untied."

"None of the painters were cut or torn." Levi's jaw tightened. "This was deliberate. Some prankster?"

Levi clearly didn't believe his own suggestion, and neither did I.

"You think this is connected to the arson," I said quietly.

"Boats loosened from the marina? Damages could have been major. And it's the sort of 'accident' that can't be pinned on anybody, except maybe poor oversight." Levi ground his teeth. "Why do I feel like someone is trying to discredit the Lodge?"

"Who would want to? It seems like a strange desire."

"I don't know." His face grew somber, and I had an impulse to smooth his forehead with my fingers. "But I need to find out."

"I'm following a few leads," I offered. I didn't have much, but giving Levi information might assuage my desire to touch his face, which I heartily disapproved of. "Nothing concrete yet, but I'll let you know what I find."

I left Levi to tie the boats more securely to the dock

while I wandered to the bunkhouse to change into my cleaning clothes. I got a few strange looks from guests as I dripped by.

"Did you fall into the water?" one older lady asked. She was clearly human, given her physical features and her shock. "It might be summer, but that ocean water is always freezing."

It hadn't occurred to me to be cold—my body didn't process ocean temperatures as anything other than pleasant—but I wrapped my arms around myself and shook my shoulders to pretend to shiver.

"I'm going to get changed," I said, and the woman clucked but let me go.

At the empty bunkhouse, I stripped off my sodden clothes and wig and left them hanging on a bathroom rack, then I slipped on my cleaning uniform and a ballcap. If I were quick, I'd still be able to catch the end of lunch before my next shift. I thought longingly of the Grace Levi had promised me tomorrow night, a reward for my extra work today. Maybe I could take just a little of it before I tucked the rest away for Branc.

Like thinking of Branc had summoned him somehow, my phone rang. My heart sank as I answered.

"Hi, Branc."

"Lune." Branc's smooth voice flowed over my eardrums like an oil slick. "Your target arrives tomorrow afternoon. He's an upper echelon siren straight from the Seamount. An older man, old enough to be your father. When he visited before, he went by the name Tyrell. Find him tomorrow tonight and ask him about the Grace supply chain and the political environment that affects

103

it." He paused. "Got it?"

"Yes," I said tonelessly.

"Make sure you take some Grace before you siren him. I want top-quality information."

The line went dead, and I cursed and slammed the phone on my bunk. There went my evening tomorrow. Instead of a night swim with Squirter, Grace pulsing through my veins, I would have to extract information from an unsuspecting visitor.

My stomach squirmed. I wouldn't win any employee of the month award by sirening a guest of the Lodge. I pushed aside Levi's accusing face in my mind and took a deep breath. I wouldn't make Tyrell do anything terrible. All I was getting was information. Then I would walk away and he would be none the wiser.

My brain tried to agree, but my heart knew better. Sirening was a part of my past that I didn't like to resurrect. Too often, I'd been forced to do things against my will by the songs of stronger sirens. I didn't want to embrace that side of my heritage.

I squashed down my guilt. I didn't have much more of this to do. A few more weeks, and I'd have enough money to pay Branc. I could manage a few more objectionable tasks.

I was almost home free. Hopefully, Branc wouldn't make the cost too high to pay the next time he asked for a favor.

The next day, Sheila put me to work scrubbing after telling me that Martin was on his days off. With no one to question, I focused on my work, and it was with tired but contented steps that I wandered to the dining hall for dinner. Hades regaled me with stories of the pale folk he'd guided to a mining museum—including their horrified reaction to the tour operator's suggestion to get into a replica mining cart on rails—and Byssa nearly spit out her salmon with laughter.

"My groups didn't do anything that ridiculous today," she said with a gasp, wiping her streaming eyes. "The last one only wanted help getting jam from the corner store. Said he'd been here before and really liked strawberry. He always stays in room five, apparently. He's a repeat customer who knows what he wants."

My hands stilled on their knife and fork. As casually as I could, I asked, "Do your groups tend to give themselves human names? My two yesterday morning wanted me to call them Jill and Bob."

"Oh, yeah." Byssa chuckled. "The older guy at the end of the day, he'd chosen Tyrell as his name."

Kim leaned over from a nearby bench with bright eyes. "I heard about one that wanted to be called Slug. He couldn't be convinced that his true name didn't translate well into English."

"If they don't have a name chosen already, I do it for them." Hades stabbed a prawn with a flourish and used it to gesticulate. "Today I guided Jack Sparrow and Davy Jones to a wine tasting."

I laughed with the others, but my heart sank. Finding Tyrell had been too easy. Now, I had no excuse not to complete my task tonight. Vents, I hated Branc.

I stayed with Byssa and Hades to play cards for an hour with Kim and a few other employees. Halfway through, Levi entered the noisy dining hall and beckoned me to join him.

"Your extra pay." He slipped an envelope into my hand, along with a small package. "And your Grace. I can't thank you enough for helping out yesterday."

I tried to smile, but it slipped off my face quickly when I remembered what I was planning to use the Grace for.

"Glad it worked out." I nodded toward the card game. "Are you going to join us?"

Levi looked wistfully at the laughing group. "I wish. But I still have paperwork to do. And I'm checking the employment records for a full list of staff, mainly so I can cross off those with an alibi for the night of the arson. My parents are planning to retire, but I didn't think they would hand over the reins this soon. It's a lot to juggle." He shook his head as if to shake his thoughts away. "It's fine. Go, enjoy yourself."

Levi left, and I returned to the others, my mind swirling with thoughts of Levi growing up here, and what must have changed with his increased responsibility. Had he used to be a fixture in this dining hall?

After a few hands of rummy—I was a terrible card player at the best of times, even more so when distracted—I made my excuses and walked to the bunkhouse to change. It felt wrong to siren a guest wearing Lodge clothing. If I were to do this, I wanted it to be separate from my duties here. It was a distinction only in my mind, but it made me feel better, nonetheless.

Clothed in my favorite jean skirt, boots, and a tee-shirt with the illustration of a flowing jellyfish on it, I left the bunkhouse. I let my feet take me on a meandering path to avoid suspicion, but no one was watching. Guests sat on the lit patio enjoying late-evening drinks, but dusk had fallen over the beachfront.

With one last glance around, I walked along the dock to the pale folk rooms and pulled open the nautilus shell doorhandle. My eyes scoured the doors for room numbers in the dim blue lighting. Number five was on the left side, three doors down. I took the package of Grace out of my pocket and stared at it. It contained enough for one solid dose. To get the answers I needed tonight, I would have to take it all.

I blew air out forcefully through pursed lips, then tipped the envelope into my mouth without hesitating further. This Grace was freshly dried, and it tasted better than the stuff I was used to these days. Flavors exploded on my tongue, and I suppressed a groan of pleasure.

Soon enough, I swallowed and only the aftertaste remained. A hum of strength built up inside me little by little until I was confident in my power. With a clenched fist, I raised my arm and knocked.

A moment later, the door opened inward. An older man, his skin and hair colorless with his full-blooded pale folk heritage, stared at me. His eyes raked over my body, and I sighed inwardly. Maybe I hadn't needed to take the

Grace after all. I could have relied on my feminine powers of persuasion.

But sirening was easier, and then I could leave quickly and try to forget about this.

"Hi, there," I purred in English. I reached out and touched his shoulder to better transmit my hums of compulsion. I wanted to get this over with. "Can I come in?"

I didn't want any witnesses. A full-blooded female siren would spot my antics immediately, and she'd be powerful enough to stop me. Another man, not so much—women held the power in the Seamount, given their greater sirening abilities—but I still didn't want to advertise what I was doing.

A dazed look came over Tyrell. He stepped aside to allow me to enter. I slid inside and closed the door with a click.

"Thanks," I said, still touching his shoulder. "I have a few questions for you. Why don't we sit?"

He led the way to the couch and sank onto it. I followed, leaning into him with my chest against his arm and my face close to his. The couch's fabric was soft against my bare arm.

"Tell me," I whispered, my lips near his cheek. My breath against his skin made him shiver. "The supply chain of Grace from the Seamount. What troubles does it face?"

Tyrell took a deep, shuddering breath, then he started to talk. "It's under jeopardy from a coalition of pale and mer folk. The Grace-Harvest is looking slim this year, and this faction doesn't want to see any Grace leaving the Seamount. There is enough to go around, I'm sure, but distrust of half-humans is driving the sentiment. I'm doing what I can to mitigate, but they are persistent." He turned his face toward me, so his mouth was close to mine. "But Driftwood is a problem. He takes too much and doesn't distribute Grace fairly. Not the way the other distributors do. The land-based supply chain wants to squeeze him out of the equation, and soon."

He leaned forward, and I drew back to avoid his lips. I was done. I didn't understand everything Tyrell had said, but I'd found information for Branc, and that was enough for me.

"You won't remember me," I said, my vibrations shaking through our contact between chest and arm. "Once I leave, you will forget this conversation ever happened."

Tyrell nodded, confusion wreathing his face. I pushed up and nearly ran from the couch. I had enough presence of mind to check for hall occupants before I burst from his room and shut the door firmly behind me.

It was done. I could text Branc my findings, then finish my stint at the Lodge and wash my hands of this mess. This assignment was borderline ethical, but it was only information. A quiet voice inside warned me that Branc wasn't known for his philanthropy, and any information he wanted would likely be used for questionable purposes. I pushed the voice away. I was doing what I had to do and drawing lines when I could. My best was all I could manage.

I pushed open the door and breathed the warm evening air deeply. Grace still coursed through my veins, and I didn't want to waste it. It was time for a swim with Squirter.

Tyrell's confessions ran through my mind, and I stopped short. Supply issues were coming to a head. Did this have anything to do with the arson at the Gracehouse? It was possible, but I didn't understand how. I wanted to discuss it with Levi, but then I'd have to say where I'd found the information, and that wasn't an option. I scowled and turned left to find a quiet place to stash my clothes.

"Lune?"

I froze, then whirled around.

CHAPTER 11

Levi stood at the shoreline, silhouetted against the starry night with his head tilted in question.

"Levi," I said with a hand to my chest. "You startled me."

"Sorry." He glanced curiously at the dockside rooms. "What were you doing in there?"

Before his curiosity could morph into suspicion, I spat out the first lie I could conjure.

"I was cleaning today, and I thought I'd left my sponge," I babbled. "I didn't want to leave it lying around for guests to see. I must not have, though, because I couldn't see it. Maybe Sheila grabbed it."

Levi nodded, apparently satisfied with my explanation. My shoulders relaxed.

"Your hair looks good," he said suddenly. "I don't see you without your wig much. Your natural color suits you."

I touched my hair at Levi's mention. I wished he hadn't said anything—I was already self-conscious enough about its glaring paleness attracting attention—but my cheeks warmed at his compliment.

"Thanks."

Levi cleared his throat and looked at his feet. "Any leads on the investigation?"

I shook my head, wishing I could mention my most recent findings. "Not yet. But William's grandson told me about Martin, who works in the kitchen, how he disappeared during the arson attempt. I'm not sure what he looks like yet, but he's supposed to be back from his weekend break tomorrow. I'll let you know what I find."

"He has spiky green hair," Levi said. "He's hard to miss."

Levi sighed and ran his hands through his own hair. This time, it didn't fluff up as it had before, because it was wet.

"Did you go for a swim?" I asked. "It's a gorgeous night for it. You're half-siren, right? Do you feel the cold like a human?"

"No, I—had a shower." Levi gave me a wry smile. "I'm adopted."

"Oh." I looked him over. He didn't have any physical attributes that indicated pale folk heritage, but I'd thought he took after his human father. "I didn't realize."

"I know. It's strange that someone like me is running this place. My parents adopted me, then my brother Austin came along as a surprise."

"I was—well, not adopted, exactly—taken in by someone. I guess you'd call him my foster father." I smiled at the memory of Eelway, then the smile dropped from my face. I'd likely never see him again, and my chest ached at the thought. "My mother wasn't interested in raising a half-human."

Levi's mouth twisted in sympathy. "That's rough."

I waved his comment off, not wanting to dive into my sordid past. "I'm off for a swim. See you tomorrow."

He said goodbye, and I passed him on my way to the shore. My sensitive nose caught the scent of salt from his wet hair, and I frowned. Unless his shower piped in seawater, he'd been swimming. Why had he lied? And what, exactly, had he lied about?

I put the mystery of Levi's wet hair out of my mind, along with the sensation of uncleanliness after sirening for Branc. In the shadow of a sweeping cedar, I stripped off my outer layers and stuffed them into the crook of a branch. Land concerns could stay on land. Right now, I had Grace to enjoy, and a friend to swim with.

From a rock on the shore, I pushed off in an arcing dive. My body sliced into the water, and the extra edge the Grace gave me thrilled through my system. Sensations flowing across my skin heightened, the blackness of my surroundings lightened, and my legs kicked with strength. I wanted to breathe the water deeply. Was it worth it, for a short swim? I weighed the discomfort of switching between water and air against the joy of immersing myself fully in the ocean.

The ocean won. I opened my mouth and exhaled all air from my lungs, then drew water in.

My gut seized with involuntary spasms until my lungs expelled all air and my body remembered the steady pull in and out that water required. Air flushed through my lungs so quickly on land. Down here, breathing took a slower pace.

Once my breaths were calm, I sent out a call for Squirter. It was too much to ask that he would hang around and wait for the off chance that I would turn up, but I still had hope.

While I waited, my undulations carried me along the seafloor. I brushed against anemones, enjoying their sticky tickle against my bare skin, and chased a lazy lingcod for fun. It gave an irritated growl as it floated deeper, and I chuckled.

The water of my element washed away my sirening antics. Down here, I could relax and forget for a moment about the complications above. Was there anywhere without people wanting to control me? If it hadn't been for Byssa and Hades, I would have run away with Squirter months ago.

A tiny body jetted toward me, and I grinned in anticipation of Squirter's arrival. When he came level with my face and spread his arms out to stop, I reached out my hand to tickle his tentacle.

He must have mistaken my motion because he immediately made a gesture mimicking mine. The sweeping movement looked like the beginning of a prayer dance to Ramu, goddess of the sea. Automatically, I floated my other arm to follow the expected sequence.

My fists clenched. What was I doing? I hadn't prayed to Ramu for a year. She, along with the Seamount, was a part of my history, not my present. She had no place or purpose on dry land, and for better or for worse, that was my home now.

My face must have grown despondent, because Squirter jetted toward me and laid his tentacle over my cheek. His tiny suction cups gripped onto my skin, and I closed my eyes.

There was no point mourning for something that I couldn't change. I could never return to the Seamount and my old life, even if I wanted to. I might be in exile, but at least I wasn't sundered from Ramu. That was the fate awaiting me because of the crime I'd committed, that and death. Sundering before death—essentially excommunication from our spiritual beliefs—meant I would never join Ramu in her blessed whirlpool of souls after my last breath. I couldn't risk that, no matter how disconnected I felt from the goddess these days.

Sad? Squirter asked.

I shook my head and gave him a wobbly smile. *No. I have you.*

He positioned himself above my eyes and released a tiny cloud of black ink then jetted away. That was Squirter wanting to play tag. I laughed and gave chase, pushing my wistful sadness deep within.

Two mornings later, Byssa and I walked to the dining hall. We were a little late—I'd slept in and Byssa had curled her hair—and I was teasing Byssa about her vanity when she stopped and put her hand on my arm.

"Look," she said. "What's happening?"

Shouts of surprise and disgust filtered out of the open windows of the dining hall below and the restaurant above. A door slammed open, and two people stumbled out. One fell to his knees, and the other clutched the doorframe. Both vomited spectacularly onto the grass.

I turned away, my stomach roiling. Another door opened, this time onto the balcony of the restaurant.

Three guests hurtled out and released the contents of their stomachs to the balcony floor.

"Ugh," I said. "What the vents is happening? You know it'll be me that has to clean that all up."

"It has to be food poisoning," Byssa said in a hushed voice. "A virus wouldn't affect so many people so quickly."

Hades edged past the man clutching the doorframe and picked his way through clean grass to get to us. His brow was furrowed, an odd look on my usually carefree friend.

"Something was off," he said. "People are blaming spoiled kippers. Luckily, I hadn't started breakfast yet. Come on, let's borrow a Lodge van and run to the corner store for something to eat. I'm starving."

"Hades." Byssa glared at her brother. "Don't you think we should help these people? They need care, and Levi will want all hands on deck to deal with the fallout. Guests are ill, too."

Hades gave a long-suffering sigh, but he draped his arm over his petite sister's shoulders. "Fine, you and your sense of responsibility win. But you bet your blowfish that I'm going to submit my food receipt to the Lodge when I buy something at the market this morning."

I followed the siblings, my mind racing. This was too much, after the fire and the untied boats. This food poisoning wasn't an accident. My heartbeat sped up. Finn had said Martin had disappeared during the arson attempt. Was this my proof? He would have been in the perfect position to tamper with everyone's breakfast.

I almost stepped on Hades's heel in my eagerness to

find Martin and solve this mystery. I didn't know what his motivation could possibly be, but I didn't need it, if I had a proven suspect. Levi would be overjoyed to put these accidents to rest.

"Watch it, Lune." Hades raised an eyebrow at me. "I didn't know you liked cleaning so much. Is the Lodge work rubbing off on you?"

"Ha, ha," I said absently. My eyes scanned the windows of the dining hall, searching for Martin's telltale green hair. "Who doesn't love vomit?"

Byssa broke away to lead a new victim from the door to a bench nearby with a convenient flowerpot adjacent. I shuddered at the surprises waiting for William and Finn this afternoon.

Hades took an exaggerated breath and held it when he entered the dining hall. I followed him then wished I'd done the same. The stench of vomit hung heavy in the air, sour and sharp. At least a third of the breakfasters showed signs of sickness, and the rest around them looked green by association.

"What should we do?" Hades forced out through his held breath. "Corral the actively vomiting ones in one section?"

I had no idea. At least it wasn't likely contagious.

"Get them outside," I said. "No one can feel well with this stink."

"Everyone out," Hades bellowed. "Get fresh air."

There was a stampede toward the door, led by the healthy ones. The sick people limped toward the exit, holding their stomachs and occasionally pausing to expel their breakfasts.

I was ready to follow them outside—I needed to get cleaning supplies from the shed—but my eye caught on a young guy with spiky green hair. My heart sank. Martin's shirt was splattered with illness, and as I watched, he bent over with a grimace.

He was my only lead. As dedicated as the arsonist might be, I doubted he would poison himself to prove his innocence.

Now who would I investigate?

CHAPTER 12

I returned to the scene of the crime laden with cleaning supplies. Sheila marched ahead of me, armed with mops and bottles of bleach, and calling to anyone not currently bent over at the middle to help her.

A dark-haired young man ran out from a private door at the far end of the Lodge, closely followed by Levi. At Sheila's call, both men glanced toward her. Levi's eyes widened when he noticed the tumult, and he dragged the younger man along behind him. They met Sheila on the lawn and had a brief, passionate discussion which ended with Sheila patting Levi on the back and directing him to the front desk. Presumably, he needed to placate angry guests. I didn't envy him.

Levi grabbed the dark-haired man's arm again when he tried to slink away and pointed him toward the dining hall with a hard look. The other man looked sulky but complied. When I caught up with Sheila, I nodded at the retreating man.

"Who was that?"

"Austin," Sheila said in a resigned voice. "Levi's younger brother. Getting him to do anything productive around here is the bane of Levi's existence. And then Austin has the gall to get in a huff about Levi managing the Lodge." Sheila snorted. "This place would fall into shambles within a month of Austin at the helm. But what are we doing here gabbing away? That dining hall won't clean itself."

She sailed away, but I darted to the side when I

spotted Byssa walking toward the front of the Lodge. I dropped my mop to speak with her.

"Byssa," I said. "This wasn't an accident."

"They said it was spoiled fish, I think." She waved vaguely at the Lodge behind her. "It's too bad that so many guests and employees like seafood, otherwise not as many people would be affected."

"That's what I'm telling you. It was planned sabotage. First the fire, then the marina, and now food poisoning. They're trying to discredit the Lodge."

"But why?" Byssa screwed up her face. "And who?"

"That's what I don't know." I refrained from stamping my foot, but it was a near thing. "Levi and I are trying to figure it out, but I just lost my only lead, and I don't know where to go from here."

"I talked to the man I guided the other day," she said. "You know, the one who bought a lantern, and I didn't show him how it worked. Apparently, he was with his partner all that evening in their room, so I doubt it was him."

"Thanks for asking." I worried my bottom lip, aggravated at all the dead ends. "Now I don't know where to look for clues."

"I'm sure Levi can help you with ideas." Byssa's wide eyes narrowed with a sly look. "You're spending lots of quality time 'investigating' with him."

I scoffed. "You have an unhealthy obsession with my nonexistent love life. Get your own, you little lamprey."

Byssa giggled, and my heart lightened despite my annoyance at my lack of leads. I picked up my mop again, but before I could step forward, Byssa put up her hand.

"Wait, I wanted to ask you. Can you show me the Grace-Harvest dance moves tonight? The ceremony is coming up, and I really want to participate."

"Sure, I can run through the moves with you if you want. But you're on your own for the actual ceremony."

Byssa gave me a look that was too understanding, although her disappointment also shone through. "Okay, tonight then. Hey, have you and Squirter seen any grunt sculpins on your swims around here? I'm dying to get a close-up picture of one in a giant barnacle."

I had a tedious, disgusting morning cleaning the dining hall and restaurant. Sheila was in fine form, directing her minions to scrub the restaurant until it was spotless and no taint of the stench remained. I was itching to swim, or at least take a shower, but before I could disappear to the bunkhouse for a pre-lunch wash, Levi hailed me from across the lawn. He loped toward me, his face pinched with stress. The silver discoloration at his neck glinted in the sun. I stopped and waited for him.

"I'm glad I caught you," he panted. "Smoothing over this incident has been hell. We've never had so many complaints before." He gripped his hair in one hand and took a deep breath. "But we both know the food poisoning isn't an isolated incident, and I'm positive it's related to the other sabotage."

"What do your parents think now?" Seafoam's

dismissive face floated in my mind's eye, and I banished it before my annoyance could show on my face.

"It's too much for them." Levi waved the notion away. "They're getting old, they don't want to deal with the Lodge anymore. These 'unfortunate disasters'," Levi gave exaggerated quotes with his fingers, "were the last straw for them. They're drawing up the paperwork to transfer management of the Lodge to me earlier than expected. So, it doesn't matter what they think. It'll be on me soon."

I stared, my heart squeezing for him. He wasn't having a good week.

"We need to find the culprit behind all this," I said. "That's the only way you'll get back to normal."

"That's what I wanted to ask. Did you have any luck with your lead from yesterday?"

I shook my head. "I had my eye on Martin, but when he started puking along with the rest, I ruled him out. Unless he's truly dedicated to his cause and is willing to throw off suspicion."

Levi shuddered. "I think it's safe to assume he's not our man. Look, I can't carve out the time to handle this the way it needs to be handled, but I can't afford to ignore it. I thought about getting the police involved, but it's too risky with our Seamount guests. Too many questions we can't answer. My brother Austin said he would help, but I have a hard enough time getting him to do his regular duties. He doesn't need the distraction. If you're willing, I'd like you to take the afternoon and snoop around for clues. I've already cleared it with Sheila. You can take around a broom or something for your cover, pretend to clean."

He looked so desperate, so hopeful, that I couldn't say no. Besides, I wanted this mystery solved as much as he did. Grace was in jeopardy, and the way things were going downhill, I didn't want the Lodge bankrupt and unable to pay my salary.

And after this morning's cleaning job, I was more than happy to hang up my mop for the day.

"Yes, of course," I told him. "But where do I start? Any suggestions?"

"I do have one, actually. Austin said that Liam, one of our maintenance workers, has a sister who got pregnant from a Seamount guest." Levi looked pained. "I had no idea. We give guidelines to our guests, but it's a free world. As far as I know, it was consensual, but with pale folk, well, you know."

I did know. It was a simple matter for me to force my will on anyone. Males weren't quite as adept, but against a human, it would be no problem. I turned into the warm ocean breeze and shivered despite the summer's heat.

"Liam blames the Lodge for his family's newest addition?"

"Maybe." Levi crossed his arms. "Austin thought it might be true. I wish he'd said something to me. I hate to think of his family suffering in silence for something I was responsible for."

"How are you responsible?" A seagull cried overhead, but I ignored it to study Levi's face. "You can't control the guests."

"But I provide an opportunity for them to come to shore and interact with humans. I can take some blame for my part in it." He looked so despondent that I nearly reached out to touch his shoulder, but humans wouldn't touch their new boss after only a week of work, I was fairly certain. "I'll have to reach out, help with compensation."

I stared at him, flummoxed by his level of concern. It wasn't what I'd expected from the Lodge. Maybe it was because Levi was human, but I would have thought that being raised by Seafoam and surrounded by upper echelon pale folk growing up would have rubbed off the disdain that upper echelon Seamount inhabitants felt toward half-humans. Were the pale folk who visited the Lodge different from those I grew up with underneath? If so, where had they been when I was treated like the scum of the sea?

"Don't beat yourself up," I said at last. "For all you know, they had a torrid love affair, and she's happily holding her new bundle of joy." Privately, I agreed with Levi's assessment, but he didn't need to hear that right now. "The situation is worth checking out, though. Where can I find Liam?"

"He's working today down by the marina. After that, though, I don't know who to look at." He spread his arms helplessly. The idyllic Lodge behind him, its cedar shake siding homey and welcoming, contrasted with the tension radiating off Levi.

"I got this," I said with more confidence than I felt. "I'll let you know this evening what I find."

My shower would have to wait. I had an enjoyable lunch with Hades in the dining hall—Byssa was busy guiding guests to a restaurant in the next town—then I grabbed a broom for an excuse and struck out for the marina.

A wide path led me to the second cove I'd discovered yesterday. As before, a few guests lounged on the plant-surrounded patio, although William and Finn weren't present this time. Instead, the sound of drills and hammers drowned out the clinking of cables on masts.

I strolled over to a pile of wood next to two men and a woman bent over an octagonal frame on the ground. I gazed at it with curiosity, and when one of the men stood and walked closer, I greeted him.

"Hi, there," I said with a cheery wave. "What are you building?"

"A new gazebo." He reached up and stretched his arms far above his black hair, silver eyes following his hands to gaze at the blue sky above. "It's supposed to be picturesque. The guests are cooing over it already."

"They do like places to hang out, I've noticed." I swept my hand toward the patio, where multiple groups gathered around tables despite the construction noise.

He chuckled. "That they do. Anything to keep the guests happy."

He didn't say this with any kind of animosity, but my instincts pegged him for Liam.

"I'm Lune." I thrust out my hand for a human handshake. "I just started as a cleaner."

"Liam." He returned my gesture with a hearty grip.

"It's a great place to work. I'm sure you'll like it here."

Was everyone taking happy pills? Why couldn't I find anyone with something bad to say about the Lodge?

"It seems good so far," I allowed. Time for some sleuthing. "But I'm a little nervous around the guests. I don't have any sirening powers myself, but I've heard about them. What if someone makes me do something I don't want to do?"

I expected his face to darken at this blatant potential parallel to his sister's scenario. Instead, his face creased in a half-smile.

"I could see how you'd be worried about that, but I've never heard of a single guest taking advantage in that way. Don't get me wrong, things happen." He sighed and shook his head. "My sister had a fling with a guest last year, and now I have a baby nephew, but she wasn't forced into anything. She's just impulsive. Always has been. The Lodge has a zero-tolerance policy for sirening, and guests would never be allowed to stay again if they disobeyed. Since this is the only place like it on this stretch of coast, the pale folk are happy to comply to keep their vacationing options open."

"That's good to know," I murmured, both relieved and disappointed. Liam's sister hadn't been sirened, but now I had no clues to follow. I flapped my hand at the gazebo. "Don't let me keep you. I'll come back in a few days and let you know how picturesque it's becoming."

He flashed me a grin. "You do that."

Interviewing potential leads was getting me nowhere, and I'd run out of subjects. It was time to polish off my old break-and-enter skills and snoop around.

At the Seamount, food and Grace didn't filter down to the half-human ghetto often enough for us. The only way to supplement our pitiful harvests was to steal from higher in the Seamount. I'd grown particularly adept at sneaking into upper echelon dwellings and finding what we needed. I had no doubt that my foster father Eelway loved me, but even he wouldn't have denied that my skills eased our lives substantially.

Until I'd been caught at the scene of a crime, of course. I scowled and marched up the path toward the Lodge. Everything had fallen apart, and I'd ended up here. It was better on land, marginally, but I missed Eelway and my friends below. Luckily, Byssa and Hades had welcomed me with open arms, even if I didn't share my past with them. They put up with a lot, and I was grateful for their friendship.

The bunkhouse caught my eye when I emerged from the trees, so I directed my steps there. It was a good starting point to reacquaint myself with sneaking around since I had every right to be there.

I let myself in and started in the female dorms. My trained eyes gave them a cursory pass, but few spots could hide anything in the sparse rooms. I felt under pillows and mattresses, but nothing turned up except Byssa's journal. I declined to open it to respect her privacy. With anyone else, I would have glanced through it, but Byssa was my friend, and her being behind the incidents was a laughable notion.

The bathroom was similarly empty of clues, so I crossed the hall and carefully pushed open the first men's dorm. It was empty, so I closed the door behind me and scanned the room. It was as sparse as the women's dorms, though not as tidy. Hades's bunk was obvious from a book about bouldering strewn across the rumpled sheets. Rachel, the aquarist Hades had his eye on in Vancouver, was intensely interested in rock climbing, as Hades had mentioned time and again.

I tucked my hand under pillows and mattresses, but aside from a phone, I came up empty-handed. I wasn't surprised. A communal bedroom was a terrible place to hide evidence. Still, I had to cross places off my list.

The storage rooms on the maintenance dock contained only cleaning supplies. A red can caught my eye in the last one, but it was paint thinner, not gasoline. I grabbed the nearest broom for a prop.

I closed the door and gazed at the main Lodge. Rooms for longer-term employees were on the bottom floor, I knew, and the upper floors housed human guests and the restaurant. I debated where to look first. Human guests seemed like a dead end. What visitors would be vengeful enough to rent a room while they sabotaged the place they were currently paying for? The restaurant was worth poking around, although I'd have to focus on speaking with employees instead of snooping since the kitchen was busy all day.

Employee rooms, on the other hand, could prove enlightening. I still had no concrete motives for anyone that I hadn't already disproved, but that didn't mean a disgruntled worker didn't have a shell to crack with the Lodge.

How to get into the rooms, though? Human doors were usually locked, so I needed keys. I tapped my fingers on my thigh, then directed my steps up the sloped lawn toward the front desk. Sandy would have access to keys, surely. I only needed to swipe her master set while she wasn't looking.

"Lune," Sandy greeted me when I entered the front desk area from the parking lot. I averted my eyes from the horrifying fireplace. "Lovely to see you. Can I help you with something?"

"I just saw Levi on the lawn," I said, my forehead wrinkling. "He's run off his feet, isn't he?"

"Poor boy, yes." Sandy shook her head. "It's been a rough week for him, what with everything going wrong. Well, things often come in threes. Hopefully, the bad luck has run its course."

Threes? That must be a human superstition. Bad things came in whatever number they felt like, in my experience. Usually more than three.

"Hopefully." I held up my broom. "Although Levi says he dropped a glass in his room. Shattered everywhere, by the sounds of it. He asked me to clean it up, but then he rushed off without giving me his key. Do you have it handy? I can run and sweep it up and get your keys back to you as quick as I can."

I smiled sweetly at Sandy, and she clucked and nodded while she unclipped the jingling keychain attached to her belt.

"Of course. Poor dear. Stepping on glass after a long

day would be a nasty shock. Mind you skip back here as soon as you can."

I nodded and took the keys before she could change her mind. The hallway swallowed me up, and I found the downstairs stairwell around a dark corner out of the way of guests.

A windowless hallway ran the length of the building, lined with numbered doors on one side. I must have been below ground level on this side, and since the Lodge was built on a slope, the rooms would open to the lawn below. The dining hall was in the middle section without doors, but it had its own stairwell to connect it to the kitchen above, keeping this underground hallway quiet and dim.

I had no idea which room was Levi's, but it didn't matter. My broom was only an excuse. I intended to examine each room as quickly as I could before dropping the keys off with Sandy.

I ran with light feet to the rightmost door and fumbled with the keys. After a quick knock to make sure no one was inside, I looked down at the keychain. There were at least twenty jangling in my hands, but only ten were gold like the lock. I shoved each into the hole with sweaty fingers until one slid easily in and turned. My mouth curved in satisfaction, and I slipped inside the room.

This suite was homey. Comfortable leather couches overlooked large windows facing the sea. A kitchen ran along one wall, small but serviceable, and through an open door, a large bed covered in a duvet of mottled green and blue peeked out.

On the wall hung a large, framed photo of Seafoam and Kane, with a younger Levi and Austin, all four smiling on a rocky beach. Was this the suite of Levi's parents? I crept around the tidy rooms for a minute but wasn't sure what I was looking for. Eventually, I backed out of the suite and locked the door. What motive could the owners of the Lodge have for burning down the Grace-house? Insurance claims might have made sense if the main building had caught fire, but not a small outbuilding.

The next room was the gardener William's, according to the carelessly tossed mail on his kitchen table. It was a smaller suite with only a kitchenette. William must eat in the dining hall most days. I poked around his belongings for a few minutes, not sure what I was looking for. Among the cardigans, newspapers, and half-drunk cups of tea, nothing jumped out as suspicious.

I ground my teeth. Clues were far and few between in this investigation, and it was wearing on me. I was glad I worked at an aquarium and not as a detective. The stress of not knowing the answers would eat me alive.

I inhaled deeply when I opened the next door along. My sensitive nose picked up faint hints of salt and stormy seas and something tantalizingly deeper. I shook my head and stalked into the room. The layout was identical to William's suite, but it was clear that a younger man lived here. A tee-shirt was carelessly slung over a worn plaid couch, a tablet hung precariously over the edge of a side table, and a box of breakfast cereal stood open on the kitchenette counter. A shirt I recognized lay on the kitchen table, and I froze. Was this Levi's suite?

131

I definitely didn't need to search his rooms, but I couldn't resist a quick look around. I peered into the bathroom, where two towels hung to dry. One was a plain green bathroom towel, and the other was clearly a beach towel with blue and orange zigzag stripes across its expanse.

The bedroom, despite clothes strewn over a chair and the unmade bed, didn't hold any hints of Levi's inner self, so I backtracked to the hallway, my heart pumping more forcefully than usual.

When I came out of Levi's suite, William's door stood open. My heart leaped into my throat, but before I could collect myself, a young woman in a cleaning uniform came out, whistling. She jumped when she saw me and put a hand on her chest with a laugh.

"Sorry, you scared me. Are you on cleaning duty down here today, too?"

"Just a broken cup in Levi's room." I held up my trusty broom. "He asked me to deal with it. I guess he didn't want you to cut yourself on the glass if you didn't know it was there."

"He's so sweet." She smiled fondly. "This whole place is great. They take care of their own. You know, they gave me a scholarship to go to university in the fall, just because I'm a seasonal employee."

"That's amazing," I said faintly. I was getting tired of hearing from contented workers. Where were the ones with a grudge? I needed motives and suspects, not glowing reviews. And while a scholarship sounded great on the surface, wasn't it another form of control, this time in the guise of help? Now this cleaner would feel obliged to the Lodge. It was a slippery slope, in my opinion.

She checked her watch. "Wow, it's getting on. I'd better get moving if I want to catch dinner. See you around."

She disappeared into the room and half-shut the door behind her. I sighed and walked to the last door. Sandy would be wondering where I was, but deception and misdirection were an old game for me. I could handle the front desk worker.

A cursory knock, then my fingers fumbled for the correct key. Before I could fit one into the lock, the door swung open. My heart nearly stopped. After four unoccupied rooms, I hadn't expected anyone to answer my quiet knock.

CHAPTER 13

A somewhat familiar young man gazed out at me from the open door of his suite, his hair and eyes dark but his skin as colorless as any pale folk.

"Hi," I said when it was clear he wasn't going to speak. "I'm supposed to clean up something in Levi's room, but I wasn't sure which one it was." I held up Sandy's overfull keychain to illustrate my point.

"It's next door." He tilted his head and studied me, then he smiled. "You're Lune, aren't you? Levi mentioned you. I'm his brother, Austin."

Right, I recognized him from the vomiting incident. Levi had mentioned me to his brother? I didn't know what to say to that.

"Nice to meet you." The human words came out automatically while I cast around for something to say. My clue about Liam and his sister had come from Austin. He knew about our investigation. Maybe he had other leads for me. "Do you know that I'm working with Levi on figuring out the arson? I followed up on your tip about Liam, but I think that's a dead end. Any thoughts on next steps? I'm coming up empty-handed."

Austin looked thoughtful and leaned against the doorframe. "Not off the top of my head. But didn't Levi say the so-called arsonist dived into the water? That sounds like someone who's comfortable swimming in the ocean. If you really think it's arson and not just an accident, I'd look at the pale folk in residence."

My lips tightened. I'd been afraid my investigations

would lead me in that direction. I'd managed to avoid recognition so far, but questioning the pale folk visitors was surely baiting the shark.

"Okay, thanks," I said, frustrated but trying not to show it. "I guess I'll have to."

Levi's shoulders slumped when I delivered the news of my failed investigation. He was in his office surrounded by papers, and he leaned back in his chair with a heartfelt sigh.

"I'll talk to some guests tomorrow," I promised. "If I wear a guide outfit, they might be willing to chat." At Levi's wide eyes, I said, "Don't worry, I can be discreet when I need to be."

"Please don't ruffle any feathers." His tanned complexion turned pale at the thought of disturbing customers. "I don't want anyone to feel they are under investigation."

"Discretion is my middle name." At Levi's raised eyebrow, I said, "Well, maybe not. But I know how to turn it on when needed."

"Okay," he said. "Thanks, Lune. I'll tell Sheila you're busy again tomorrow afternoon. You should join her in the morning, though. I don't think I can steal her cleaners for any longer than that. She'll have my hide."

I stayed in the dining hall after a dinner of clam chowder to hang out with Byssa. Kim waved at us when she wandered through the door with bottles under her arm.

"Hi Byssa, Lune," she called out. "I brought ciders. We totally deserve it after today's disgusting fiasco."

Byssa shuddered. "Don't remind me."

Kim slid onto the bench across from us, and I gratefully accepted a bottle from her.

"You have nothing to complain about, guide," I said to Byssa with a playful push of my shoulder against hers. "Who do you think was the one doing the mopping?"

Kim grinned. "Then you've more than earned your cider. Cheers to the housekeepers, our unsung heroes."

I spent my evening with the other two, and when a few others joined us, the evening grew even more lively. I hadn't had such lighthearted fun for months, maybe years, and it loosened something inside me. I found myself grinning without reason, simply happy to be in the moment among new friends. This group of misfits, cast off from the Seamount for various reasons, had been growing on me for the past week during our communal meals and evenings.

When Byssa finally yawned and said she was tired, I shook off my strange euphoria and accompanied her to the dorm. After my hard work cleaning in the morning and my dispiriting lack of progress in the afternoon, I was done. All I wanted was to sleep and dream of waves and jellyfish, not fires and vomit.

When I pulled back my blanket, a black chunk of something unidentifiable sat on my pillow. I wrinkled my nose and picked it up gingerly. What was it? I peered closer.

The piece of translucent green looked suspiciously like a strip of dried Grace, but one end was singed with soot, like it had been exposed to a fire. The scent of burning drifted into my nose.

My stomach curdled. This piece of burned Grace was no accident. It was a message. Someone knew I was investigating the fire, and whoever it was wanted to warn me off the job.

"Shower's free," Byssa said brightly from behind me. I shoved the Grace under my pillow and grabbed my towel. Byssa didn't need to see the warning. She would only worry.

But I wasn't stopping. If anything, this message sped up the current I was riding. Now, I was determined to get to the bottom of this mystery. This went beyond getting money to pay Branc or helping Levi.

If someone was threatening me, they would meet my teeth, not my tail.

I didn't sleep well—surprise, surprise—and it was with a growl that I greeted Byssa's cheery nudge in the morning.

"Look lively," she crowed. "Those toilets won't clean themselves."

Kim laughed from across the room, and I threw my pillow toward my retreating friend.

"I can't believe you convinced me to come here," I grumbled.

"It was your choice not to guide." Byssa threw my pillow back, and I buried my face in it. "Honestly, it's quite fun. I'm enjoying talking to the guests. I hardly remember the Seamount, so it's nice to hear about it from people who live there. It's not like you tell me anything."

This dig was gentle, as all comments by Byssa were, but it still burrowed deep. I'd told her hardly anything about my previous life, even after a year of friendship.

But what was there to tell that wasn't depressing, aggravating, or incriminating?

I dragged myself out of bed and slouched into a fresh cleaning uniform I'd grabbed yesterday. I had no intention of smelling like vomit for two days in a row.

Byssa and I ate breakfast with the others in the dining hall, during which I tried to peel my eyes open. I wished for a lick of the green nudibranchs with stimulant slime found only at the Seamount to wake me up. Humans drank coffee, as Hades frequently wafted at me, but I'd tried it once and nearly threw it across the room. Its acrid, burned flavor had gripped my tongue for hours after, and I'd convinced myself that I didn't need any help staying alert.

Mornings like this made me question that resolve.

Sheila greeted me at the door of the dockside rooms.

"Eliza is already working on the right-side suites," she informed me. "You can do the left. Suites 3 and 7 will need a full clean for new occupants arriving this afternoon. The others can do with the usual room freshening."

I accepted my cleaning supplies and assignment and trudged to the first room. Now that I'd done this for a week, the chores were routine enough that I could let my thoughts wander. They inevitably focused on my dead-in-the-water investigation.

I dreaded approaching the pale folk this afternoon. Maybe I could take over Levi's paperwork so he could question his guests. I snorted and stripped off my outer clothing so only my undergarments remained. No, I would have to bite the oyster and talk to the pale folk myself. I would wear my sunglasses and wig, that was all. Maybe my ballcap, too. I couldn't be too careful.

I slipped into the water of the lower room with my sponge. The blue lights were soothing, and I scrubbed walls in mindless contentment, happy to be immersed. I'd almost finished when a whirring noise interrupted my thoughts.

A panel moved on the seaward side, and I backed into a corner in shock. Two pale folk swam in, their kelp-like clothes flowing freely with their movement. My eyes widened. The slight woman with short-cut white hair clutched her arm, and blackish blood seeped from a ragged wound.

She's hurt, the taller woman said in an authoritative manner. *Help us.*

I nodded with a jerky motion and swam to a nook in the wall. There, I knew, the Lodge provided a first aid kit specifically designed for underwater guests. I rummaged inside the kelp sack and finally extracted a pouch of soothing sponge paste and a wrap of seaweed.

The hurt woman held out her arm, and I gingerly applied the paste to her wound. She grimaced, and the other woman winced.

What happened? I asked while I worked.

Shark, the unhurt woman replied. *It came right at us, slashed her arm before we could react.*

Why didn't you siren it? I asked. Little in the sea could harm us if our voices were intact.

I tried, she said indignantly. *But it didn't respond. It was like the shark was already being controlled by someone else.*

I tied the wrap around the slighter woman's wound, my mind whirling. This stank of the "accidents" on land, and it pointed strongly to one of the pale folk masterminding the events. What was the connection? Who wanted the Lodge discredited so badly?

Thank you, the hurt woman said once I'd finished my ministrations. *I hope we didn't take you away from your work. Will your supervisors be upset?*

It's fine, I assured her, surprised she would care about any trouble I got in. *Helping guests is our priority.* While no one had specifically stated this, the sentiment was abundantly clear from Levi's words and actions.

My pale hair floated in front of my face, and I brushed it away impatiently. The unhurt woman peered at me.

You look familiar, she said with a frown. *Do I know you?*

I don't think so. My heart thundered wildly, and I groped around for my sponge. I felt naked and exposed without my wig and sunglasses. Had my year of hiding just unraveled? *Your room is clean, so I'll leave you two in peace. Have a good day.*

I swam to the opening and propelled myself out of

the water. That was too close. I vowed to avoid pale folk contact until I was properly attired.

Both Byssa and Hades weren't due to return to the Lodge until dinner, and I didn't feel like making small talk with the other workers after my brush with inquisitive pale folk. Squirter must have been wondering where I was, so when the lunch hour arrived, I darted to the bunkhouse to pick up the half-burned bit of Grace from under my pillow and raced to the quiet south beach for a swim. I could crack an urchin to eat for lunch while I was underwater.

My teeth chewed the piece of Grace while I stripped off my shirt, skirt, and wig. The burned flavor was disgusting, reminding me of a charred burger I'd tried once at a barbecue party of one of Hades's friends, but I had no intention of wasting this precious morsel.

Squirter joined me after a few minutes of floating over eelgrass beds and running my hands through their flowing strands. He crawled over my arm in greeting. It tickled, and I rubbed his mantle in return.

Squirter lifted off me and drifted to the seafloor, where three purple sea urchins clustered along a ridge of rock. With deft tentacles, he flipped one on its back. Spines and tube feet waved with languid motions, but Squirter looked at me and waited.

Hungry, I said to him. *Thanks.*

I grabbed a loose rock and cracked open the hapless

creature with a firm whack. With practiced fingers, I dug inside the delicate shell and pulled out the animal's white flesh. I carefully pressed the meat between my lips and chewed in satisfaction.

Squirter tucked his tentacle into the shell and extracted his own morsel. It disappeared under the webbing between his arms where his beak and mouth resided.

My eyes traveled around the seafloor while I chewed another piece. I didn't expect to see anything extraordinary—my skin sense would tell me if something approached—so the disturbed anemones gave me pause. I frowned. Something had brushed against them recently, and it hadn't been me. Other sea creatures usually gave anemones a wide enough berth that they didn't pull into themselves.

When Squirter had cleaned out the urchin fully, I drifted over the anemones—now starting to unfurl— and scanned the seafloor for clues. Silt beyond the anemones had been dug out in a divot. It wasn't anything too strange, but in conjunction with the anemones, it made me question who had been down here before me.

I shook my head. Of course, this beach would be popular with Lodge guests and employees alike. Some half-human probably had the same idea for a lunchtime swim and had recently passed this way.

The signs triggered my old tracking skills I'd honed at the Seamount. It had been my job to follow upper echelon folk and steal their Grace from them. Sometimes they had tried to shake me off, but I'd learned over the years how to track them from only the faintest signs.

Squirter pointed out the next clue, a broken giant barnacle shell, and I shook my head in disapproval at the sloppy swimming of my quarry. If they didn't have control, they should swim higher in the water column.

The water grew darker to our right until a cliff face loomed out of the murk. Squirter jetted ahead, and I swam more slowly into the rock's shadow. The face was pitted and jagged, and dark shadows clung in ragged splotches across the surface.

I ran delicate fingers over a bryozoan colony—a colorful, encrusting life form clinging to rock—and used my skin sense to track Squirter's movements. His small form crawled over a rock then disappeared.

I pursed my lips then clicked to call him out. Where had the little cephalopod gone? I hoped he had checked out the crevasse beforehand. I wouldn't want him to fall foul of some larger creature. Squirter was only a little octopus, after all, and the ocean was full of predators.

With that concerning thought, I propelled myself forward. A large shadow under a rocky overhang caught my attention. This was where Squirter had disappeared. I clicked again, but he didn't answer.

If I hadn't been holding my breath, I would have sighed. How did Squirter expect me to follow him into a crevasse? I was twenty times his size.

I poked my head into the darkness, then my skin sense kicked in. This was no narrow gap between rocks. A much larger opening beckoned.

The cave was worthy of exploring, but I needed a breath before going further. I hadn't bothered with transitioning to breathing water, not for a short swim like this, but needing to surface every ten minutes was frustrating.

Once I'd gulped a few lungfuls of air, I flipped upside down and kicked to the cave. With trepidation, I pulled myself through the rocks on either side of the entrance and pushed forward.

Without my skin sense, I would have been hopelessly untethered. My eyes closed, and I focused on feeling my way. A narrow tunnel lined with jagged rocks led through the rocky cliff. A few hardy sponges clung to the tunnel, but with little water flow and no sunlight, life was restricted.

Movement ahead made my heart pound, but it was only Squirter. He gave an excited hum and latched onto the top of my head. I pretended to shake him off, but wearing him like a hat gave me a sense of security. At least I wasn't alone in this darkness.

Gloomy light pressed against my closed eyelids, and I blinked them open. The end of the tunnel greeted my gaze. With one final pull forward, I floated into the cave.

It was only a little larger than my outstretched arms, and its walls were made of the same jagged rock that the tunnel had been filled with. Fissures in the ceiling let light filter through, enough to see the contents of the cave.

A bag was tied to a rock. My heart squeezed. It was so familiar. The kelp-woven pouch was the same design as countless bags that filled Seamount homes. On land, I could place my keys on the counter, and they would be there when I returned. In the ocean, anything lighter than a rock would drift away.

I pushed myself closer to the bag and pulled gingerly

at the drawstring. I might have worried that the usual inhabitant of this cave would notice my intrusion, but from their clumsy passage through the water, tracking was not their strong suit.

The mouth yawned open, and I carefully pulled out the top item. It was a black hoodie that matched the one the arsonist had worn. My heartbeat sped up. Was this the lair of my culprit? I shoved my hand in the bag, heedless of disturbances.

As my fingers groped in the bag, I wondered at the inclusion of the hoodie down here. Why hadn't the culprit taken it to shore, or even thrown it out? Then I recalled the clear bags I'd seen maintenance workers hauling out of garbage cans on the property, and I nodded. He hadn't wanted to risk exposure. Black hoodies weren't uncommon, but he probably wanted to remove all suspicion from himself. A dripping wet hoodie after the arson incident would have been a red flag to anyone watching, and even the private employee rooms were cleaned by Lodge workers. If the arsonist had a handy cave to stash his evidence in, why wouldn't he?

Smoothness met my questing fingers. I drew out a wide, flat bone from the bag. This, too, was familiar. We used these in the Seamount to write on. The scavenged bones of furods, small swimming horse-like creatures that lived only at the Seamount, were very soft. With a stylus made from a ligan tooth or a sharp rock if no stylus were available, anyone could scratch Seamount-script easily into a flat scapula. Better yet, the surface could be ground down with sandstone and re-written on many times before the bone grew too thin to carve.

I grabbed a handful of silty mud from the bottom of the cave and smeared it over the bone. When residual silt cleared from the water, not helped by Squirter swimming through the cloud with playful jets, mud-etched scratches showed clearly.

The next Grace shipment travels soon, but it must be stopped. Shut down the Lodge before the swordfish moon, or you will regret our alliance.

The bone was neither addressed nor signed. I checked the back, but that was the only message on the translucent scapula. I stared at the script again. Somehow, the arson was connected to the Grace shipments I'd heard about from Tyrell, my target for Branc. Who were these people? Why did they want the Lodge shut down, and what did it have to do with Grace shipments?

One thing I knew for certain: all the full moons had names, and the one in midsummer was called the swordfish moon. It was named for the migration of swordfish past the Seamount every year.

The swordfish moon would rise in two days.

CHAPTER 14

I didn't know what to make of this information, but it was the most I'd found so far. Levi needed to hear it, and soon. The unknown writer of the script wanted Grace shipments to stop, and they wanted the Lodge shut down. That meant less Grace for me to pay Branc what I owed. This mystery needed to be solved now, and if Levi and I put our heads together, maybe we could figure out who the arsonist was. My chest tightened with intense resolve.

No, wait. I needed oxygen.

I inwardly cursed my need for air, but there was no point in switching to water breathing now, not when I had urgent news for Levi. I hummed to Squirter and threaded my body through the tunnel. I had a minute or two before my desire for air turned into a desperate need.

Squirter followed me out, brushing against my skin as he squeezed past me. I was too slow for the little octopus. We emerged into open water, and my shoulders relaxed. I didn't mind tight spaces, but having only one entrance gave me a tingly neck.

I brushed my hair impatiently away from my face and turned toward the beach. I barely had time to register two figures barreling my way before they were on me.

Strong arms grabbed me around the middle and forced me against the rock. My leg scraped against sharp protrusions, and jolting pain nearly made me gulp seawater.

A man wearing a black costume mask and swim

shorts embroidered with the Lodge logo pushed me against the rocks again, and my arm received the brunt of damage this time. I clutched it and tried to push myself sideways, away from the man, but he followed with clear intent.

A large, gray body slid past, and my heart leaped into my throat. The second figure was a shark, and now I was bleeding. I gathered myself to siren the animal, but the man leaped at me.

I released a distress hum without thinking and dodged him, thinking frantically. The shark took another pass, closer this time. It hadn't attacked yet, which meant that it likely wasn't hungry, but surely it would take the plunge and test the bleeding goods soon. My heart pounded unbearably, and I winced at the oxygen my body was using up. I didn't dare take the time to switch to water breathing. The shark hadn't attacked yet, but it wouldn't hold back for much longer.

A lithe body streaked past me, right at the man. It rammed him in the chest, then circled around for another attack. When the creature faced me, I recognized the puffy gray face of a wolf eel. At the same time, Squirter glommed onto the man's arm. I could imagine the damage his small but sharp beak would do to the tender skin underneath.

Relief coursed through me at the creatures' help, but it didn't last long. Before I could swim further than three kicks, the man had ripped Squirter roughly off his arm and hit the wolf eel away.

Now that I was away from the melee, the shark twisted in midwater and gazed at me with intense eyes. I suddenly regretted leaving the man, as much as he wanted to hurt me. Being pushed around by another person was less terrifying than being mauled by a shark.

Luckily, I wasn't without skills. I gathered my wits and sent out a hum of control to calm the shark long enough for me to escape. Being a siren had its benefits. Communicating with creatures in the sea was one of them.

The shark didn't change its swim pattern in the slightest. If anything, it drew closer on its next pass. My heart shrank into a wizened ball of fear. That could only mean that the shark was being controlled by someone else already. It couldn't be the masked man—half-human though I was, no male could out-siren me—so someone else must be on his side.

I was outclassed. If a female full pale folk had sirened the shark, I couldn't fight the animal's compulsion. And, with my bleeding limbs, I was practically asking to be eaten. Why hadn't the shark attacked yet? Either it was waiting for me to bleed out to become easier prey, or it was being controlled to scare me until the masked man came for me.

Through my terror, my skin sense picked up movement. Not far away, two siren-shaped figures swam with leisurely undulations. Maybe they were on the masked man's side, but I was out of options. It was a risk to encounter pale folk without a disguise again, but it was a greater risk to swim with a bloody leg and arm in front of a shark. If I didn't try reaching out to these passersby, I might as well say goodbye to Squirter right now.

I wasn't ready for that.

My distress call was as loud as I could make it. I backed into the cliff face in a futile attempt to escape from the predator before me. It swam within an arm's length of me, and I winced. This was it. Surely, with one more pass it would arch its back and rush me with its mouth open wide, siren control or not.

The shark turned. White, pointed teeth gleamed in its cavernous maw. I squeezed my eyes shut, but nothing could stop me from feeling the scene with my skin sense. I waited for the end.

A vibration thrummed through the water, but it wasn't targeted at me. The shark twisted and swam with unhurried motions toward deeper water. I cracked open my eyes and gazed after it in disbelief. To my right, the frantic motions of Squirter and the wolf eel calmed as the man dived deeper, away from the animals. To my left, the two pale folk who I'd sensed earlier drew closer.

Are you all right? The woman stared at me with a creased brow. She must have been the one to break the compulsion on the shark.

Her companion narrowed his eyes toward the fleeing masked man but didn't pursue. I nodded with jerky motions, then a spasming in my chest alerted me to my need for air. I thrust my body upward, never gladder to surface in my life.

Once my desperate need for air had been satiated, I dived again into the depths to thank my saviors. Although I didn't want to give them another good look at my face, I couldn't leave without acknowledging their help. I certainly hadn't expected them to aid me. I'd been in tight situations at the Seamount, and no upper echelon pale folk had ever deigned to stir themselves. Had I misjudged them? Obviously, plenty of pale folk were snobbish and cruel, but were they all like that? Having someone to reach out to in my hour of need sent tickles of cool pleasure from my hair to the stunted webbing between my toes. Maybe there was something to this Lodge place. Maybe Byssa wasn't completely crazy to want to be connected to the community here.

But, still, I didn't want to be a part of the whole scene badly enough to give up the autonomy I strived for. I appreciated the help of these pale folk, but all in all, I was better off without the Seamount, Branc, and that whole world in general.

But maybe I wouldn't tease Byssa quite so much anymore.

Thank you, I said once I reached the pair. My bleeding had almost stopped—the joys of siren blood coagulating properties—but I was sore and shaken. I wanted to return to land, as strange as the sentiment was, and gather myself once more. I tried a smile, though, as these two had certainly earned one. *You saved me.*

Of course, the woman said. She frowned as she absentmindedly stroked the wolf eel's flank. It appeared unharmed, and I made a gesture of thanks toward it. The woman said, *Why was the shark attacking you?*

I spread my hands helplessly, although it was less of a mystery to me than to them.

Someone was controlling it. I don't know why.

Before they could question me further—or get a better look at my features, which I deliberately obscured behind my floating hair—I thanked them again and swam toward the beach. Squirter joined me on the way, and I was intensely relieved to see him unharmed.

Bathtub? I said to him before I reached the surface. I didn't want to leave Squirter down here alone. He could look after himself well enough, but I wanted to keep him close until we solved the arson mystery. Squirter could avoid predators, but would he know how to stay safe against attackers who targeted us specifically? I didn't want to take that chance.

Squirter clicked his beak in approval, and my shoulders slumped in relief. I left him floating in the shallows while I pulled on my uniform with its handy absorbent layer and then waded out to get the little octopus.

He tolerated being lifted out of the water, but I hated to see him squishy and limp in my hands. Even though he could stay above water for many minutes, I quickly walked with long strides down the path. I had no idea how I would explain my odd cargo to any human I passed, so it was lucky the path was deserted.

I popped him in our small bathtub in the bunkhouse, then I ran to the supply room for a container. Four large buckets of seawater later, Squirter happily drifted in the tub. I threw in Byssa's travel soap holder and my toothbrush for him to play with, then I shoved a Lodge ballcap over my white hair and left the bunkhouse. Dealing with Squirter had distracted me for a few minutes, but I had a mission and no time to fuss about with a wig. I'd almost died for the secrets of the arson, and Levi needed to know.

Delayed fury heated my chest as I strode toward the

Lodge. The arsonist wasn't only interested in discrediting the Lodge. He wasn't above assault, and I had no idea if he'd been angling for murder. I'd been beyond lucky that the pale folk had rescued me.

My stomach squirmed at that thought. Apparently, the upper echelon folk who visited the Lodge weren't all bad, although I questioned whether they would have reached out a hand if they'd known who I was. I didn't believe that their community goodwill would extend to a half-human criminal. They might be all right with half-humans at the Lodge, but that didn't mean their prejudices wouldn't surface when put to the test.

No, I needed to rely on myself. It was lucky the pale folk had been there, but I shouldn't have put myself in a situation that called for rescue. Now that I knew the arsonist was out for blood, I would step carefully.

I stomped up the slope to the front desk. Sandy looked up from her computer and smiled at me, but her expression faltered when she saw my stony face.

"Lune. What's wrong?"

"I need to speak to Levi," I said. The door slammed behind me for emphasis. "Now. Do you know where he is?"

"In his office, I think. But he's pretty busy right now—"

I ignored the rest of Sandy's sentence and blew past her into the hallway. A few twisting turns later, I stood outside Levi's office. I gave a perfunctory knock then pushed my way in.

Levi looked up in the office just big enough for a large desk across from two chairs. Tall windows let the westerly light inside. He frowned at me, but it was in confusion, not annoyance.

"Lune." He stood up. "Hi. I'm pretty busy right now. Can this wait?" At my withering glare, he wilted and said, "It's fine. Any news?"

"You could say that." I eyed a chair in front of his desk then decided I was too amped up to sit. Instead, I paced the area behind it. "I went for a swim at lunch and found a secret cave."

Levi's eyebrows rose, but he waited for me to continue.

"In this cave was a Seamount-style bag with a black hoodie that matched the one I saw the arsonist wearing." I let this sink in for Levi, then I put up my finger. "And I found a note in Seamount-script. It said that the recipient needed to shut down the Lodge before the swordfish moon in two days. They want to stop the next Grace shipment."

Levi sat on the edge of his desk and released his breath in a long sigh. "So, this is all about Grace distribution. Damn it! Is this Driftwood or a third party?"

"I'll let you ruminate on that, because my story isn't done." I tilted my head and stared at Levi. "When I came out of the cave, a man wearing employee swim shorts and a black mask attacked me. He hurt me." For the first time since surfacing, I remembered my wounds, and the pain flared anew. I twisted my arm and leg to show Levi, and he winced.

"Let me get the first aid kit." He stood, but I waved him back.

"It's not bleeding anymore. I was only saved because two guests were swimming by and heard my distress call. The attacker got away, but it's clear he's the culprit. He has at least some pale-folk heritage, and he works at the Lodge."

Levi's shoulders slumped, and he gazed at the wall with unseeing eyes.

"I don't understand," he muttered. "All the employees are like family. I can't think of anyone I would suspect."

Levi's dejection hit a chord in me. He truly had no idea who was behind the attack. The tight-knit but inclusive community spirit of the Lodge struck me again. Maybe there was something to this place, after all.

But someone was behind the crimes. I didn't have the same sentimental blinders that Levi wore. It was up to me to expose the culprit, and I would have an easier time of it without the ties of friendship that Levi was entangled in.

Before, I was invested because I didn't want my money and Grace jeopardized before I had a chance to earn it. With an attack on me specifically—not to mention the warning of burned Grace—this was personal.

Now that my life was in danger, I needed to step up my investigation. I hadn't wanted to approach the pale folk guests for fear that one would recognize me. But now that I knew the culprit was an employee, their unbiased observations could point me in the right direction. Everything was risky now, and I had to choose the risk with the highest reward. Solving the mystery and not dying felt like a reasonable decision compared to possibly being recognized and dying.

What had happened to my life?

"I'm sorry," I said, because I truly was. Levi's horror was infectious. "We need to move fast since the swordfish moon is only two days away. With your permission, I'll start interviewing guests. They'll give us an unbiased opinion of what's been happening here."

"Yes," he said with distraction, then his blue eyes zeroed in on me. "Be as discreet as you can, please. I know the Lodge is falling apart, but the guests don't need to know what's going on."

Shouts filled the air outside. Levi and I looked at each other, then we both lunged for the window.

CHAPTER 15

Employees and guests ranged along the shoreline, pointing and gesticulating at a sailboat in the bay whose deck listed at a dangerous angle. The mast tilted precariously. A few people clung to the far edge of the boat, eying the ocean with hesitation. Their shouts carried across the water of the bay with piercing clarity.

Levi cursed and spun around to dash out the door. I followed close behind, and we thundered down the hall, out the front door, and down the grassy slope toward a growing crowd. He skidded to a halt at the water's edge and scanned the watchers.

"Ila, Sam," he barked.

Two people looked up, the woman with bleach-blond hair in a ponytail, the man with a uniform shirt clearly chosen tighter than necessary for ease of showing off his physique. Next to them, a young man with long hair tied back in a low ponytail was smirking and trying to hide it. I narrowed my eyes and earmarked him for further investigation. Unless he were devoid of compassion, humor at this spectacle might indicate involvement with its source.

The boat shifted as something in its hull filled with water, and the humans clinging to the edge shrieked and cried. Watchers on the shore pointed at the spectacle with wide eyes and gaping mouths. Had nobody thought to help the victims yet?

"Swim out there and help the people off the boat," Levi said. "I don't know how well they can swim." He looked significantly at Sam and Ila, indicating that the passengers were human. It didn't matter how good they were at swimming—the water was cold for a human, and distances were hard to judge across water. They would need help.

"I'll go too," I said. I stripped off my shirt—modesty wouldn't help the passengers survive—and the other two followed. Levi nodded tightly.

"I'll get a boat from the marina, but it might take me a few minutes."

He raced off, and I splashed into the shallows. When I was deep enough, I dived into cool waves. My skin sense told me that Sam and Ila followed close behind.

It took us no longer than two minutes to reach the faltering vessel, but in that time, the deck was half-submerged. A man had jumped into the ocean with his lifejacket on and was gesturing at his friends to join him. A young girl screamed off and on, and her mother clung to her with a tight embrace while also holding onto the edge of the listing deck. At another jolt of the boat's hull, the humans aboard shouted as one.

I shouted to get her attention. "Jump in. I'll take the child to shore."

The mother stared at me with wild eyes, then she said something to the girl and gave her a gentle push. The girl clung to her mother, so the woman took one last agonized glance at the waterlogged white sail and rolled over the edge. Both she and the girl fell into the water with a splash, the girl's scream truncated on impact.

I kicked furiously to reach the pair. In the furor, the mother had released her grip on her daughter, and now both flailed at the surface. They wore lifejackets, but no one had fitted the girl's jacket properly, and she slipped out. Her frantic movements were ineffectual, and the mother tried to swim closer to her daughter.

The girl scrambled on top of her mother. With the extra weight, the pair sank under the surface.

I shook my head and angled my body to come at them from underneath. If I attempted to help them at the surface, they would simply climb on me. Byssa had taught me that panicking humans in water were predictable. Instead, I grabbed the mother's waist and kicked upward. I tucked my head into her side to avoid the girl's flailing feet and concentrated on supporting the two above water.

It took a minute, but the mother's brain finally snapped out of her panicking state. She must have calmed her daughter, because I suddenly wasn't in danger of being kicked in the teeth.

Sam swam toward us and popped his head out of the water so I could only see his truncated torso and legs. He must have convinced the girl to come with him, because she gripped his neck in a piggyback carry and he turned toward the shore. Gently, I released the mother's waist until she bobbed in the waves, supported by the lifejacket. I swam up and surfaced.

"Are you okay?" I asked the woman.

She stared at me with wide eyes. "Yes, I think so." She glanced at her daughter, growing smaller as she approached the shore. "I need to follow her."

"Of course." I glanced around. Ila had found a rope from somewhere, and the other boat occupants were tethered together in a line of bobbing lifejackets. She tugged them in the direction of the beach, so I nodded at the woman. "Lie on your back and I'll tow you."

She was tired enough to not protest, so I grabbed the shoulder of her lifejacket and kicked to shore. A seagull perched on a floating piece of driftwood eyed me warily, and I tugged the woman sideways to avoid a collision.

"What happened?" I said after a moment. She was at the scene of the crime, after all. And I had no doubt that it was a crime. We had passed the realm of coincidences ages ago.

"There was a big bang," she said. "The skipper said we must have hit something, but the depth finder didn't show any rocks. When the crew looked in the cabin, it was filling up with water." She swallowed and glanced at the sailboat, whose mast was now the only part sticking up from the water's surface. "The skipper yelled something about the hull getting hit. That's all I know."

An engine roared, and a motorboat appeared around the point. It rocketed toward us and slowed down when it approached. Levi put the boat into neutral and waved us closer, so I tugged my cargo toward his outstretched hand.

Together, we tugged and pushed the woman on board. Before Levi left to pull in the other boat occupants, he bent over the edge of his boat to speak to me.

"Lune," he said in an urgent whisper. "Can you look at the boat for clues? I—" He swallowed. "I can't swim."

I blinked at him. He'd lived at the Lodge his whole life and had a siren for an adoptive mother. How had he never learned to swim?

"Yeah, of course," I said automatically. "I'll come see you once I'm done."

Levi nodded tightly and returned to the outboard motor's tiller. I watched him putter toward the bobbing line of lifejackets with wonder. I couldn't imagine not swimming. What a strange life humans led.

With a shake of my head, I dived under the waves once more. The sailboat loomed in my skin sense as a hulking form on the shallow seafloor, the mast poking out of the mirrored water's surface. I swam deeper to examine the hull.

On the far side, a gash exposed the innards of the boat. I winced at the impact this must have created. Then, I frowned and examined the hole further.

The gash was lined with flakes of white bone. I knew that substance. A creature known as a callo with a dense skeleton was scavenged when it died, and its bones fashioned into sharp objects. Callo bone was a common material to make spearheads out of at the Seamount. Sirens didn't use them much—mer folk were the aggressive defenders of the Seamount, not the pale folk—but I'd still seen them around. They were ideal for ripping apart wood and metal hulls, according to the mer folk who occasionally practiced the sport of salvage. Some of the upper echelons paid handsomely for treasures from a wrecked ship.

I shook my head. If we'd needed more evidence that the arsonist was in league with some unknown pale folk, here it was.

I swam around the boat once for form's sake, but

nothing else was amiss, so I turned in the direction of the shore and my pile of clothes waiting for me.

The crowd had dispersed by the time I arrived at the beach. I dripped toward my clothes, mercifully undisturbed, and climbed into them, thankful for the absorbent layer of my uniform. I needed to figure out how to put one in my regular clothes. Did Byssa know how to sew? I would have to ask her.

Levi appeared in the trees, leading the shivering humans wrapped in blankets. He passed them off to Sandy, who had hurried down to join them, and the line toddled off to the Lodge to warm up. Levi strode toward me, his handsome face grim.

"Not an accident," I said once he was in earshot. He glanced around, but no one was around to hear us. I waved vaguely at the water. "Someone punctured the hull with the kind of spear that mer folk use. I saw traces of callo bone from the spear's impact. The arsonist is definitely working with Seamount folk, like the note suggested."

"Did pale folk do this, then?" Levi's jaw was tight.

I shook my head. "I doubt it, not from that note we read. The arsonist's job is to discredit and close the Lodge for the pale folk. They might have given him tools to work with, but they aren't getting their own hands dirty. That's his job."

Levi let out an explosive sigh and raked his hands through his hair. It was a nice glossy dark mahogany, I decided. I still preferred blonds, but if I had to choose second-best, Levi's hair color would probably win.

"We stick to the plan," he said at last. "Question the

guests without awakening suspicion if you can. We need to get to the bottom of this. I'm going through all employment records and finances to see if there's anything that stands out. I wish we could catch the arsonist in the act, somehow."

"Like a trap," I murmured, my mind racing. "Wait, what if we marked him?"

"How?"

I held up my finger as I thought. "We know the underwater cave is his hangout, right? He knows I know where it is, but after the attack, why would he suspect me of going back there?" Squirter and his playful ink crossed my mind, and I smiled. "We put something in the tunnel to mark him once he's on land again."

"Yes," Levi said slowly, his gaze turned inward. "Permanent pen ink wouldn't work, not underwater. What about something that would scratch him, or leave a rash?"

"Jellyfish tentacles?" I asked. "I could collect some, I suppose. He would probably sense them through his skin sense, though, and know what they are."

"I was thinking stinging nettle," Levi said with a glint in his eye. "It would be harder to recognize underwater—not something you usually see down there—and the plants would be easier to attach to the cave sides."

"Then all we have to do is wait and watch for someone jumping around in pain."

Levi nodded, a light of hope filling his face. He chuckled. "Simple yet ingenious. Nice one. But how do we get him back to the cave? He saw you there. He'll expect you to return with reinforcements."

"It's his touchpoint for communicating with the pale folk. He'll need to come back at least once to warn them about my interference. I should set the trap right away."

Levi checked his watch. "I have to go into town this afternoon anyway, so I'll find some nettles in the forest while I'm out." He glanced at me with a furrowed brow. "But I don't like you going back there. He attacked you, and you nearly didn't make it back. No, I'll have to get someone else."

"We don't know who to trust," I argued. "At least I know the dangers. Look, I'll take Byssa and Hades with me, okay? Three against one, even with a shark. And I'll bring a weapon."

Levi's lips thinned, but we needed to set this trap, and he knew it. He wanted to go himself, I could tell, but this wasn't a job for a human. Especially one that couldn't swim.

How could someone not swim? Maybe I should offer to teach him. A vision of Levi without his shirt warmed my cheeks, and I cursed the inheritance of human skin tone from my unknown father.

I frowned. Why did Levi have a beach towel drying in his room if he didn't swim? Was he trying to practice when no one else was watching? My heart squeezed for him, and I wished he would let me help. Although, I couldn't exactly mention the beach towel to him without admitting I'd snooped in his suite.

"Okay," he said finally. "As long as both your friends go. Are you certain Hades isn't the arsonist?"

I barked out a laugh. "Considering he's never been

here before, and he's as eager as I am to earn his wages, I don't see any motivation. Besides, he's a good guy."

"I would have said that about all my employees," Levi muttered, then he waved off his comment. "No, I don't think it's Hades. I trust you. And I'll let you know when I get back from town with the supplies."

He turned toward the Lodge and left me with an odd feeling deep in my gut. He was willing to trust my word on something this important when he barely knew me. I couldn't imagine putting that much faith in anyone, let alone a near-stranger.

On my way to the marina to find pale folk guests to question, I twisted my hair up and tucked it under my ball cap. My sunglasses sat in my pocket, so I unfolded them and pushed them onto my face. Hopefully, my features would be obscured enough even without my wig. We needed answers, and they were worth the risk of exposure.

I was in luck. Three groups of pale folk sat under wide umbrellas and wider sunhats on the patio overlooking the tiny marina. I took a deep breath and gathered my thoughts. How would I approach these people delicately? Subtlety wasn't my forte. I wished Byssa were here with her sweet demeanor or Hades with his easygoing charm.

For some reason, Levi had trusted me with this. My shoulders straightened. I would try my best to get the answers we both desperately needed.

Enough thinking. I would make it up as I went. My feet strode forward of their own accord, and I found myself next to the table of the nearest pale folk.

"Good afternoon," I said. The two men looked up at me in surprise, colorful drinks in their hands. Both sported heads of white hair and pale skin, and one had a round, almost cherubic face, while the other had angular cheekbones and a hooked nose. Within the relative sanctity of the Lodge, they must have felt comfortable wandering around undisguised. I wondered what the human guests thought of them. I tried for a breezy smile and raised my hands to place them on their shoulders.

"We speak English," said Cherub. "A little."

"Wonderful." I smiled more warmly this time. "I hope you're enjoying your stay so far."

"Yes, very good."

"We're doing a customer survey," I blurted out. It was the first idea that popped into my head. "Can I ask, do you often sit on the patio here?" I pointed my finger down in case their English wasn't great.

"Yes," Cherub said. "Every day. It is nice." He wrinkled his nose until a happy expression crossed his face when he found the word he searched for. "Peaceful."

"Great, wonderful." I nodded vigorously. "And when you were here, say, four days ago, did you notice the people who work here? We want to keep the workers in the background, hard to see."

Cherub frowned in thought. "Maybe some."

"Two working in the dirt," Hook Nose supplied.

"Yes, two over there." Cherub pointed at the surrounding gardens, and I nodded. William and Finn had been here then. "And three with the boats."

My attention zeroed in on Cherub.

"Could you describe them?" At Cherub's confused look, I said hastily, "So we can tell if you noticed them a lot or a little."

"One man had short hair, and one was dark-haired but pale," he said. I recognized the buzzcut of Frank from the bunkhouse—Hades had pointed him out before—and the other might be Austin, Levi's brother. "And the other one had long hair tied back."

Had I really solved this? I inwardly marveled. The chuckler at the boat accident wore his hair long. Laughing at your crime was a sure giveaway.

"Thank you so much," I said. "You've been very helpful. Enjoy your stay."

I left the patio, determined to find the chuckler, or at least discover his name and where he usually worked. I didn't meet anyone on my way to the front desk, and before long, I stood in front of Sandy.

"I'm looking for a young man with a long ponytail," I said to the older woman. "He dropped something, and I want to return it to him."

"Oh, that's Henry," she said. "He works maintenance in the summers, has done ever since he started university. He's the son of one of my bridge club members, Rosa. Lovely boy, if a bit wild." She held out her hand. "Here, if you give me what he dropped, I can make sure it gets to him."

"I left it in the bunkhouse," I invented quickly. At

Sandy's furrowed brow, I said, "I figured I would catch him after work."

I exited the front lobby quickly and sighed at my close escape. Luckily, I was good at concocting falsehoods at the flick of a foot. That talent had squeezed me out of a few narrow scrapes in the past.

Where would a maintenance worker be in the late afternoon? As I pondered this question, a vehicle zipped by in the parking lot and slammed on its brakes in a reserved spot. Levi leaped out of a pickup truck with the Lodge logo on the side and ran my way.

"I got the supplies," he said once he landed next to me. I liked hearing him breathless. Wait, what? I focused on Levi's words instead of my errant thoughts.

"Great, good," I said.

"Let's assemble them right now, before dinner. I have a few minutes, but after dinner, I have to meet with the head cook."

"Lead the way."

I followed Levi back into the Lodge, admiring the cling of his pants over his backside. I shook my head vigorously and fixed my eyes on his shoulder blades instead. It wasn't much of a distraction, surrounded as it was by broad shoulders, but it was a more socially acceptable place to rest my eyes. What was wrong with me? I needed to get out of this place. Maybe I should relax, release my fear of control for just one night to relieve my unruly body.

Back in the city, I would consider it. For now, I needed to focus on solving this mystery with my good-looking partner.

Vents. Focus, Lune.

Levi closed the door behind me and emptied his bag onto the desk. A package of glue, some twine, two pairs of gloves, and a bag of plants fell out.

"If we tie bundles of nettles with the twine, then you can use this underwater epoxy to fasten the twine to the tunnel walls." Levi offered me a pair of gloves. "I thought the glue made more sense than trying to hammer nails into rock, even if you have extra strength underwater." He gave a wistful glance at my arms. I crossed them.

"Why can't you swim?" I asked, too worn out from the day to ask more tactfully, and too curious to keep silent. "If you want me to teach you, I can. I can't imagine not swimming, ever. I know it's cold for a human, but they do make wetsuits."

Levi's mouth twisted, and I didn't know if he was trying to suppress laughter or sadness.

"I appreciate the offer," he said quietly. "It's not from a lack of desire, I promise you. It's a bit of a sore point. I'd rather not discuss it."

If he'd said the words with anger, I would have pushed back for more, but his gentle sadness stopped my mouth.

"Sure," I said. "That's fine. Let's set up this trap."

We got to work, but I couldn't help glancing from time to time at Levi's bent head and wondering what venting reason could possibly stop someone from swimming.

CHAPTER 16

We finished the traps before dinner, and I traipsed downstairs with my bag full of tied plant bundles. Both Byssa and Hades were present, and thankfully sitting only with each other. I grabbed a plate of barbequed salmon and slid beside Hades.

"Hi, stranger," he said. "How are the toilets today?"

"Ha, ha," I said, shoving salmon into my mouth. "That was this morning. At lunch, I was attacked underwater near a secret cave where the arsonist hangs out, then someone punched a hole in a boat in the bay with a mer folk spear and I had to rescue the guests aboard. Then I did some sleuthing, and Levi and I made a trap to identify the arsonist. I need to install it underwater tonight, and I was hoping you two could come with me."

I put another forkful of fish in my mouth while Byssa and Hades gaped at me.

"Busy day," Hades finally croaked. "Makes me wonder if I should have signed up for toilet duty instead." He wrinkled his nose. "Forget I said that."

"Lune." Byssa reached over and grabbed my hand with a grip like a crab's pincers. "Are you okay? I can't believe you were in danger."

"A few scrapes, but I'll survive." I shrugged and poked my fork into another morsel. "I don't know what would have happened if some pale folk guests hadn't been swimming by. A controlled shark was about to take a bite out of me, and Squirter was fending off the arsonist

170

with only a wolf eel to help."

Byssa's already pale face grew even more bloodless. She withdrew her hand from mine and passed it over her forehead.

"Of course we'll come with you," Hades said firmly. "I'll bring my dive knife, too. No one's going to take us down."

We finished our dinner, Byssa taking her time because she always liked to savor each mouthful, and I led the way to the bunkhouse. With a start, I remembered Squirter.

"I need to grab Squirter," I said. "I brought him to our dorm bathroom so he wouldn't fall foul of the arsonist."

"Oh, I want to say hi." Byssa hurried ahead of me. "I love that little guy."

"Here's hoping your roommates don't mind bathing with a cephalopod," said Hades. "It's a little strange, but to each her own."

I pushed his shoulder playfully. "Don't be weird. Get your towel. We'll meet you outside in a few minutes."

I entered our dorm room after Byssa. Kim was in her bunk reading a book and smiled when she noticed me.

"Feeling more comfortable these days?" she said. When I frowned, she waved at my head. "You're losing the wig and contacts more frequently. It's a good look on you."

"Thanks," I said slowly. I'd been ditching my disguising accessories lately, despite the danger of recognition by pale folk guests. They felt more cumbersome than usual, and it was freeing to be myself.

At the Lodge, I was surrounded by half-sirens who didn't look twice at white hair and pale eyes.

Byssa was already in the bathroom, but she hadn't yet emitted any squeals of delight, which was unusual for her upon meeting Squirter. Her head twisted and turned as if searching.

"Where did you put him?" she said.

I frowned and joined her in the doorway. "In the bathtub with buckets of seawater. Why, isn't he there?"

"No." Byssa sank onto her hands and knees and peered under the sink cabinet. She glanced at the toilet bowl with a grimace. "He wouldn't go in there, would he?"

"I hope not." I peeked just in case, but the bowl was empty. So too was the counter except for two different-sized loofah sponges that someone had left beside the sink. I wasn't seriously worried—Squirter could take care of himself—but I was curious about which crack he'd squeezed himself into.

Byssa stood with her hands on her hips. She rummaged in the cupboard, then ran her hands over the counter. When her fingers encountered the first loofah sponge, she lifted it to check underneath.

"He's not that small," I said, laughing despite my niggling concern.

Byssa glared at me. "I'm not leaving anything unturned until we find Squirter." She reached for the second sponge, then she shrieked.

At the sound, the sponge turned a vibrant red and unfurled eight arms. I laughed again even harder and scooped up the little octopus.

Funny, I hummed to him, and he vibrated back with happiness.

"You're a menace," Byssa said aloud, rubbing him on his mantle. He reached out a tentacle and wrapped it gently around her finger.

"I'll take him in the backpack," I said to Byssa, placing Squirter gently into the bath. "So guests don't see him. Hold on."

I grabbed my specially reinforced backpack, filled the insert with Squirter's bathwater, and tucked the octopus inside. He hummed happily against my back. Byssa took two towels from the bathroom, then we said goodbye to Kim and met Hades outside. Together, the three of us traipsed down to the small south beach and disrobed on the shore.

My toes curled around pebbles on the beach, and I tipped Squirter out while the other two chewed small pieces of Grace. Byssa frowned at me.

"Aren't you going to have some?" she said. "I hate swimming without that boost."

"I forgot," I lied. Most of my spare Grace was earmarked for Branc, but my friends still didn't know about him. I was too embarrassed to admit how naïve I'd been when I'd first arrived, and I didn't want to have them offer charity for my stupid mistake. "It's fine. The cave isn't far."

Hades eyed me but didn't comment. Byssa ripped her piece of dried Grace between her teeth and offered it to me. To my surprise, my eyes prickled.

"You don't have to—" I began, but Byssa shook her head.

173

"Just take it," she said. "Come on, Squirter is waiting."

Byssa shoved the Grace in my hand and turned to wade into the waves. I hesitated for a moment, but the lure of Grace won me over. I chewed it greedily and closed my eyes as sensations tore through my body like being tossed in a powerful wave of my favorite things.

The sea beckoned, and I walked into the water that glimmered gold in the sunset. After a deep breath, I dived into an oncoming wave.

My skin sense blossomed, clearer and more vibrant than usual, thanks to the Grace in my veins. I emptied my lungs of air and endured the uncomfortable hacking until they filled with seawater. Byssa and Hades were directly ahead, waiting for me, and Squirter gripped Byssa's shoulder with his suction cups. The little octopus was a sucker for her tickles.

I caught up, despite the drag from my unwieldy package of stinging nettles, and led the way toward the secret cave. On the way, I sensed the wolf eel who had come to my rescue. I stopped and made a sound of gratitude.

The eel twined her way around a rock and eyed me. Wolf eels were well-known for staying within their territory, and I wondered if she had seen the arsonist. I tried a simple question.

Bad swimmer here. Looks?

The wolf eel twisted around my legs. Her answer came a moment later.

Big. Dark. Pale face. She twisted around my stomach. *Also, big animal here sometimes. Long. Don't know it.*

She streamed away, back to her den, and my shoulders

slumped. I hadn't expected much—all humans likely looked alike to a wolf eel—but I had hoped. Still, the culprit likely had dark hair and pale skin, so that was something.

What was her comment about the long animal? I would have dismissed it, except for the memory of the large, sinuous creature at the edge of my skin sense last week.

I shook my head. One mystery at a time.

I continued to lead the way until the cliff face loomed over us. Hades and I waited for Byssa to take a breath of air at the surface. When she returned, Hades unsheathed a diving knife he'd strapped to his leg and held it out before him. When his legs disappeared into the hole, I followed.

Byssa's body drew near to my legs, and the three of us traversed the dark tunnel in a line. When we emerged into the cave, Hades looked around with interest.

Kind of small, he said. *Let's get a scent.*

He opened his mouth and allowed seawater to flow inside. I cursed my ineptitude. I'd swum so often without Grace in the past year that I'd forgotten the information available in water. Taste could give huge insight. I opened my mouth wide.

Hades and Byssa were the predominant flavors of the water. Hades was peppery, and Byssa tasted like the sweetness of honey. I closed my eyes and tried to detect fainter signals. After a moment, a hazy but distinctive flavor of cloves mingled with the others in my mouth.

Once I'd memorized the taste, I closed my mouth and looked around. Squirter jetted happily around the small space, loving the company.

Any more clues? I asked.

Look here. Hades waved us over. *A note.*

I sighed in disappointment. *There was a note last time, too. Here, pass it over. I'll check it.*

Hades handed it to me with a twisted mouth—he wanted to read Seamount-script better, but it was complicated—and my eyes glanced over the words. It was a different note than last time, and I gripped the scapular bone hard. The arsonist must have scrubbed out the last note and written this new one in its place.

What does it say? Byssa said with impatience.

The Lodge is almost closed, I read aloud. *Give me another day, and your Grace won't have anywhere to land. And don't use this cave for messages again—it's being watched.*

It was written in poorly formed script, as if by a child, which was more evidence of the arsonist being half-siren.

Who is the note for? Hades asked.

I shoved the bone back in the bag. *Whoever the arsonist is working for. Pale folk who don't want Grace coming to land.* I pointed at the tunnel. *Come on, let's set this trap. You two guard outside, and I'll glue on the nettles.*

I left Byssa and Hades dripping at the bunkhouse door and sought out Levi in the Lodge. I twisted my wet hair into a bun at the nape of my neck to stop it from dribbling water down my back, then entered the dining hall from the bottom lawn.

Levi wasn't there—not that I'd expected him to be—so I wandered upstairs into the restaurant, empty at this late hour, and into a hallway. Where should I look for him? I now knew where his suite was downstairs, but I balked at invading Levi's privacy so blatantly. His whole life was centered around the Lodge. Surely, he deserved a break from it occasionally. If his rooms weren't sacred, where else would be?

He'd said he had things to work on this evening. Maybe he was in his office. Happy to have a destination, I strode purposefully down the staff hallway toward a half-open door. Rustling and murmured voices filtered through, and I pushed it open further.

Levi and his brother Austin sat on either side of the wide desk, flipping through copious piles of papers that littered the desktop. I cleared my throat gently to announce my presence, and both men glanced up.

"Lune," Levi said with gladness in his voice. "You're back. How did it go?"

"What were you doing?" Austin asked in his lighter voice. He brushed a lock of floppy hair out of his eyes and stared at me.

I glanced at Levi. How widespread did we want this information to go? He didn't look at me, instead shuffling his papers around to search for something.

"Lune found a cave underwater with the arsonist's belongings inside, then she was attacked by him." Levi picked up a paper in triumph. Austin continued to look at me. "Here it is. Anyway, so she set up stinging nettles in the tunnel leading to the cave so we can identify the culprit by his rashes once he visits the cave again. Clever, right?"

"Very," Austin murmured. When I glanced at him, he gave me a small smile. "Nicely done."

My mouth twisted. "Unfortunately, the arsonist already visited the cave. I found a new note warning the pale folk not to return there. How do we get him to go back to his hideout?"

Levi's brow creased, and Austin's head tilted.

"Won't the arsonist return to clear out the cave once the pale folk read their message?" Austin said. "I can't imagine he would leave evidence behind for long. He knows we're onto him."

"I hope you're right," I said. "I'm ready to solve this mystery."

"That's what we're doing tonight, too," Levi said. He waved the paper he'd found. "We're looking for irregularities in the finances in case the culprit is using Lodge money oddly. It's a slim chance, but I have to turn over every stone."

"What did you find?" Austin said, his eyes on the paper.

"The April credit card statement for card three." He glanced over the numbers, but his face fell when his eyes reached the bottom. He threw it down in disgust. "Nothing strange. I wish I knew where the card two July statement was. That's the only one we're missing."

"Let's check again," Austin suggested, and the two brothers bent their heads over the papers.

"I'll let you get on with it," I said. "Oh, one more thing. I saw Henry smirking at the sinking boat today—you know, the guy with the ponytail—so he's a suspect on my list now. I confirmed with some guests that he was at the marina the day the boats drifted away. Austin, you were there too. Did you notice Henry acting oddly?"

"Not that I remember." Austin's brow furrowed. "Wait, he might have run back to grab forgotten tools after we'd already left the marina. I think that was him. Worth investigating, anyway."

"Henry?" Levi said in disbelief. "I can't imagine him ever doing all this. And why?"

"You don't think anyone at the Lodge could do this," Austin said. "That's why it's so hard to investigate."

Levi's shoulders slumped. "I know. I can't believe it of anybody."

He rubbed his eyes. I wondered how much sleep he'd been getting the past week, with all the chaos. He blinked, and something fell into his outstretched hand.

"Damn it," he muttered, keeping one eye closed. "My contact fell out."

Without looking at either of us, he rushed out the door. As he passed, I glimpsed the contact in his hand. To my surprise, it was an opaque blue. Why would Levi wear colored contacts?

"I'm glad my eyes are good," Austin said behind me. "My pale folk blood does something right. Have you ever heard of pale folk wearing glasses?"

"It's handy that our eyes are used to changing diffractive distance," I said automatically, but my mind was on Levi's eyes.

"Sucks to be human," Austin said with emphasis.

I awoke the next morning to Kim squealing.

"It's Grace payment day!"

Something landed on my stomach, and I patted it with my hand to find out what. A crinkly package met my questing fingers, and I cracked open my eyes.

In my hand was a plump waxed envelope of dried Grace. My stomach squeezed with anticipation.

"Amazing," Byssa said in a thick, sleepy voice from above me. She hung her head over the edge. "Want to go for a swim later? I'm so taking a double dose."

"Yeah." I would save most of the package for Branc, but a little wouldn't set me back in my debt repayment too much, I hoped. "That sounds great."

Byssa climbed down from her bunk and put her arms up in an elegant arc. "Wait. if yesterday was Friday, that means today is Saturday."

"Congrats." I tucked my head into my pillow and spoke in a muffled voice. "You know the days of the week."

A pillow thumped against my backside.

"Saturday means Grace-Harvest," Byssa said with glee. "Finally. I've been waiting for this for weeks. For years, actually, ever since I left the Seamount. It's going to be amazing. Please say you'll come."

I frowned into my pillow. Why wouldn't Byssa let this go? I had no desire to dredge up my past. Land was my home now.

"I'm not going," I said. "And I recommend you don't,

either. Getting involved in all that will only bring you heartache, especially when you can never go back to the Seamount and partake in the proper ceremony."

Byssa's eyes bored a hole in the side of my head. I groaned and faced her accusing eyes.

"Why would you say that?" she said, her hands on her hips. "You don't need to rub it in that I can't breathe properly underwater. I know perfectly well why Hades and I came to land when we were five."

My stomach shriveled. I hadn't been thinking of Byssa when I'd said what I had. I'd been thinking of myself.

"I'm sorry. I didn't mean it like that."

"And I think you're wrong." Byssa turned to a nearby dresser and pulled out clothes with jerky motions. "Why is it all-or-nothing? Why can't we celebrate one of the most important days of our calendar wherever we are? Why can't the misfits gather and celebrate what makes us who we are? I wouldn't miss it for the world."

She turned her back on me, slipped into her clothes, and followed Kim into the communal bathroom. I closed my eyes, and my mouth tightened. I wanted to take the words to Byssa back—hurting my sweet friend was like a bone spear in my gut—but they were out in the world now. And I meant them.

Didn't I?

CHAPTER 17

Byssa's manner was stiff when she emerged from the bathroom, but she waited for me before leaving for breakfast. I tried to talk about light, normal things—how murky the water was this time of year, whether the jellyfish were blooming yet or not, how long before Hades would dye his hair a different color—and by the time we reached the dining hall, she was almost back to her usual self.

We were the first to arrive for breakfast, and kitchen staff were laying out the first dishes on the buffet table. I rubbed my hands together.

"I'm starving," I said. "Dinner was good yesterday, but lunch was one lonely little sea urchin. Time to eat properly today."

Byssa spooned porridge into her bowl then lifted it to her nose. She sniffed with her eyes closed. "Mmm, warm porridge reminds me of my aunt's cooking."

I ladled porridge into my own bowl. The stuff was odd at best, gloopy at worst, but it was the only dish out this early.

Byssa turned her head when two young men entered the dining hall, rubbing their eyes and yawning. My own eyes widened, and I looked quickly down at my bowl to compose myself. The one with the ponytail was Henry, and this was my chance to interrogate him.

Byssa greeted the duo with her usual peppy cheer, and they wandered our way. My eyes raked over their bodies—if one of them were the culprit, surely I would see evidence of stinging nettle rashes—but both were distressingly smooth-skinned and content.

"You're up early," she said.

"Jess has a project she wants done today." Henry groaned. "I shouldn't have finished that tequila last night with Quentin." He elbowed his friend next to him.

"Is there a good pub in town?" I asked as a prelude to my more searching questions.

"Oh, yeah, the Singing Seahorse is great," said Quentin. "We go there all the time; it's super lively. Their pool cues are bent, but the beer is good."

"What's the best night to go?" I grabbed a spoon to cover my interest. "Fridays must be good."

"I didn't go yesterday, but last Friday was raucous," Quentin said. "Remember, Henry? We had dinner there and didn't leave until closing time."

"Because you were too busy chatting up the bartender." Henry chuckled. "It's tough being a wingman. We get no credit. And since Nolan was being weird and didn't come with us that night, I had to follow you around."

"You're here to watch and learn, young grasshopper," Quentin said in a pretentious tone. Henry shoved him on the shoulder, and Quentin laughed and grabbed a bowl.

Byssa and I moved away to find a table. I slid onto a bench, wilting with disappointment that yet another suspect had struck himself off my list. Then my head perked up. Their friend Nolan hadn't been with them, which they'd considered strange. Could he be my next target? With no other leads, Nolan was my next best hope.

Our bunkmate Kim burst into the dining hall from the hallway that led to the kitchen and stairs. Her eyes were wild, and she glanced around with jerky motions of her head.

"I need a knife," she rasped out. Her hands patted the buffet table, but it held only the porridge pot. She spun and ran toward the kitchen door. I looked at Byssa, and she shook her head.

"What's up with her?" I said.

"She must need help with something. Come on."

Byssa jumped up and I followed. Shouts punctuated music filtering through the kitchen's open doorway, and we sped up.

Kim waved a huge meat cleaver in the air, and the head cook held out her hands as she backed away. Martin and Otto were frozen against the walk-in fridge door. Martin's spiky green hair crushed into the metal, and Otto's scarred face was twisted further with fear.

"Put down the knife," the head cook said in a shaking voice. "I don't know what you're doing, but you need to stop."

"They all need to die!" Kim shrieked. She gestured at the ceiling with the cleaver. "Every guest here is a traitor. I'm going upstairs whether you're in the way or not."

I gaped at our usually calm and pleasant bunkmate. Had she snapped? Was she finally exposing a seedy underbelly of the Lodge?

Kim rushed at us, and Byssa and I pressed against the hallway wall. The crazed woman darted toward the stairs to the guest restaurant above.

"Lune," Byssa hissed. "What do we do?"

I ran after Kim, my mind sorting through my options. I could tackle her, but I didn't like the look of that knife. I could shout ahead to warn the diners, but Levi's horrified reaction at disturbing guests sprang to mind.

Luckily, I was half-siren. If I could reach Kim, I had a good chance of controlling her, assuming she wasn't under the influence of some illegal drug that I couldn't break through or being controlled by a more powerful siren than me.

Kim was halfway up the stairs when I grabbed her around the waist. We fell forward, and the meat cleaver thudded against the step. I clutched her body to my chest and hummed desperately.

Kim stiffened, then she melted against the stairs, compliant with the power of my calming hum. I relaxed and halted my song, ready to turn it on again the instant Kim returned to her crazed state. Byssa snatched the meat cleaver and backed down the steps.

"Lune?" Kim said in a muffled voice. "What's going on? Can you get up? You're squashing my hip into the step."

I pushed to my feet. Kim rolled over and wobbled to a standing position. She passed a trembling hand over her face.

"What was I doing?" she murmured. "I don't understand."

"I think I do." I glanced at Byssa meaningfully. "Someone sirened you to attack guests. Remember the arson attempt, and the poisoning, and the boat incident? Someone is trying to sabotage the Lodge, and you were the most recent victim."

Kim swallowed. "I was going to hurt people." Her voice shook. "With that knife."

"Come to the dining hall," Byssa said in a soothing tone. She passed me the meat cleaver and drew Kim down the stairs with an arm around her shoulders. "Have some breakfast. Food makes everything better."

I stared at the meat cleaver in my trembling hands. The arsonist wasn't holding back. If he'd been successful this morning, Kim might have hurt someone and gone to jail or a psychiatric ward. The Lodge certainly would have suffered alongside her.

The arsonist could siren others, that was clear. He would have been in this hallway this morning to come across a defenseless Kim, who had no siren abilities of her own. The kitchen staff was well-placed to administer Kim's treatment. If I hadn't already ruled out Martin, my money would be squarely on him.

Considering Kim had threatened the head cook, Martin, and Otto first, it was unlikely that any of them were the culprit. All had looked genuinely shocked, and none showed signs of nettle rash. Were they excellent actors or innocent?

Either way, the arsonist wasn't letting up. I needed to solve this mystery before anyone else got hurt. Nolan might have been skulking around this morning, out of sight. Barring any new leads, he was my next suspect.

Sheila cornered me after breakfast with narrowed

eyes.

"I don't know what special task Levi has you down for," she said. "But it will have to wait. Gerri called in sick, and I need the dockside rooms cleaned this morning."

I sighed inwardly but nodded my agreement. Sheila stalked off.

I turned to Byssa. "If you figure out which one Nolan is, let me know, okay?"

"Of course." Byssa bit her lip. "We'll figure this out."

I hoped she was right, but our leads were as rare as an angelfish in northern seas. Hopefully, the nettle trap would work, and we'd see the arsonist covered in rashes this afternoon.

Heartened by this thought, I gathered Squirter into my backpack from the dorm bathroom. He could play in the undersea rooms while I cleaned. I grabbed cleaning supplies from the supply house, then entered the dockside suites and began to work.

The monotonous chores lulled me into a meditative state, only broken by Squirter's antics underwater. He liked to chase my sponge around and occasionally mimic its shape and texture. I pretended to grab him a few times, and he clicked in delight at my teasing.

At the third room, the door swung open at my knock.

"Sorry," I muttered, also making an apologetic hand signal to the familiar-looking man from yesterday. Today, Cherub wore an orange buttoned shirt, long pants that fit loosely, and bare feet. "I'll come back later."

He beckoned me inside. "You are cleaning? Stay, please."

I eyed him as I entered. "We spoke at the patio yesterday," I said finally.

"Yes." Cherub smiled and walked over to the couch. He flopped onto it after a glance at the open trapdoor filled with water. "You asked about workers. Is it okay?"

Not much was okay, but I remembered Levi's desire to keep guests in the dark, so I smiled brightly.

"Yes, everything's fine."

I started to sweep, conscious of Cherub's eyes on me. He appeared curious more than anything, and I found myself contrasting his pale locks and round cheeks to Levi's silky dark hair and large eyes, flat blue though they were. Although apparently, he wore colored contacts. Intense desire to see his real eyes swept over me.

Whoa. What was I thinking about? I swept more vigorously, but it didn't sweep the images of Levi from my mind. In desperation, I spoke to the guest.

"Were you here eight nights ago? Do you remember where you were that evening?"

When I glanced Cherub's way, he was frowning at me. Maybe I was too direct with my questions, but if he gave me answers, it would be worth it.

"At an eating place," he said finally. "Away from here. We ate cow in bread."

I suppressed my giggle. Had they visited a burger joint? Still, any questioning about the night of the arson wouldn't be helpful, and he'd already spoken about the marina incident. A thought occurred to me.

"You saw workers at the marina five days ago. Do you remember one coming back to the marina after they had finished?"

He frowned and shook his head. "We left. I didn't see."

"Okay, thanks."

He stood and walked over to me. I leaned on my broom and considered him.

"Something is going on," he said. "You are worried. I can feel it."

With a start, I ceased the unconscious faint hum of distress from deep in my chest. How had he picked up on it from across the room?

"Humming moves in the floor," he said, correctly answering my unspoken question. "If you do it louder, you could siren me or anyone."

"It's too far away," I said. Surely, I needed physical contact for my song to be effective.

He shook his head and pointed at the floor. "Touch, not hearing. It is a land thing. You did not know?"

I stared at him. Was he right? When I'd sirened others in the past, I'd either chosen a quiet environment or had touched them. Could my vibrations travel through hard surfaces without my target needing to hear them? Air was so strange. Water vibrated easily, and it was everywhere when living under the sea.

"Thanks." I smiled at him, grateful for the tip. I didn't know how I could use it in the future, but it was good to understand the extent of my capabilities. "I didn't know that."

Cherub nodded and returned to his couch. I finished sweeping and wiped the window, but my thoughts raced. Here was yet another pleasant and helpful Seamount inhabitant. Apparently, the good ones weren't as much

189

of an anomaly as I'd first believed. But where had they been when I was a bottom feeder under the sea?

A loud creak startled me out of my ruminations. I glanced at Cherub, who looked confused at the sound.

"I think it came from outside," I said. "I'll go investigate."

"Use our entrance." He pointed at the trapdoor. "My partner is a good sleeper. He won't notice you."

I nodded and slipped out of my uniform, then pulled my backpack closer to the trapdoor. With a guilty glance at Cherub—would he mind Squirter swimming in his lower room?—I pulled the little octopus from the inner container and dropped him into the water, then slid in after him. The hook-nosed man who had been on the patio floated on the far side of the room, strapped to the wall. I swam gently to the outer door, careful not to disturb his slumber. When the sliding door glided open, I beckoned to Squirter and floated outside.

When we were both in the murky bottom of the bay, I closed the door and looked around. Pilings thrust deep into the sand anchored the floating dockside rooms, which nearly brushed the ground during low tide.

Weird noise, I said to Squirter when he made a formless sound of question. *Find.*

Squirter floated, motionless, in the gentle wave action. A creak vibrated through my body. My head whipped around, and Squirter jetted in that direction. I followed, curious about the source.

A piling at the end of the dock loomed into sight. I stopped, appalled. Without a generous helping of Grace, my skin sense hadn't felt the sort of detail that my eyes could see.

My side of the piling was intact, but the oceanside wood was eaten away, chopped by some sharp instrument until barely a third of the piling's diameter was anchoring the building above.

Without the piling anchors, nothing would stop the dockside rooms from floating out to sea.

CHAPTER 18

The creaking noise pulsed through my body again, and the piling visibly wobbled. Squirter darted back to me from his inspection of the piling and attached himself to my bare shoulder with firm suction cups.

Another creak sounded from a short distance away. I kicked closer. The other piling that anchored the dockside rooms in their place on the shore was in even worse shape. Without the pilings' stabilization, the dockside rooms would drift away, causing extensive damage and ruining half the Lodge's rooms, specifically rooms meant for pale folk. I took one last, horrified glance, then kicked back to the room I'd entered the sea from.

I swam quietly past the sleeping siren and hauled myself onto the upper floor. Cherub glanced at me with curiosity.

"You found it?" he asked.

"Nothing to worry about," I said with a bright smile plastered to my face. I scooped up Squirter with one hand and dropped him in my backpack. "Some routine maintenance needed, that's all."

I pulled on my absorbent uniform, wiped water marks off the floor, and fled the room. Straight to the Lodge I jogged, my backpack uncomfortably heavy on my shoulders. Squirter hummed his displeasure at our fast pace, but I needed to tell Levi the news.

When I burst into the front lobby, Levi was mercifully speaking with Sandy and a customer. I beckoned him with frantic motions, and he made his excuses and walked toward me.

"The dockside rooms are about to drift into the strait," I hissed once he was near enough. "Someone's hacked at the pilings. There's hardly anything left."

Levi's face grew pale.

"Find Jess," he said hoarsely. "She and her maintenance crew should be behind the bunkhouse this morning. Tell them to bring tools. I'll clear out the dockside rooms."

I nodded and raced away, my boots thudding on the gravel outside. Jess and three others were resetting loose stones of the front entry gateposts. I skidded to a halt at the maintenance crew leader's side.

"Emergency maintenance needed at the dockside rooms," I gasped. "Underwater. Levi said to come with tools right away."

To her credit, Jess dropped what she was doing and corralled her crew with a few urgent words. I left them to run to the supply shed while I slipped into the bunkhouse. The bathtub was still filled with seawater, so I dumped a grumpy Squirter into it. I threw in my hairbrush and a few hair ties for toys, gave him a quick mantle tickle as an apology, then raced outside.

Levi held the door of the dockside rooms open as disgruntled customers exited.

"Please make your way to the restaurant for a complimentary meal," he called out. "And thank you for your patience while we sort out this inconvenience."

I stood beside him and translated his message for a few confused-looking pale folk. When their eyes lighted on the restaurant and the final guests had filed out of the ocean wing, Levi's shoulders slumped.

"I don't know how long this can go on for." He passed a shaking hand over his eyes. "If I can't get to the bottom of this, guests will be hurt, our reputation will be shot, and we might have to close the Lodge."

Was the Lodge's existence that fragile? I had been about to tell Levi of Kim's misadventure this morning, but I couldn't bring myself to burden him more. My heart squeezed at his anguish. Then it nearly stopped as the implications sank in. If Levi closed the Lodge, was that it for my dreams of freedom? Were my cash and Grace slipping out of reach?

"I haven't seen anyone with stinging nettle rashes, but I have one more lead." I placed my hand on Levi's firm forearm. "I'll follow it up today."

I still needed to figure out who Nolan was. It was almost lunchtime, so I wandered to the dining hall in search of him. Hopefully, he ate with everyone else.

My distraction made me dribble butter onto the serving table when I dished out well-salted carrots and peas. My eyes scanned the room and raked across every face.

When I saw an unfamiliar pale young man with messy brown dreadlocks laughing with ponytailed Henry near a window, my stomach squeezed in triumph. I casually walked over to Kim and placed my plate across from hers. Her cheeks were a healthy pink—a far cry from her pale wildness this morning—and her eyes were bright.

"Hey," I said. "Busy day?"

"Always," she said through a mouthful of seafood lasagna. "Had a rough start, of course, but it went up from there." She dropped her voice to a whisper. "I've been wearing ear buds and blaring music when I'm not serving customers. It's the best defense I can think of to avoid being sirened again."

"Levi is on it," I assured her. "He'll figure out who did this to you." I hadn't told Levi about Kim yet, but the arsonist was clearly behind her attack. I rested my elbows on the table and leaned forward to hear Kim's suspicions. It wasn't like I had many other ideas to go on. "Do you think someone's disgruntled with the Lodge?"

"I have no idea." Kim sipped her water. "I can't see how. We're treated really well here." She grimaced. "But after this morning, I don't know what to believe."

Her face fell, and I changed the subject to brighten her spirits.

"You've been here longer than I have." I nodded toward my target of interest. "What's that guy's name, the one with the dreads?"

Kim glanced over. "Nolan?" she asked with a raised eyebrow at me. "Why, are you interested in him?"

"Maybe." I shrugged and pretended to look shy. Interest was a good cover for my questions. I didn't want Kim to turn her suspicions on everyone at the Lodge. For a trusting person, it would be demoralizing. "Is he human or half-siren? Do you think he'd come for a swim? I'm always more natural underwater."

Kim snorted and dug her fork into her lasagna. "Good luck. He technically has some siren in him way back, but otherwise human all the way. I've seen him 'swim'. You'd think he was a dying seal with all the flailing and splashing."

My heart sank like a rock to the seafloor. If Nolan wasn't the arsonist, who was? I had no more leads.

"Too bad," I said with real regret. "Maybe he's not for me."

We passed the rest of lunch speaking about trivial things, and I tried not to dwell on my disappointment and growing anxiety. With no leads, how could I discover the arsonist? With no culprit caught, how could the Lodge stay open? Were my dreams of independence drifting into silt before my eyes?

With no leads to follow, and a grumpy Sheila to appease, I cleaned rooms for the first part of the afternoon until it was time for the Grace-Harvest celebration. When I returned to the bunkhouse to change out of my dirty, damp clothes, I surprised Byssa with her arms outstretched in the middle of the dorm room.

"Lune." Byssa flopped her arms against her sides with a doleful expression. "I can't remember the moves for the Grace-Harvest dances tonight. I really wanted to take part, not just be a spectator."

She looked ready to cry. Despite my distaste for anything to do with the upcoming celebration, her distress moved me. I couldn't let my friend swim to Grace-Harvest unprepared, not when it meant so much to her. A wave of guilt washed over me. I'd promised to show her the moves earlier, and I hadn't fulfilled that promise.

"Start like this." I took her wrists and lifted them into position, then stood across from her with my arms similarly raised. "And sweep them around."

Slowly, haltingly, we stepped through the motions of the main Grace-Harvest dance. It was necessarily awkward since we were limited to two-dimensional movements. With every minute that passed, Byssa's moves grew surer, and her eyes brightened.

"Are you sure you won't come this afternoon?" Byssa said when we finished. "Dancing, fresh Grace, and all that. I'll really miss you there."

"No," I said automatically, but my voice lacked the conviction of before. Dancing with Byssa had brought back happy memories of joining in with the vast, city-wide dance of the Seamount's Grace-Harvest, when for one night we were all equal under Ramu's grace. Dancing beside my friends Pelagia and Cetus, next to my foster father Eelway… my throat closed as I remembered anew that I would likely never see them again.

But dancing no longer pierced me with a bone blade of memories. Instead, I remembered Pelagia's laughing mouth and Cetus's eyes closed in ecstasy with a piece of fresh Grace on his lips. My heart squeezed, and I opened my mouth to change my answer, but Byssa had already turned away in disappointment. My lips snapped shut. It was for the better. I wanted to move on, embrace my land-based life. And one of the pale folk might recognize me. It wasn't worth the risk. My excuses sounded hollow, even to my ears.

Kim returned to the bunkhouse, along with four other women. They changed into their best swimsuits—Kim's had glittering rhinestones embedded along the bodice— and one woman donned a flowy chiffon dress that mimicked a Seamount style. It wasn't made of prepared seaweed, but it would drift around her in a similar fashion.

Byssa hugged me goodbye, and the group joined Hades and the others in the hall. Then, laughing and chattering, they traipsed out of the building. The door swung shut with a heavy finality, closing me off from everyone else.

I took out my contacts in the bathroom and blinked to remove the dry sensation that I never got used to. To take my mind off my aloneness, I sat next to the bathtub and ran my fingers through the water. Squirter wrapped a tentacle around my smallest finger, and my eyes grew hot.

"Maybe I made a mistake," I whispered to the little octopus. He wouldn't understand me, but I needed to talk to someone. "None of the pale folk has recognized me yet. Maybe I'm not as infamous as I fear."

Squirter squeezed my finger, clearly sensing my distress. I leaned my head back and blinked furiously. Through a big sniff, I heard a knock on the dorm door.

"Levi?" I said when I opened the door. "What are you doing here?"

"Your friend Byssa mentioned you weren't planning to go to the Grace-Harvest celebrations." He shifted from foot to foot, then held out a waxed envelope. "I thought you might like some of the fresh Grace they'll be handing out down below."

I stared at the bulging envelope. My mouth watered, and my mind whirled. Levi's thoughtfulness overwhelmed me, but the notion of eating fresh Grace by myself in my room was repulsive. I'd never spent Grace-Harvest alone—except for last year, during my escape—and I didn't want to start now. Vents, no one had recognized me yet. I wanted to celebrate alongside my friends on the most important day of the year. I might live on land now, but that didn't mean I had to forget everything from my life before. Much of it wasn't worth remembering, but some of it was. I didn't want to toss the shark out with the remoras.

"Thanks for thinking of me," I said, my voice thick with emotion. "Truly. But I think I'll join the others, after all."

Levi nodded. He searched my face, then he gave me a smile that didn't reach his sad eyes.

"You're lucky to be a part of it," he said softly. "It's smart to not take your inclusion for granted."

I bit my lip. Did Levi think of me as a petulant child who didn't know a good thing when it was in front of her? The longing in his voice told me otherwise. He wanted to experience Grace-Harvest, but as a human, he had no chance at joining the underwater celebrations.

How difficult had his upbringing been? His parents seemed loving, and they clearly trusted him as a son, but he was not of their blood and could never be fully like them. What other activities had he not been included in, especially living at the Lodge? His lack of swimming ability couldn't have helped, and I wondered again how he could avoid the water here, of all places.

I didn't know what to say, so I placed my hand on his arm and squeezed it gently. A quick hum of understanding, too low to hear, vibrated through my chest by accident. His face cleared, and he gazed at me with a vulnerable expression.

"See you after the celebration?" I said quietly. "Plan our next moves and all that?"

"Yeah." He cleared his throat and moved toward the door. My hand slipped off his arm. "See you then."

I quickly changed into an actual swimsuit for the occasion—too bad my kelp dress was back in Vancouver—threw a towel around my body, packed Squirter in his backpack, and slunk out the door. No human guests were wandering the paths today, and I followed unobtrusive temporary signs written in Seamount-script toward the quiet cove to the south.

Once at the shore, I threw my towel into a pile of

others, tipped Squirter into the water, waded in after him, and submerged.

I wanted to do this right, so I breathed out fully then sucked back a lungful of water. My diaphragm seized and cramped with a coughing fit, but soon enough, I expelled all air from my body and breathed salty water once more. The cool green sea was murky with algae, but my path was clear. Humming drew me forward, the sound welcoming and familiar. Homesickness lanced through me with physical pangs, and Squirter jetted close to me for comfort.

My skin sense felt the people before my eyes saw them. A group of thirty, forty, maybe fifty pale folk gathered in a cluster above the seafloor. A rocky outcrop topped with anemones jutted upward in the center, and figures danced around it.

I swam closer and floated behind the nearest group of spectators. The water wasn't clear enough to see anything but the nearest edge of the dance circle, but my skin sense gathered impressions of the dancers' beautiful movements. With satisfaction, I saw a flash of Byssa's black hair and tasted her scent in my open mouth as she passed. She was dancing. Although she occasionally raised the wrong arm or twisted the other way, her movements were graceful and sure, and her joy was palpable.

Byssa had been dreaming of this day for weeks, and I smiled at her delight. I wished my own feelings for the celebration were as simple as hers. I disliked rubbing shoulders with the entitled pale folk from the Seamount, here for a vacation, uncaring about the lower levels in their home, disdainful of half-humans.

Not all of them were like that, I reminded myself. The pale folk I'd met here showed no sign of snobbery toward me or the other workers. They didn't fight for us at the Seamount, but maybe they were ignorant. Could the Lodge act as a place of enlightenment for the upper echelons? Suddenly, I saw the Lodge in a whole new light.

Nostalgia was my predominant feeling, though. Maybe I had been wrong to banish everything related to the Seamount from my life. Times had been hard there, but my heritage, experiences, and friends had surrounded me, and I didn't want to forget them all. I closed my eyes and basked in the collective vibrating song of my people.

Thank Ramu for the Grace that sustains us...

A familiar scent of cloves filled my mouth as a group of spectators passed me by. My eyes blinked open, and I scanned the faces. Most were workers from the Lodge—Nolan, Austin, Otto, and others whose names I didn't know—and I frowned. Where had I tasted that scent before?

The humming changed cadence, and I put the mystery from my mind. The final dance was about to begin, then they would hand out fresh Grace. A shiver ran down my spine with anticipation.

Byssa floated by again, but this time she spotted me. She darted my way and pulled me by the arm toward the circle of dancers.

You're here, she said happily in our language of hums, clicks, and gestures. *We need one more. Eliza was hurt at the boat accident. Please, step in for her. We need an even number of people, otherwise, I can't dance.*

I wavered. Attending was one thing, but dancing was a whole other level of commitment. Did I really want to dive in with everything I had, as well as expose myself to all the visiting pale folk?

Byssa's beseeching face won me over.

Okay, I said with reluctance. *I'll do it.*

Byssa threw her arms around me, and we twisted in midwater.

Yes! she said. *Come on, we're about to start.*

As soon as my limbs moved to the lilting calls of callo whistles and the collective songs of my people, I was transformed. No longer was I Lune Seafields, aquarium worker and perennial debtor. I was Moongleam, proud siren of the sea.

My eyes closed, and I performed the moves almost without thinking, so ingrained in my psyche were they. The movements of the other dancers flowed over my skin in a sensual way, and our fluid motions ran together in a circle of perfect harmony. Byssa missed a few moves, but it didn't matter. We were all connected under Ramu's Grace, and for the first time in a very long year, I was part of something greater than myself. It was intoxicating, and time ceased to exist as I swam, floated, and twisted around the spire of anemone-blanketed rock.

Finally, the song ended. I opened my eyes, both exhilarated and sheepish at my previous trance-like state. Byssa slipped her hand into mine, and I squeezed back, happy for the contact.

Levi's mother Seafoam swam around the circle,

distributing fresh Grace to each dancer first before the spectators. When she came to me, I opened my mouth, and she placed a slice of Grace on my tongue. When I closed my mouth on the chewy morsel, flavor exploded. A groan of ecstasy escaped me, and Byssa's hand clenched in mine as she received her own Grace.

My limbs, previously tired from the dance, grew strong again. Scents in the water flowed across my tongue with vibrant pungency. Facial features of other dancers grew clearer as my eyesight sharpened. My legs and arms practically moved on their own as we whirled around the circle in the closing dance. Byssa's eyes shone when I caught her gaze.

Once the dance ended and the sensation of fresh Grace had faded in intensity, I followed a giddy Byssa and satisfied Hades back to the beach. As much as I hated to admit that I might be wrong, I wondered if there were something to being part of the Lodge after all. I hadn't felt this peaceful since I'd arrived on land. Maybe I'd been wrong to write off my entire history just because of how a few upper echelons had treated me. I had many parts, and maybe it was time to embrace them all.

CHAPTER 19

I left Squirter underwater with the admonishment to be careful. He tickled my ear before darting away, and I smiled with a squeeze of my heart. He needed some playtime in the ocean, but it was hard to see him go.

When Byssa, Hades, and I emerged, dripping, from the water onto the tiny beach I'd started from, Levi was waiting in the tree line. His worried face was lit orange with the setting sun, and he waved at me.

I grabbed my towel and wrapped it around myself before trudging up the pebbly beach toward him.

"What's up?" I asked. Byssa and Hades joined us, and their warmth radiated against my back.

"I found a clue." Levi's eyes raked over the others surfacing in the water and toweling themselves off on the rocks, but no one was close enough to hear his words. He focused on me again. "I was at the water's edge this evening, and I found a gas can washed up on shore. It has to be the same one. I'll get you to confirm later—I left it behind the bunkhouse—but how many gas containers are floating near the Lodge this week?"

"But we already knew the arsonist took the gas can with him in the water," Hades said. "Is it so strange that you'd eventually find it on the beach?"

"That's not all." Levi dug into his pocket and extracted a crinkly waxed envelope. He held it out for us to inspect.

"It's an envelope," Byssa said, her slender fingers plucking it from Levi's palm. "It looks like the kind we get Grace in."

"Close." Levi's face was grim. "Notice the mark on the corner? We don't only distribute Grace at the Lodge, although that is the majority of our products. No, this envelope held tube worm casings from the Seamount."

"You mean the stuff that increases oxygen retention?" Hades glanced at Byssa. "They used to give that to you, didn't they? Didn't work very well."

"Not for me, no," Byssa agreed. She dug her toes into a patch of sand between pebbles. "But I'm sure it works for half-sirens who need a little boost, not a complete overhaul."

"Yeah, it does." Levi ran a hand through his hair, making it stand up on end. The odd silvery scars on his neck caught the evening light and stood out in stark relief. "Austin uses it sometimes. Lots of half-sirens do here. Not only does it allow you to breathe underwater better, but you can hold your breath for longer, too."

"So, you're saying that the arsonist is a half-siren who uses casings," I said. My heart pounded. Did we finally have a clue that would lead us to the culprit? "How do we find out who uses this stuff?"

"I checked the sales ledgers, and only four men bought some this month." Levi raised a hand at my questioning face. "I know, someone could have bought it for someone else, or the arsonist could have purchased casings last month and only used them now, but we have to start somewhere."

"Brilliant," Byssa said firmly. "Progress is valuable."

"Who are they?" I said with narrowed eyes. "Give us some names, and we can follow them to watch for suspicious activity."

Levi gave a small sigh of relief and his face relaxed. "Thanks, Lune. The guys who bought casings this month are Darren, Frank, Otto, and Sam."

"I'll follow Darren," Hades offered. He glanced down the beach at the disappearing festivalgoers. "We're in the same dorm room."

"Do you think he actually did it?" Byssa whispered. "His girlfriend Kim would surely know, wouldn't she? And she doesn't seem like the type to be okay with arson."

"I thought that about everybody at the Lodge," Levi said, his jaw tightening. "But somebody is doing all this damage."

"I'll follow Frank," Byssa said.

"Wait, doesn't Otto work in the kitchen?" My shoulders straightened. "One of our 'accidents' was an attempted poisoning, and Kim's episode happened near the kitchen. He might be our guy. Does he have any reason to despise the Lodge?"

"Not that I know of." Levi shrugged helplessly. His eyes were bright in the dark shadows of his sunset-hued face. "But I've said that about everybody."

"I'll follow Otto," I said with a nod. "There's a good chance he's the one, and I'm tired of coming up empty-handed."

Byssa and I rushed into our dorm to change. I threw

a ballcap on my head to remain inconspicuous, but for the first time, it pained me to cover up my hair. After Grace-Harvest, I didn't want to hide anymore.

I pulled the cap more firmly on my head. If I caught Otto in the act tonight, any sacrifice was worth it. I had a good feeling about Otto's guilt. He was pale with dark hair, just like the wolf eel had described. The poisoning and Kim's sirening would have been simple for him, and he could have instrumented the boat and marina disasters during work breaks. In fact, I didn't recall seeing him among the spectators at the boat fiasco, nor vomiting during the food poisoning situation. The destroyed pilings could certainly have been the work of an evening. The arson itself was tricky, given that it had been during dinner, but surely the kitchen staff took breaks. Maybe it had been Otto's day off.

I passed Darren and Kim once outside. Hades skulked in the shadows a distance away, and I tried not to look at him.

"Hey," I said once in earshot of the two. "Do you know where Otto is hanging out this evening? I wanted to ask him something."

My brain was too preoccupied to come up with a reasonable explanation, but Kim didn't blink.

"He's in the dining hall. It's a tradition among a few of the wilder guys to have an afterparty after Grace-Harvest." She tucked her arm more securely through Darren's. "We have better things to do, though."

Darren winked at me, and they continued on their way. I shook my head and pointed my feet toward the dining hall. If Otto was partying, then so was I.

When I entered the dining hall, a chorus of raucous cheers greeted me.

"Lune!" someone shouted. "Join the party."

I smiled tightly and walked toward the group of ten at a central table. I recognized many of them—ponytailed Henry, bleach-blond Ila, silver-eyed Liam, and dreadlocked Nolan—and I waved at Liam when he greeted me. He patted the bench beside him, and I climbed in. Otto was close, on the other side of the table, which suited my goals perfectly.

"Do you play strolia-secrets?" Henry called over to me.

"Course she does," Ila said. "She's from the Seamount. Right, Lune?"

I nodded, and my eyes absorbed the contents of the table for the first time. Amid glasses and bottles of heavy drinking already well underway, familiar shells littered the table. A tall spire—a *strolia* fish horn affixed to a squat cylinder of wood—stood in the center.

"I haven't drunk nearly enough to play yet," I said. Henry whooped at my response. "Pour me a stiff one, will you?"

Liam pushed a cup of rum into my hand with alacrity, and I poured it down my throat while the others cheered. I didn't want to drink too much—my focus was on watching Otto, after all—but no one would believe that I'd play this game without loosening up a little. At the

Seamount, we would lick the ground-up residue of a certain local snail, which gave a similar reaction to alcohol. We'd have to manage with rum tonight. No one bothered to smuggle snails out of the Seamount, not when Grace shipments were the priority.

Strolia-secrets originated at the Seamount, and I'd played it many times before. Players each held a cluster of shells in their hand, hidden from other players. In unison, everyone would reveal a shell to the group. If any were of the same variety, those players had to make a grab for the horn. Whoever won collected the revealed shells and chose another player to ask a question to. Normally, the unlucky person would be forced to reveal a secret. If it were dark or shameful, the players would donate a shell to the revealer.

Luckily, I was quicker than most. I rarely lost a game of strolia-secrets, and tonight I had no intention of revealing any of my own secrets. Otto gave me a handful of small shells, and I palmed them in preparation for game play.

The others were fast—the ones who weren't entirely sloshed, anyway—but I was faster. Soon, I'd impressed them with my winnings, and they were cheering me on.

"Ila," I said when I held the horn again. "Have you ever stolen something?"

"Gummy worms from the corner store when I was eight," she said. The others groaned, and she chuckled. "Sorry, I'm not that criminally minded."

I didn't care about her answer, only that I asked a few people questions before I targeted Otto. Before the game could resume, Sam walked in, closely followed by Levi.

Sam was greeted with happy shouts, but Levi's presence sparked delight. A cacophony of voices chimed together.

"I haven't seen you darken this door in months."

"Come to mingle with the staff again?"

"Finally! Grab a drink."

Levi grinned, and I had a glimpse of what his life must have been like in the past before the weight of responsibilities had landed on his shoulders. He glanced at me briefly, and I nodded. We both had jobs to do.

Sam sat on the opposite side of the table, and Levi climbed over the bench to sit next to me. He was close enough that warmth radiated from him like a warm current. I shivered and tried to focus on the game, but his presence was distracting.

Otto gave Levi and Sam their own shells, then the game resumed. A few rounds passed without my involvement. Levi scored three rounds in, and he held up the horn in triumph.

"Sam," he said. "Where were you on Friday night, not yesterday but last week?"

I blinked in surprise, although I kept my gaze fastened on Sam, not Levi. The question was so blatant, I wondered who would see through Levi's façade.

Luckily, everyone was too drunk to pay attention to nuance. Even Otto only sorted shells in his hand. Did I imagine his shoulders were stiff with tension?

Sam coughed, his eyes not meeting Levi's. "Um, well, out, I guess."

"Got to give us more than that," someone shouted.

"Fine." Sam took a swig of rum then blurted out, "I was with Belinda from the market after work. All night, too."

Someone whistled, and Otto slapped him on the back. "I had no idea you were into sexy older ladies."

Sam coughed and reddened, and the rest laughed. Under the cover of noise, I grabbed a bottle of rum and poured more into Levi's glass.

"Looks like you're off the hook," I whispered. "Sam could be lying, but I doubt it. And his alibi is easy enough to check."

Levi stared at his glass, his lips tight. "We have so few suspects left," he said quietly. "Now what?"

"We'll figure it out." I bumped my shoulder against his. "I still haven't ruled out my target. Your job is done tonight. For once in what looks like a long while, have some fun."

Levi gave me a swift smile then gulped his rum and prepared for the game. Despite his worry over the arsonist, every round of strolia-secrets released tension from his shoulders, and his rapport with the others grew livelier. Even through my preoccupation with watching my target and my distraction with Levi's closeness, I was happy to see him relax.

The next time I won the horn, my gaze fell on Otto. I stared at him. "What are you more afraid of, burning alive or being buried alive?"

"Buried alive," he said without a trace of hesitation. When the game resumed, I snuck a triumphant glance at Levi. Otto's words weren't conclusive by any stretch, but someone who wasn't fearful of fire would make an excellent candidate for arson.

The shells didn't fall my way for quite a while after

that, and I chafed at the delay to my questions. Eventually, Henry won the horn and put Levi on the spot.

"The most shameful thing I own?" Levi repeated. He looked thoughtful. "Definitely my Aquaman boxers."

Hoots of laughter followed this pronouncement. Levi grinned and gulped his rum.

Before the game gave me another opportunity to ask Otto more questions, we stopped playing in favor of a card game. I sipped at my rum more frequently than I should have, frustrated at my inability to get more answers out of Otto. Only my acute awareness of Levi's body close to mine and his enthralling scent tempered my annoyance.

Finally, Otto stood on unsteady feet and said his goodbyes. I gave him a minute's head start then followed. Otto didn't live in the dorms, so I guessed he would leave via the road. From the front porch of the Lodge, I watched Otto wobble away on his bicycle, my jaw tight. I hadn't ruled him out as a culprit, but he hadn't done or said anything conclusive, either. Now, he looked too drunk to get home, let alone engage in nefarious plans.

I sighed then jumped at a low voice.

"We're no closer to solving this, are we?"

Levi stood close behind me on the Lodge's porch. The swing invited me to sit, but I feared that if I accepted, I would fall asleep there. The weight of my long day and recent failure pressed on my shoulders.

"At least we know it's not Sam," I said. "And Otto is still suspect number one."

Levi trained his gaze on Otto's retreating taillight, then ran a hand through his hair. I stepped closer involuntarily, filled with a desire to reach for his hair with my own fingers.

"You were so good at the game this evening," Levi said quietly. His eyes, dark in the shadows of night, stared into mine. "You never spilled any secrets."

"You want a deep, dark secret?" I stepped forward and touched Levi's chest with a light finger. He shivered, and the motion stirred a desire in me. I wouldn't have dared in daylight, but the night and alcohol loosened my inhibitions. I ran my finger down his chest and sideways until my fingertip rested on the hip of his jean's waistband. "Like your choice of boxers?"

Levi huffed a breathless chuckle. "Those boxers are absolutely one of my deepest shames, even if Austin bought them as a joke for me last year. Come on, there has to be something you were going to share."

I considered him, my fingertip still tucked into his waistband. My heart pounded in a steady rhythm. A sense of recklessness washed over me and pushed me to speak.

"I'm on the run," I whispered. "For a crime of self-defense. An upper echelon man attacked me, and I killed him." Black blood and sightless eyes swam in my vision. "It all went wrong. I can never return to the Seamount." My breath caught. "But now, I don't know that I even want to."

I couldn't believe that I'd just unfolded my darkest secret to a man I'd only known for a week. Was it the alcohol speaking, or was it something about him? If he'd been pale folk, I'd be convinced he'd sirened me. But he was only human.

It was so freeing to speak aloud what I hadn't dared say to any living soul before. I'd escaped my crime at the Seamount before I could say goodbye to my friends

215

there, and I hadn't spoken a word to Byssa or Hades. Levi's expression, what I could see of it in the darkness, was devoid of censure. The nearly full moon illuminated the mottled skin at his neck, and it gleamed with a mesmerizing silvery sheen.

An owl hooted from a nearby tree, and the sound awakened me from my odd mood. A sensation like cool water trickled down my back, and I jumped away from Levi. Why had I told him that? What would he do with that information? It was stupid to open up to a near-stranger.

"It's late," I said. "I should go."

Before Levi could say anything, I strode away as fast as I could without breaking into a run. I pushed Levi and my indiscretions out of my mind, instead focusing on my mission. Keeping up with the afterparty had been a struggle for me, and my head pounded with tiredness and alcohol. Clearly, Otto wasn't up to anything nefarious, at least not this evening. He wasn't off the hook, though. Too many signs pointed to his guilt, and I'd have to follow up further in the morning.

I crept to my own door, exhausted beyond measure. Averting a murderous rampage, cleaning all morning, evacuating the dockside rooms, Grace-Harvest, then pretending to enjoy myself while watching a suspect—I needed to pass out in my bed. Maybe tomorrow Levi would have a brilliant idea because I was fresh out of them. Hopefully, I could brush my incriminating words off as rum-fueled nonsense in the morning.

I peeled off my clothes, tugged on a shirt to sleep in, and crawled into my bed. Byssa was a lump on the top bunk, so clearly her quarry had retired far earlier than Otto had. I was asleep in seconds. Not even the lingering questions of the arsonist could keep me awake tonight.

Something tickled my nose in my sleep, and I sniffed awake. Darkness still reigned, and a figure was silhouetted against the curtained window where the moon shone through. A muffled curse, then lights flicked on.

"Wake up, everyone," Kim shouted, her voice shrill. "There's a fire!"

CHAPTER 20

Every muscle in my sleepy body seized in alarm. What should I do? My brain wouldn't move fast enough. Fire was not my element. Water. We needed water. Should I go to the bathroom to fetch some? Would my legs carry my terrified body there? What would it feel like to burn?

"Come on, Lune." Byssa swung down from her top bunk and hauled at my arm. "We need to get out. Fires can spread quickly."

Byssa's familiar voice snapped me out of my horrified trance. She yanked me out of bed, and I followed her out the door on stumbling feet. Outside, we joined Hades and the others. They mingled and shouted to each other.

"Where's it coming from?"

"Did anyone see it?"

"Where's the fire extinguisher?"

"Here," a voice shouted. Kim's boyfriend Darren burst out of the bunkhouse with a red fire extinguisher clutched in his hand. He glanced around wildly. "Where do I point it?"

Kim grabbed his shoulder and swung him around.

"It's pretty obvious," she screeched. Flames licked the ledge of the hall's window, beside the door. "Get it!"

Darren pulled the fire extinguisher's pin and pointed the nozzle at the base of the fire. With steady sweeps, he shot a stream of yellow powder at the flames. I grabbed Byssa's hand and Hades's forearm so tightly that it must have hurt them, but they didn't complain after they glanced at my wide-eyed face.

I didn't trust fire—its unpredictable nature, its terrifying heat—and I didn't know it well enough to understand it. Byssa and Hades had lived on land since they were children, but I didn't even own a candle.

"It's a tough one," someone murmured beside us. "How did it start, with a slug of gasoline?"

I exchanged a glance with Hades. The arsonist had struck again, but this time, his target had been us. If not me specifically, then at least people in general. He wanted the Lodge closed, and what better way than to threaten lives?

Just as Darren shot the final spurt of chemical powder on the smoldering wreck of the windowsill, Levi, Austin, and their parents arrived. Kane was pale but appeared in good health beside Seafoam, who wore a burgundy silk housecoat wrapped around her willowy frame. Levi had pulled on jeans and a sweater over his sleeping attire. I took a moment to imagine what that attire might be— the thought of Aquaman boxers over muscled legs was a welcome respite from my fear of the fire—then I schooled my mind to recall the gravity of the moment.

"What happened?" Levi barked.

A babble of voices broke out, explaining what we'd experienced, and Levi's face grew grimmer as he listened. Seafoam put her hand over her mouth, and Kane wrapped his arm around her. Austin shook his head with grave concern.

"The fire's out, but the bunkhouse isn't fit for sleeping in," Levi said finally. "Grab your blankets and pillows. You can sleep in the dining hall for tonight, and we'll sort beds out in the morning."

Seafoam stepped forward.

"The Lodge is finished," she said in a quavering voice. "Too many accidents have happened. We need to think about the safety of our workers and guests. We will close the Lodge in the morning. Everyone will receive their full contract pay before they leave."

Levi's mouth dropped open. His mother clearly hadn't discussed her decision with him.

"Wait a minute," he said, speaking in a low voice that nonetheless carried through the subdued chatter that had erupted at Seafoam's announcement. "That's too drastic. We need to talk about this first."

"It's too late." Seafoam waved her hand through the air. "One thing after another. We can't survive this. What if a guest or worker died next? The Lodge is clearly cursed. No, we can't carry on." She took Levi's hand in hers and stroked the back of it. "I'm sorry, minnow, I don't want this any more than you do, but it's the right thing."

She squeezed his hand then turned and led Kane away. Levi stared after his retreating parents, and Austin stepped toward him.

"You've tried," he said. "So hard. But if we can't find the culprit, what are we going to do? Mom's right. It could be a body we find next. We can't let it get that far."

Levi's shoulders slumped at his brother's words. Then he nodded and turned to us.

"Come on, everyone," he called. "Grab your blankets and head to the dining hall."

I didn't sleep any more that night. Levi's crestfallen face swam in my mind's eye, and every time I drifted, fire crept into the edges of sleep and drove it away. Instead, I listened to the others breathe and waited for daylight.

This was it. The Lodge was done. All my efforts to find the arsonist had failed. I'd finally come to see how valuable the Lodge was to half-sirens, to Byssa, and to myself, and now it was gone. I wondered what Levi would do now. He poured everything of himself into the Lodge, and it was strange and unnatural to imagine him in a different setting. He belonged here.

The only good thing to come out of this debacle was the promised paycheck in the morning. The thought of paying off my debt to Branc didn't taste as sweet when stacked against the loss of the Lodge. I would rather have worked my full contract, found the arsonist, and returned later to Vancouver.

But if my twenty-five years had taught me anything, it was that life wasn't fair, and I had to grab what I could get before opportunities slipped through my fingers. I would leave the Lodge with my money, Grace, and a lingering sense of loss.

When light finally brightened the curtainless windows of the dining hall, I rose, rolled up my blanket, and padded quietly out the door. The morning air was still and the water calm as a light rain pattered on its surface. I recalled Squirter in the waves, and I turned in the direction of the water. No one was up at this hour, so I waded in still wearing my sleeping shirt.

It took only a few minutes of humming for Squirter to find me. He landed on my head and wrapped tentacles around my ears. His antics cracked a smile from me despite everything.

Leaving soon, I said.

Today?

Probably. See you south.

Squirter stroked my cheek, then he darted away until I lost him in the gloom. My skin sense followed him until he disappeared from sensing.

I emerged from the water and dripped over to the bunkhouse. The stench of burned wood made me gag, and I pressed my wet sleeve against my nose to dampen the smell.

Quickly, I threw on my jean skirt and a tee-shirt that read "the ocean made me salty". My wig and contacts remained in my bag, but I slipped my ballcap over my hair. I gathered my belongings into my backpack, then I did the same for Byssa and Hades. With all three bags in my arms, I stumbled back to the dining hall. The windows gleamed in the dawn light, and my eyes blinked back tears that threatened to spill over. I didn't want to leave.

Fiercely, I imagined handing over my money to Branc. I pictured his shiny black hair and shark-dead gaze, and how happy I would feel to be rid of him from my life forever. It wasn't as strong a consolation as I'd thought it would be, but it was all I had.

People were stirring from their cocoons and rolling blankets when I entered the dining hall. Kitchen staff were clanging pots and pans, preparing breakfast. I headed straight for Byssa and Hades and dropped their bags at their feet.

"That's everything," I said. "No need to go back to the bunkhouse."

"Good morning to you, too." Hades stretched his hands over his head and yawned hugely. "I do not recommend the floor for a good night's sleep."

"Is this it?" Byssa sat on her blanket with arms on her folded knees. "We just leave now? The Lodge is over."

My stomach shriveled at the reality that I'd been trying to avoid thinking about. It sounded worse out loud. I steeled myself to answer Byssa.

"There's nothing we can do, not anymore," I said. I took off my ballcap and pulled my pale hair back in a messy ponytail to give my hands something to do. "It's done. We take our money and split."

Hades sighed. "It was a good gig. I wish it could have been longer. But I still have holidays to use up. Hey, Byssa, what do you say about visiting Cindi in Gibson? It's on the way, and we haven't seen her for ages."

Byssa nodded slowly. "That would be nice." She stood and reached for her blanket to fold. "It would make this ending easier to swallow."

"You're welcome to come with us," Hades said to me. "Cindi doesn't mind extra guests."

"Thanks," I said. "But I want to get back to the city."

Once I had my money and Grace, I didn't want to wait to give it to Branc. If it were in my possession for too long, I would start to like having it there, and it would be that much harder to give it up. And the satisfaction of

223

paying off my debt? I couldn't wait.

"We'll give you a ride to the bus station," Byssa said.

Seafoam entered the dining hall with a tray of envelopes, Levi trailing behind her. Gloom radiated off him in waves, but he tried to smile at the friends and employees he'd worked with so closely.

"Please form a line," Seafoam called out in a stronger voice than that of last night. "And I'll distribute your paycheck and Grace. Thank you for your service."

Each envelope had a name on it. I shuffled forward with the rest, and when I reached the front, I said my name. Seafoam glanced at me closely, gave me a fleeting smile, then passed over a large envelope with my name on it.

I clutched the fat envelope to my chest, afraid of losing it. This package was the key to my future independence, and I would fight anyone who tried to take it from me.

Levi's forlorn figure caught my eye, and I walked toward him into his faint, warm scent. A strong desire to taste his scent underwater washed over me.

Leaving now also meant leaving him. I shook myself. Where had that thought come from? It wasn't as if we were an item or had even made moves in that direction. Besides, I preferred blonds.

That line was getting tired, even to myself. I longed to stroke the silky mahogany hair off his forehead.

"I'm sorry we couldn't solve the mystery," I said when I was close enough. "It shouldn't have ended this way."

Levi gave me a pained grimace that might have been an attempt at a smile.

"No, it shouldn't have." He ran his hands through that hair I wanted to touch.

"What will you do now?" I tried to imagine him anywhere else but couldn't.

"I don't know." He looked around helplessly then visibly gathered himself. "I have certificates in hotel management and plenty of experience. I'll have to polish my resumé and start job-hunting, I guess."

"Is there nothing we can do anymore?" I said, surprising myself. Didn't I want to get back to the city right away, pay Branc, and start my new life of freedom? "What if I stayed, and we looked for more clues?"

"Thanks for the offer." Levi tightened his lips with suppressed emotion. "I wish I had some idea of where to look. But that's exactly why I couldn't convince my parents to reverse their decision to close. I have nothing to work with, no leads, nobody to point fingers at. Even if you stayed, what would we look for?"

I shrugged, feeling the weight of insurmountable odds on my shoulders, knowing it was only a fraction of what Levi must have been feeling himself. I didn't want the Lodge to close. I'd only started to realize what it represented—a link to the heritage I didn't know I needed, a chance to connect with those like me—and now that opportunity was disappearing forever.

And I'd failed Levi. He had tried so hard to prop up the floundering Lodge in the face of fires, disasters, and poisonings, and he still hadn't prevailed. I'd promised to help him uncover the arsonist, and we'd come up empty-handed.

"No." Levi straightened his shoulders. "The Lodge is

finished. The arsonist got what he wanted, so I hope he's happy. I'll find a job, you'll go back to your regular life, and everything will be fine."

I gave him a tight smile, then spontaneously threw my arms around him for a swift hug. He wrapped his own arms around me and squeezed tightly. He felt good and smelled better, and I wanted to stay in this Levi cocoon for far longer.

I broke away and patted his arm.

"Take care, Levi," I said with one last look into his contact-blue eyes.

He nodded with a tight jaw. "You too, Lune."

I stared out the bus window, rain streaking its glass. Byssa and Hades had dropped me off at the bus station an hour ago, and now I was almost at the ferry to take me to Vancouver from this isolated stretch of mainland.

My stomach weighed me down like a heavy lump of discontent. Guilt flashed through me in a hot wave every time I thought of Levi's dejected face. With nothing better to do, I ran through everything I knew about the arsonist. How had I found out so much and discovered nothing?

That first evening, I'd seen the arsonist at the dock carrying a gas can and lighting the Grace-house on fire. He'd clearly been male, slender but reasonably built.

Otto passed through my mind. He was dark-haired and pale, just as the wolf eel had described. As a cook, he'd been well placed to tamper with food. His whereabouts were suspicious for many of the incidents, and he bought worm casings to improve his oxygen retention. I didn't know what sort of motive might spur Otto to discredit the Lodge, but he was worthy of looking into further.

I reached for my phone, ready to text Levi my suspicions—maybe he could question Otto before he left, for Levi's peace of mind, if nothing else—then a different dark-haired pale man jumped into my mind's eye.

Austin.

CHAPTER 21

My eyes widened, and I sat up straight in my bus seat with a pounding heart. Austin was the right size and gender. I sifted clues through my feverish mind. Austin had been at the marina the day that the boats were loosened. He knew the Lodge inside and out, just like his brother, so slipping poison into food and sirening Kim wouldn't have been difficult. He was a competent swimmer, as a half-siren himself, and he could have easily borrowed a bone spear from his pale folk allies to sabotage the sunken boat.

Levi hadn't found the document he'd been looking for, but Austin had been searching with him, hadn't he? He could have slipped any offending paperwork into a drawer when Levi looked the other way. And after I'd encountered Austin in his room during my search, the warning piece of burned Grace had landed on my pillow that night. Even the scent I'd tasted in the cave matched the clove scent when Austin had passed me at Grace-harvest.

It all fit. How had I not seen where the evidence pointed before? Fire coursed through my body at the memory of Austin's pretend concern over the disastrous events, how he'd spent evenings with Levi pouring over documents. What an actor. Although, it had been the perfect task to cover his tracks.

My fingernails dug into my palms. How could I have been so blind? Levi had even mentioned that Austin took the worm supplements sometimes to increase oxygen retention. I didn't blame Levi. It was only natural that he'd never included his brother in our list of suspects.

My heart squeezed. His own brother. Levi would be devastated.

But what was Austin's motive? Sheila's words came back to me.

Austin, Levi's younger brother. Getting him to do anything productive around here is the bane of Levi's existence. And then Austin has the gall to get in a huff about Levi managing the Lodge.

I sat back, winded by my revelations. What would I do with this information? My first instinct was to call Levi, but my hand froze at my pocket. What good would the truth do him? The Lodge was closed—reopenable, sure, but not without difficulty—but he would have to learn of his brother's duplicity. Would he rather remain ignorant in brotherly love, or shattered by the truth?

I tightened my jaw. I knew what I would want, and that was the only guidance I had. Selfishly, I also wanted a chance for the Lodge to reopen. I wanted to know that there was a place where I was respected for everything I was, as well as a connection to that life I thought I'd left behind for good.

My sense of justice also prevailed. I'd been in danger of punishment my whole life for crimes I'd only committed to survive. It was galling to see someone get away with attempted murder for a motivation other than pure need. Austin shouldn't get away unpunished.

I pulled out my phone and called the Lodge. An answering service picked up, and I listened to the automated options with a sinking heart. How could I contact Levi? I didn't have his personal number.

"For emergencies," the smooth female voice intoned. "Please dial the following number."

It rattled off a phone number, and I quickly dialed it before I forgot the string of digits. Hopefully, whoever answered would know how to contact Levi.

"Hello?" Levi's solid voice filled my ear with welcome warmth. He sounded tired.

"Levi? It's Lune." I swallowed. Was I ready to bring his world crashing down?

"Lune." Pleasure filtered through the speaker. "What's up? Is everything okay?"

"No." I took a deep breath. "I figured out who the arsonist is."

Levi gasped. "Who?"

"It's Austin," I said quietly. "I can't see how else to interpret the clues."

Levi was silent for a long while. I let him digest the news as I covered the facts and stared blindly out the rain-strewn window.

"I wish it didn't fit," he said finally, his voice thick with suppressed emotion. "But it does. He's hated my parents' decision to leave management of the Lodge to me. Vocally so. Even though he's never worked hard enough in his life to show he could handle it." He paused. "It doesn't help that I'm adopted. He feels passed over, the rightful biological heir. If he'd ever shown initiative, my parents would have pegged him for co-management." He gave a heartfelt sigh. "My parents. They'll be devastated."

I gave a sigh in turn, but Levi interrupted me before I could answer.

"Hold on, I have another call from Sandy coming in. I'll be right back, okay?"

The bus geared up for a hill while I waited. When Levi returned, his anger practically melted my phone.

"Sandy found one of the cooks dead on the dock. Everyone else is gone—even my parents drove to my aunt's place today—and Sandy was just heading out when she found Otto. He'd been at the Lodge for the last ten years, ever since he dropped out of high school. We were his second family." He breathed heavily. "His throat was slit. Sandy thinks it was from a bone knife."

I cursed. "Was it Austin?" I checked myself. Levi wouldn't want to think about his brother being a murderer. "Sorry. No. It was probably the pale folk he's working for. Why would Austin use a bone knife?"

"I hope you're right." Levi's voice was grim. "Otto was a friend. I can't believe Austin would do this. Was Otto in the way? Damn it! I need to find him and get some answers. He'll be at the Lodge, I'm sure of it."

"Where are you?"

"In town. I had to get away for a bit. But I'll head back right now. Austin has to answer for his crimes. It's one thing to be irresponsible, but destruction and murder are another thing entirely." When Levi spoke next, his voice was more composed. "Look, thanks for calling and letting me know. I'll handle it and text you later."

"Yeah, sure," I said in distraction. He signed off before I could say more.

I clutched the phone in my hands and stared at it unseeing. Levi was going to march back to the Lodge and confront his brother. And then what?

231

My skin prickled with foreboding. If my suspicions were correct, Austin wouldn't be alone this close to the swordfish moon and his deadline. His pale folk co-conspirators would want to check Austin's work, and maybe even remove Grace from the Grace-house. They were certainly ruthless enough to murder Otto. Unless Austin was a complete sociopath, I could count on him being unwilling to harm Levi too badly. But brotherly affection wouldn't restrain the pale folk.

If I wanted the Lodge to have more than a herring's chance in a bubble net of reopening, Levi needed backup. He was planning to confront a hostile Austin and ruthless pale folk by himself. Everyone had left the Lodge, even his parents.

Levi needed the Lodge. The half-sirens who worked there and the pale folk visitors needed the Lodge. Vents, I needed the Lodge. I needed the companionship of others like me. I wanted a reminder of my past, a link to my heritage, and a place to make future memories. I wanted to feel that connection to a greater whole that I'd been lacking for the past year.

I sat up and shoved my phone in my pocket. I had to return to the Lodge right now. No bus would take me there quickly enough, and hitchhiking might leave me stranded for hours.

The highway followed the ocean. With a few quick steps, I could be in my element. With enough Grace, I could swim swiftly. In less time than the meandering, frequently stopping bus, I could be back at the Lodge with Levi.

If I ate enough Grace.

My righteous passion shrank like a disturbed anemone. To get to the Lodge in time and with enough strength to meet whatever obstacles would thwart me, I would need to ingest nearly all the contents of my payment envelope. If I did that, I could kiss my freedom goodbye. Sure, the money would go a long way to paying off my debt, but Branc might retaliate with higher interest on the remainder. He wouldn't want to lose my valuable skills too easily. I'd been counting on presenting my entire payment at once to avoid argument and loopholes. Without the Grace, I'd be stuck under Branc's thumb for who knew how long.

My breath came in short, sharp bursts, and my hands clenched and unclenched arrhythmically. My freedom was everything I'd yearned for. I'd scrimped and saved and lived in squalor and sirened for morally questionable reasons, all leading up to this day. If I stayed on the bus, took the ferry to Vancouver, and walked up to Branc in the back office of his club, the shackles I'd been living with could be unlocked tonight.

But I would give up the chance of community I'd found at the Lodge, and any connection to my heritage so easily found there.

And I'd be failing Levi. Again.

I stood and slung my bag over my shoulder.

"Stop the bus!" I yelled and wobbled up the aisle. "Please. I need to get off here."

The driver looked at me askance but shrugged and pulled onto the shoulder.

"No refund," he warned before shutting the door behind me and peeling off in a spray of gravel.

A car whipped by, and I stuck out my thumb on a whim while I walked. I'd seen movies where hitchhiking had worked, and it would save me a bit of Grace. I debated keeping my white hair up in its ballcap or letting it fly free for attention.

I gave it three minutes with my hair fluttering in the growing wind and rain before giving up in disgust and sprinting across the ill-used highway. I didn't have time to waste. Levi needed me.

A row of houses lined the shore, but I ignored the private property signs and strode between them to the sea. With the rain had come a summer squall, and waves crashed onto the rocky beach.

One last time, I pulled out my phone and dialed Levi's number. If I could prevent him from going to the Lodge by himself, maybe even pick me up in his truck first, that would save me so much heartache. It rang and rang until voicemail clicked through. I cursed and took a deep breath. My only option was swimming.

I stripped down to my underwear and bra and shoved my clothes in my bag. I bit my lip at the stack of bills buried inside. Was I really going to leave all my hard-earned cash on the beach where anyone could find it? That money would go a long way toward paying my debt. I shook my head violently. Levi needed me. I'd have to take the chance.

I stowed the bag out of sight in a pile of driftwood after extracting my Grace envelope from the Lodge. When I shook the contents onto my hand, a palmful of thick-cut dried Grace fell in a full pile.

My mouth watered at the sight. I hadn't seen so much

Grace in one spot for most of this long, empty year. If I wanted to make it to the Lodge and be in full fighting form at the end of the journey—after depriving myself of the substance for so long, I was in deficit—I needed to eat most of this handful.

It wasn't only my debt to Branc that fueled my reluctance. I didn't want to know how good it would feel having that much Grace at once. With all this ingested, I'd be scrimping for even longer in the future, except this time with the painfully fresh memory of being satiated on Grace.

I took a deep breath, plucked a piece with my free hand, and placed it on my tongue. Flavor burst in my mouth, and I closed my eyes. When I'd swallowed the morsel, I blindly groped for more. Piece after piece entered my waiting mouth, and the sensation of pleasure and satiation intensified. When the last piece was gone from my hand, I flung myself into the water.

My skin was alive in a way that made my previous swims feel like a human blundering in the dark. The world around me hit my senses with dazzling clarity. My skin tingled with almost unbearable sensation, and water that trickled past my closed lips burst with flavors that flooded my mind with information. I wanted to gulp seawater into my lungs—so badly—but I resisted. It was uncomfortable and time-consuming to rid myself of water later. Presumably, Levi would be on land, and I needed to stay flexible to help him.

Water flowed past my limbs with almost unbearable motion, and I nearly gasped at my unexpected sensitivity. A vision of the seafloor below burst into my mind's eye with astonishing clarity. Waving anemones, meandering fish, even a crab the size of my thumbnail scuttling beside a rock, all were as clear and obvious as if I could see them with my eyes in plankton-free water. The sensation was intoxicating, and I drank it all in with greedy attention.

Every so often, I sent out a call for Squirter. I wasn't hopeful that he was still in the area, but I wanted to see the little sucker. Part of me wanted him safely away to the south, but my larger, more selfish part wanted him by my side. We'd been through a lot together, and he was good in a tight spot.

I stuck close to shore, as that was the most direct path to my destination. My skin sense was overwhelming, and with information coming from every angle at every second, I missed a crucial signal.

The sharp tap of metal on metal drew my eyes toward the sound.

CHAPTER 22

A scuba diver stared up at me, her knife out to hit her tank to alert her diving partner to my presence. He peered up from his examination of a sea star. When his eyes saw me and widened, he whipped his waterproof camera in my direction.

I was quick, but the distraction from my skin sense had cost me. Faint clicking indicated that my swimming habits were being immortalized. The woman made crude hand signals in my direction, trying to communicate the best a human could manage underwater.

I froze. Should I swim away as fast as my Grace-strengthened limbs could manage, and hope that the images weren't clear enough to identify me?

No. Staying unnoticed was too important. Pictures could be smeared over the Internet, and who knew who would see them there? My work, meddling curiosity-seekers, pale folk who knew of me...

I ignored the signing diver and kicked toward the photographer. He jerked backward, but I was too quick for him. With a swipe of my hand, I batted the camera out of his grip and pried it open with my strong fingers. The case cracked, and seawater flooded the interior. The photographer made a strangled grunting noise through his regulator, but I wasn't finished. My fingers pried open the memory card port and withdrew the storage. With a snap, the card folded in my grip.

The woman held her knife toward me now. It trembled with fear, although her eyes were determined.

Did she think she had a chance? My actions had turned me from a curiosity into a danger. I couldn't leave them like this, not if I wanted to remain anonymous. I might not like to use my siren song, but I didn't know what else to do. Luckily, there were ways to compel others while not causing harm.

I backed away and hummed deep in my chest. With Grace flowing in my veins, thick and cool, my powers were enviably strong.

Forget me, my hum told them, not in words but in the deeper understanding that ran between a siren and those she influenced. The humans would know my intent deep in their core. *This was a dream. Forget me.*

When the divers' eyes glazed over with dreamy unconcern, I slowly undulated out of their vision into the cloudy waters beyond. I tightened my lips and swam faster. Stopping the divers had been a time-consuming distraction that I couldn't afford. Was Levi at the Lodge yet? Were Austin and his allies there?

I called out for Squirter as I swam, and after a few minutes, I was rewarded by an octopus jetting toward me over a rocky outcrop. With my enhanced senses, I could feel every tentacle streaming behind him, every bump on his skin, and his wake as he moved through the water.

I greeted Squirter with a happy hum, and he circled me twice in excitement.

Bad people ahead, I told him. *Friend in danger.*

Squirter made the signs for Byssa and then Hades.

New friend, I said.

Squirter fell in beside me, and we charged forward. My limbs were filled with energy and strength from my extra doses of Grace, and Squirter had to work hard to keep up.

But it wasn't fast enough. Time was flowing too swiftly. Was Levi already at the Lodge? Had he confronted his brother yet? How close were the pale folk in league with Austin? I desperately undulated my body harder and faster, but I despaired at reaching the Lodge in time to help Levi.

But there was something I could do. I disliked sirening other creatures—Branc had me siren too often, and I'd been under the thrall of upper echelon women before—but I couldn't see how else to reach Levi in time. It was time to embrace my pale folk heritage. Especially with extra Grace in my body, getting more help wouldn't be a problem. As long as I took care of my charge, the imposition would be minimal.

For Levi, I decided. For him and the Lodge, I would embrace my heritage.

I changed my call to attract another creature. Within a few minutes, the sleek shape of a California sea lion floated toward me. I hummed a soothing tone, and the sea lion slipped between my waiting arms.

Forward, I clicked. Squirter wrapped himself around my neck, and the sea lion darted northward with me clinging to its back.

I was fast—so much quicker with Grace coursing through my veins—but the sea lion was faster. We shot through green-tinged waters of the midday strait, thick clouds of algae blooms rushing through my hair and past my searching eyes. We surfaced every few minutes for the sea lion and I to breathe, and the noise of the growing wind surprised me every time. A few times, I corrected the sea lion's course, but for the most part I let it run. The Lodge was straight up the coastline. With my heightened senses, I would be able to identify the surrounding waters with ease.

Figures emerged in the outer limits of my skin sense, and I paused the sea lion midwater. Squirter tightened his hold on my neck, and I closed my eyes to fully experience my skin sense. Four, no, five pale folk swam in my direction with leisurely movements.

There was no point hiding from them, because they would have sensed me at the same time I sensed them. Instead, I waited for the group to draw near. Would they recognize me? Were they Lodge guests, or were they the pale folk working with Austin? Would I greet them or fight them?

The three of us waited, the only movement from the sea lion's occasional flipper paddles to keep us in place. The group headed straight for us. It wasn't often that pale folk encountered each other away from the Seamount, so it was only natural that they wanted to see who I was. If I swam away, they would grow suspicious. It was better to greet them quickly and move on.

One of the group was familiar, and I'd braced myself for my previous target Tyrell's face by the time he emerged from the murk.

Greetings, he said to me with a polite hand gesture. *Where do you swim today?*

It was a rote question, and I gave it the answer he expected.

Between the waves and into the deep. To hasten him on his

way, I added, *Pleasant journeys.*

The woman next to him in an exquisite white seaweed dress peered at me.

So formal, she said. *Isn't this the woman who was in your room the other night?*

Tyrell's head whipped toward me with narrowed eyes. My heart sank. The woman must have seen me leave Tyrell's room after I'd sirened him for Branc. No one had been in the hallway when I'd left, but I hadn't checked for open doors. Tyrell didn't remember me, but as a siren himself, he knew that I could have compelled him to forget me.

Who are you? he said, his fists clenched. *What did you want with me? Wait, are you working for someone?*

Tyrell was too close to the mark. I gripped the sea lion with tight legs, and it shifted under me.

I don't know what you're talking about, I said with a toss of my hair. *I don't know you.*

It's Driftwood, isn't it? Tyrell blew water out of his mouth in a frustrated stream. *I don't know what I told you, but Driftwood can't know my involvement. What did you tell him?*

I didn't know who Driftwood was, although I was starting to have a shrewd suspicion that Branc was involved. Tyrell's face was hard, and his friends were ranged behind him, ready to act on Tyrell's lead.

I don't know who Driftwood is, I blurted. Squirter tightened his grip on my neck, maybe feeling my pulse quicken under his tentacles. I was ready to run, and I hoped the sea lion was, too.

I don't believe you, he said. *And I can't allow you to leave here with the knowledge you stole from me.*

241

He glanced at his neighbor—a leggy female with cropped hair and a hard look—and she narrowed her eyes in preparation.

I didn't know what she planned. At worst, she would kill me. At best, she would compel me to forget my meeting with Tyrell. That wouldn't be so bad, except causing forgetfulness was an inexact science. The chances of me forgetting the past few days entirely were high, and I couldn't allow that. Levi needed me, and if I forgot what I was doing, I wouldn't swim to the Lodge to help.

Before she could release whatever hum she was preparing, I sprang into action. I released a blast of panicked sound, enough to disorient the entire group. In the same moment, I squeezed the sea lion. It leaped forward and shot into the cloudy water, and I kept up my blast of sound to block any incoming compulsions. Faintly, the insidious reach of sirening drifted through the currents, but I screamed louder and urged the sea lion forward.

The group pulled together and attempted to follow me for a while, but they gave up before I lost sense of them. Pale folk swim quickly, especially those with properly formed feet, but they were no match for a sea lion. Surely, Tyrell would realize that I'd told someone his secrets before now. The eel was out of the cave at this point, and chasing after me wouldn't solve anything.

My heart took a long time to return to its normal rate, and I had to point the sea lion toward the surface a few times to catch my breath. Squirter got fidgety when the flavor of the water changed to a recognizable taste. We were close to the Lodge.

I let go of the sea lion with a hum of gratitude, and it swam south without a backward glance. I closed my eyes and opened myself to my skin sense, but no pale folk were in the water near me. With caution, I kicked my way upward and poked my head above the mirror-like surface, cracked with waves.

The Lodge lay sprawled on the shoreline, nestled among towering conifers. It was deserted, and a lump grew in my throat. That was why I was here, to reverse the damage Austin had wrought on this place of community. I would do what I could to change the Lodge's fate.

My eyes scanned the docks, and my breath caught. Levi was tied to the Grace-house with ropes around his legs and torso. His mouth was bleeding, and a bruise swelled on his cheekbone.

"Vents," I whispered. "What happened to you?"

A familiar figure walked into view from behind the dock's supply building, followed by three pale folk. My stomach clenched. Maybe I was naïve, but I didn't believe Austin would harm his brother. I had no misconceptions about the pale folk. They wanted the Lodge deserted to destroy it fully and were willing to cut down anyone in their way. Levi was in their way.

I needed to duck under the water before anyone saw me. My hair flashed white even through the rain, and it was only a matter of time before someone noticed me. I needed to get closer to free Levi.

I took a breath to sink below the waves, but a shout stopped my heart. My eyes flicked to Austin, who pointed at me with an open mouth and furrowed brow. Levi's eyes followed, and he paled at the sight of me.

Quicker than I could react, Austin whipped a rifle toward me and started shooting into the water. Before I descended to avoid being a target, three pale folk dived in from the dock.

I gestured to Squirter to get behind me—the last thing I wanted was for one of the stray bullets that whizzed through the water around me to find my little friend— then agony lashed my leg like the strongest jellyfish sting. I tucked my leg closer and squeezed my eyes shut tight at the pain. Austin had hit me, after all.

Squirter's suction cups clutched my back. For his sake, I found the strength to dive away from the bullets that my skin sense could still feel shooting through the water. I moved with numb efficiency, but panic bubbled under my surface. I'd been shot.

But I couldn't afford to fall apart. When I was deep enough to avoid the bullets, I examined my leg. Blood wept in a dark cloud, but I tried to tell myself the wound was only superficial. No bone, and barely any muscle. I'd have to push through the pain if I wanted to escape the pale folk coming for me.

I kicked closer to the seafloor with a wince, my eyes searching. When a clump of seaweed emerged in the gloom, I grabbed a few blades and quickly wrapped them around my injured leg to slow the bleeding. My trembling fingers secured them Seamount-style, and I latched onto the task to distract myself from the pain and lurking panic. I knew the bandages would hold well enough for now. They would stop the bleeding, and that was my main concern. If I wanted to hide from the pale folk coming my way, I couldn't lead them to me with the scent and sight of blood.

My skin sense alerted me to the presence of something large, but it wasn't one of the pale folk. It was a six-gill shark. It must have been swimming nearby and been drawn to this area by the scent of my blood.

My heart beat faster, but I was confident in my leg wrap. Frantically, I thought of ways to use this to my advantage, and not succumb to the sharp teeth of a predator.

With my enhanced siren abilities, I sent out a soft hum to the shark. *Stay close*, I said to it, and the huge fish paced in midwater behind me, out of sight but not out of sensing.

I kicked down to the seafloor and found a crevasse to sneak into. I tore a gash in my underwear bottoms, but I managed to wriggle out of sight, Squirter next to me. There, I waited for the pale folk to swim by. Hiding was always my foster father Eelway's advice. Better to lie low and live another day than to catch the attention of predators or the upper echelon.

The first one wasn't long in coming. A current from the movement of his body flowed over my skin, preceding his shadow darkening the crevasse. Softly, quietly, I sent out a deep hum of attraction, subtle enough that he wouldn't sense it until it was too late.

With my enhanced abilities from the extra Grace, vibrations pulsed effortlessly through my body and into the surrounding water. The shadow paused.

Quickly, on another frequency, I sent another pulse

of attraction, but this one tuned to the waiting shark. Currents over my body spoke of the shark's arrival.

Attack! I thrust my whole body into the call. The pale man's distress vibrated through the water as the shark darted forward.

Blood drifted into the crack where Squirter and I hid. I pulled myself out of the rock. Now that the pale man had sent out an alert to his fellows, my hiding spot was in jeopardy. It was time to ride a new current to Levi.

The injured man writhed nearby, his eyes frantic and focused on the sleek gray body circling him. I didn't want to kill the man, only slow him down, so I sent a call to the shark.

Stop, I said. The shark circled again but with less intensity. After one last pass, it moved with a languorous flick of its tail into the murky water beyond.

I undulated toward the Lodge dock, and Squirter followed closely. A body loomed in my skin sense, and I shied away in fear. With my heightened senses, it was too easy to tell that this was a woman. I was only a half-siren. Despite my enhanced abilities with extra Grace, I was no match for her skills.

I needed to distract her so she couldn't siren me. *Come*, I thrummed at the shark, hoping desperately that it was close enough to hear my call. I swam frantically toward the dock. It wasn't far, but the distance stretched with my need.

The shark floated beside me, and Squirter jetted to my side and attached himself to my stomach for protection. I wasn't worried about the shark, not with my enhanced abilities.

Attack, I said, and sent an impression of direction. The shark stared at me with its fathomless black eye as it passed, heading straight for the female siren.

I continued to swim toward the dock, but my attention was solely on the shark and woman. My skin sensed the shark's approach, its opening mouth, its burst of speed.

Then a hum vibrated the water, its target the shark. My heart sank as the shark twisted in midwater and swam toward the open strait. Of course, the woman had negated my instructions and sent the shark away. I might feel powerful, but a full female siren would win every time.

I put on an extra burst of speed and tuned into my surroundings with my skin sense. Too late. The bone blade sank into my arm in the same instant that I felt the male siren beside me. He wrenched his blade out of my forearm with a satisfied grin.

I clutched my injury and gritted my teeth. Black blood pulsed out of the wound and searing agony lanced through my arm. Vents, it hurt. It felt like what I imagined fire might feel like: burning that lanced into my flesh with sharp crawling pain.

I sent out a hum of furious control. This trench-dweller wouldn't get away with stabbing me.

The bone blade drifted out of his loose fingers, and I grabbed the sinking handle before it fell to the seafloor. He gazed at me with dispassionate eyes, and a fierce rush of satisfaction filled me.

His eyes blinked awake again as a hum of negation reached us. I inwardly cursed. The woman was close by and foiling my plans again.

Distract, I said to Squirter. He clicked and jetted toward the man's face. Before the man could react, my little friend wrapped his body over the man's face, covering his eyes.

I didn't waste a moment of Squirter's bravery. I darted forward and stabbed the man in his own forearm, feeling a vindictive pleasure over the act. Blood pooled above the wound. The man was distracted by pain, so he stopped trying to peel Squirter off his face.

Come, I said to Squirter. He jetted away from the man, but not before inking him. We swam away as quickly as we could. With my skin, I sensed the woman stop to tend her hurt comrade, and I relaxed my shoulders with relief. Somehow, with the help of my siren abilities, the canniness of my ghetto upbringing, and my octopus friend's bravery, we'd escaped three pale folk.

But was Levi unharmed?

Blood seeped out of the wound on my arm, but I didn't have time to bandage it. My injury would clot soon enough. And I was almost there. The pain I would have to ignore, although the water's motion over my wound made swimming a nightmare.

A piling loomed out of the murk, and I angled my body upward. Before I reached the sloshing waves above, Squirter gave a click of distress. I turned to him.

Be safe. I rubbed his mantle. *Hide. I'll be back soon.*

Squirter groaned with unhappiness, but he jetted toward the seafloor. I hoped he would find a nook to slink into, but I couldn't worry about him now. Squirter could take care of himself, but Levi needed me.

I surfaced next to the dock, gripped the edge of the tiny platform surrounding the supply house, and hauled myself up. It was lucky I had extra strength because my injured arm and leg screamed at me. I had to grit my teeth and call on every drop of enhanced strength I had to push through the pain and weakness.

I landed beside the supply house where mops and other cleaning equipment were stored. The rain had stopped, but the sky still swirled with angry purple clouds, and wind whipped into my watering eyes. I took a few deep breaths to center myself—my first in many minutes—then peeked around the corner. Levi was still tied up on the dock, but my eyes fell on the open door of the Grace-house. My mouth watered. Eating that handful of Grace on the beach before swimming here had been exquisite. Grace was sitting *right there*. I could feel that bliss again.

What was more, a few handfuls would release me from my bonds to Branc. The building full of Grace was beyond distracting, but I wrenched my attention back to Levi. I'd made my choice by eating my Grace and swimming here. Levi needed me. I'd have to pay off my debt to Branc another way.

My attention zeroed in on Austin, who had grabbed a red gas can and was splashing the walls of the Grace-house with it. My nose wrinkled in distaste as splatters of gasoline flew onto the ocean's turbulent surface with Austin's heedless motions.

Then, my eyes widened. Why else would Austin douse the Grace-house with flammable liquid if not to light it on fire?

CHAPTER 23

My blood ran hot through my veins. Lighting the Grace-house on fire was such a waste of Grace. And Levi was right there. What was Austin thinking?

"What are you doing?" I shouted at him, all thought of subterfuge forgotten. I leaped onto the dock properly, and a stormy wind hit me with a strong gust.

Austin jumped in surprise, then he scowled. He slugged the last of his gasoline on the building then tossed the can aside. It landed on the wooden dock with an empty thud.

Levi saw me and grunted through a strip of fabric that acted as a gag.

"Everything needs to burn," Austin said without acknowledging his struggling brother. His words were flat, as if he'd memorized them. "The Seamount can survive without this Grace, but the Lodge needs to end with no chance of reopening. Sirens should stay where they belong."

"Then where would you be?" I shouted. "Your own mother is a siren."

"That's given me nothing," Austin spat out with far more feeling than his previous recitation. "My pale folk heritage is worse than useless. I can hardly breathe underwater, my skin sense is pathetic, and I don't even look the part." He waved at his dark hair and eyes. "What has being a half-siren ever done for me? It's not like it got my parents to side with their own son for once. No, they gave Levi the manager position at the Lodge

250

instead."

I frowned. It sounded like Austin had some deep-seated issues with his parents. Somehow, he'd melded his issues with concerns over Lodge management. From what I'd heard, nobody thought he'd be up for the job, so Seafoam and Kane's decision hadn't been surprising to anyone except Austin, apparently.

"Maybe they cared more about choosing someone competent over nepotism," I said. "You have to earn your place in this world."

Austin flushed with anger. When I glanced at Levi, his eyes were wide as he stared at his brother.

"What do you know?" Austin snarled. "You wouldn't understand. You're practically a full siren. You don't know what it's like to be surrounded by those who look down on you, condescend to you for your weakness, pass you over because you're not worthy. That's been my life in this dump, over and over."

I almost laughed aloud. Austin could have been talking about my life at the Seamount. At least he'd had a family who loved him, even if they didn't give him everything he wanted in a pearl-rimmed bag.

Then I sobered. Austin had let the resentment of his siren side fester until it boiled over in this ludicrous scheme. If I hadn't discovered the Lodge and its connections to my heritage, I might have shriveled away into a shell of my former self, imploding instead of exploding like Austin. Too well, I understood his dilemma.

That didn't mean I condoned it.

"You're entitled in the worst way, and you don't know

251

how good you had it," I said. "And this ends here."

I stepped forward to compel him into compliance. If using my song would stop criminal acts, then that was a part of my siren side I would gladly embrace. Before I started humming, Austin opened his mouth and belted out an old sea shanty.

"On the twenty-third day of the month of June, in the year of fifty-four…"

He had a tuneful voice, not unexpected for a part-siren, but he wasn't trying to entertain us. If he were loud enough, he would be able to drown out any compulsion I tried on him.

I cursed and ran toward him when he dug into his pocket. I feared he would pull out a lighter to set the Grace-house on fire, although I figured I had a little time. Levi was still tied up to the building, after all. Surely, Austin had no plans to incinerate his brother.

I picked up a screwdriver—someone must have been fixing the dock earlier—and threw it at Austin. He dodged, still singing.

"They sent us weary whaler men, to sail for Greenland's shore, hey boys…"

I grabbed another screwdriver, hoping to distract or injure him enough to gain the advantage. Grace might give me increased strength underwater, but I was normal above. I didn't want to bet that I would win against Austin.

But speaking with the pale folk Lodge guests had taught me I didn't need Austin to hear me to fall under my spell. Vents, I didn't even need to touch him. I dropped to my knees, tossed away the screwdriver, and placed my palms on the dock boards. With every drop of strength, I forced out the loudest hum I could muster.

A hammer liberated from the supply house hit my shoulder, and I gasped as my arm grew numb. Austin must have understood what I was trying to do, and he wanted to stop the compulsion. Despite the shock of the hammer's blow, I continued my hum.

It wasn't strong enough through the wooden boards and Austin's feet to pull him fully under my control, but the next tool he threw at me missed by a long shot. He stepped forward with sluggish strides, clearly fighting my vibrations. He kneeled with the labored motions of an eighty-year-old human, and his hands clutched a loose board from the side of the dock.

Levi grunted in warning through his gag. Austin was schooling himself to push through my control. I leaped up to get away, breaking my connection to the dock, but I was too slow.

Austin's board slammed into my throat with all his considerable force. I tried to gasp, but my throat seized shut. A wheeze squeaked through my beleaguered airpipe, and I stumbled toward Levi with one hand gently clutching my empty chest.

Levi grunted, and his foot kicked a chisel toward me. I grabbed it, my breath coming more easily with practice—although not without pain—and spun toward the approaching Austin. I jabbed it at my opponent, and he cursed at the blood that blossomed on his shirt near the shoulder.

"You're crazy," he shouted, gripping his chest. "Why do you care so much, anyway? You only worked here for two weeks."

He shoved me back, and I stumbled and fell on my backside. My still-bleeding arm screamed at me, my throat was squeezed out of shape, and my mangled leg smarted under its seaweed wrap. Why did I care so much? What was the Lodge to me?

I narrowed my eyes. The Lodge was a community, a link to my heritage, and a future with more hope than I'd dared to dream of.

And it was Levi. The Lodge was his life, and in the short time I'd known him, I'd grown to respect what he did here. I'd grown to care about him, too, to my surprise.

But I would have helped anyone in Levi's state.

I had nothing left, no strength, no sirening ability, no weapons. All I had were words. Somehow, I had to remind Austin of why he should care. He might want to reject his heritage and his family, but how quickly could those ties be loosened? I'd found out that they were near impossible to break.

"I'll stop you from burning your brother alive if it's the last thing I do," I whispered. "How could I look Ramu in the eye when this life is over, if I'd been party to death by fire?"

Austin paused, his hand clutching a lighter. His horrified face stared at me, then at Levi, then back at me. He tossed the lighter to the dock with a disgusted motion.

"I would never," he gasped. "Is that what you think? I'll burn the Grace-house because the Lodge will never reopen that way. But I wouldn't hurt Levi."

"Then why is he bleeding?" I gestured at Levi, whose wild eyes darted between us.

"He got in the way." Austin squirmed. "The others had to subdue him. It wasn't me."

"But you didn't stop them." I pushed to my feet, wobbling a little at the top. I was sick of Austin's self-deception but relieved when he took a step back from the Grace-house. Levi would be safe. Now, I just needed to free him from his bonds. I didn't like the dangerous scent of gasoline that wafted past my nose.

Levi slumped his shoulders in relief, but my eyes were on the pale woman in a red seaweed dress who had appeared in the water behind Austin. After climbing effortlessly onto the dock, she swooped down and picked up Austin's discarded lighter. She wrinkled her delicate nose in distaste.

I knew what would happen before the nightmare inevitably played out. The woman flicked the lighter, stared at the flame with a mesmerized expression, then bent to touch the lighter to a stream of gasoline at her feet.

Fire ripped along the dock with dazzling swiftness. I screamed through my tortured throat. Fire was my worst nightmare, and it was traveling to swallow the Grace-house with licking tongues of heat. Levi was still tied to the building, his grunts of fear hurting my heart. He strained against his ropes, desperately trying and failing to escape.

Austin took three steps to his brother's side and bent to untie him as the fire crackled closer. A gust of wind made the flames dance and grow. The woman yanked him back.

"This wasn't part of the deal," Austin yelled, wildness flashing in his eyes. "I need to get him out of there."

The pale woman shook her head with a calm but definitive "no". Austin tried to pull his arm away.

"Get off me," he snarled. "I can't leave my brother to die."

Levi's eyes rolled to Austin, to the woman, to me. I crept closer, forcing myself toward the mesmerizing yet horrifying flames while the others were occupied. I didn't want to catch the woman's attention and join Levi's fate.

The woman grabbed Austin's shoulder. I couldn't hear anything, but Austin's eyes glazed, and his body slackened. She had sirened him. With a gentle tug, the woman led Austin to the edge of the dock. One after another, they dived into the frothy waves without a backward glance.

The flames crackled louder, and my muscles froze. I couldn't move, could hardly breathe, could only watch with sick fascination the progression of fire over the Grace-house walls. The sickening stench of burning wood and gasoline filled my nose. How could I get any closer? For sure, I would succumb to the fire. Flames would crawl over my body with burning fingers of pain, and nothing would be left of me but an inferno of hot agony.

Levi's desperate muffled calls for help woke me from my paralysis. I leaped forward, intensely aware of the orange heat behind Levi. Already, flames licked at his shirt, and his body bucked. I swallowed fear-induced nausea and yanked with trembling fingers at the ropes around his torso and the Grace-house anchor line. It took two tries, but finally, the rope unraveled. Levi bent to untie his ankles, then he kicked the rope away. He scooped me up and stumbled forward out of the flames.

"You're on fire," I gasped, shying away from his smoldering shirt. I wriggled out of his grasp and tugged his hand. "Quick, into the water."

Levi resisted my pull. Instead, he let my hand go, ripped off his gag, dropped to the dock, and rolled like a frisky seal. I watched, open-mouthed, at his antics.

"What the vents are you doing?" I rasped out. "Get in the water, you idiot."

Levi finally stopped rolling and crawled onto his knees. He pointed at his shirt which was blackened and filled with holes but fire-free. He grinned weakly at me.

"Stop, drop, and roll. Basic lesson for dry folk."

"You could have just jumped—bah." I waved in dismissal, then glanced at the burning Grace-house. I felt sick, but not only from the sight of fire. So much Grace up in flames, and we couldn't do anything to stop it. Even the stormy drizzle wasn't strong enough to dampen the flames.

"That was our entire stockpile," Levi murmured, his gaze fixed on the burning Grace-house. One whole wall burned with vigor, and the roof had streaks of orange flickers crawling over it. Gusts of wind spurred the flames to greater heights. He gave a heartfelt sigh. "Somehow, it feels like my life is going up in smoke. Is that too dramatic? I don't know. That's it for the Lodge, at any rate. The fire's too big to put out with a bucket, and the door is covered by flames. There's no saving it."

My lips tightened. I'd saved Levi, but had I failed the Lodge? Surely, I could do both. Fire and water didn't mix, so we needed lots of water. An idea rapidly formed in my mind, then was instantly squashed.

"Water doesn't work on a gasoline fire, does it?" I asked without hope. Byssa had mentioned that fact to me after she'd discovered my phobia of fire and had tried to combat it with knowledge.

Levi glanced at me then gave the burning building a critical eye. "The gas would be burned off by now," he said. "The wooden walls are what's on fire at this point."

"Wait here," I said breathlessly. "I might be able to help."

CHAPTER 24

I bolted to the dock's edge and dived in. I sent a brief, fervent prayer to Ramu that my throat had recovered enough from Austin's blow to call for help. I centered myself, closed my eyes, and hummed.

It hurt, but my sound was miraculously clear and strong. Grace must still be filling my veins. I kept up my hum for a solid thirty seconds, hoping something would answer.

My heart nearly stopped when I felt bodies through my skin sense, then it started up again in erratic bursts.

A pod of Dall's porpoises swam directly toward me, summoned by my plea for help. When they were close enough for me to see their sleek black bodies with white stomachs, I made my request.

Splash building.

The porpoises needed no further encouragement. Two even flipped in a circle underwater when they heard my call. With playful squeaks and chitters, the little pod raced to the surface and poked their heads out of the water.

I swam to the other side of the dock and surfaced. Levi stared at sheets of water splashing onto the burning building from a dry distance. I hauled myself up and joined him in contemplation of the lighthearted mammals putting out our fire.

"You did that?" he said eventually.

I nodded with a grin I couldn't hide. "They seemed quite excited by the opportunity."

Levi laughed, but it was more an expression of relief than of mirth. When his chuckles died away, he ran hands through his dark hair.

"I wonder if there's anything left," he whispered. "If there's even a portion unburned, we can open the Lodge again. If it's all ruined, we don't have enough capital to buy more, and our reputation will be shot. We won't be chosen as a distributor again. Without that seal of approval, the pale folk visitors won't trust us."

"But you have history as a vacation spot for them," I said with a frown. Would the pale folk really be that fickle?

"But trust is everything. They risk a lot coming here, and we promise to keep them safe on land. If I can't even protect the Grace, if I'm not trusted to be a distributor, how can I convince them that I will protect them? Especially since I'm a new manager. Pale folk visitors pay the bills around here, that and reselling Grace. The Lodge will be finished."

"You could just run the human side of the hotel," I suggested, although I didn't really mean it. The Lodge as a strictly human establishment held little appeal.

Levi shook his head. "My parents would never go for that, and they still own the place, even if I'm the manager. The major appeal of the Lodge was for its siren clientele. Without that niche, it's just another resort. I'd have to think long and hard whether I'd fight to keep that going or find work in another hotel."

I watched the porpoises play until the Grace-house steamed instead of smoked, and I contemplated my life without the Lodge. It would be much like before, but with the dispiriting knowledge of what could have been.

One by one, the porpoises submerged and disappeared. Levi sighed and shifted his feet.

"Let's see if anything is left," he said.

I nodded, and we picked our way across the dock strewn with the detritus of our battle. I kicked Austin's lighter, and it skittered over the boards.

Levi gingerly pushed the Grace-house door open fully and stepped inside. I followed, nearly gagging on the foul burned smell that caught in my throat.

Light filtered into the dark space through chinks in the burned wall, illuminating shelves with paper-wrapped packages. Levi stared at the burned wall, whose Grace was charred and blackened. I touched Levi's arm and drew him around to look at the untouched walls.

"Most of it is okay," I said. "Check it out. It might be a little smoky, but still tasty."

Levi's eyes raked over the untouched packages. "Think I could pass it off as ocean-land fusion?" he said with a hint of his former humor. "Smoky bacon Grace?"

I chuckled. "Speaking from experience, Grace tastes great no matter what."

Steps on the dock turned our heads. Levi listened to the murmur of voices, and his face dropped.

"It's my parents," he muttered. "Sandy must have called them about Otto. I need to tell them about Austin. Give me a minute."

I nodded, and he withdrew. Levi's calm words were muffled through the wooden walls. I tried to tune them out, but Seafoam's gasp of horror was hard to ignore. My eyes wandered over the intact packages. Would Levi miss one?

Yes, I decided. After a full quarter had burned, he would probably count the remainder with due care. And even if he didn't, stealing from Levi held no appeal. It wasn't worth paying off my debt for.

The thought surprised me. Did I really care about what Levi thought of me more than my freedom? It was hard to believe, but my hands didn't stray from my sides to grab a package.

Finally, Levi poked his head in.

"They want to thank you," he said with a jerk of his head. "Come on out."

Seafoam's eyes were rimmed with red, and Kane stood stiffly and gazed out to sea. Seafoam gripped Kane's hand.

"Thank you for solving the mystery of the arson," Seafoam said in a shaky voice. Her pale eyes blinked furiously. "I'm heartbroken that Austin felt he needed to destroy the Lodge and everything it stood for just to make a point."

"He's always been loudly discontent about us choosing Levi as manager," Kane said. "But he never followed up with taking on more responsibility to prove us wrong. We wanted to trust him with the Lodge—so much—but we never felt we could."

"Foolish boy," Seafoam said with a sniff through fresh tears. "And now the Lodge is over. We can never recover from the shame. Honestly, I don't have the energy to recreate what was lost. The Lodge's time is done."

My heart squeezed with regret. I'd only just found the

Lodge, and now it was fading into a memory. Levi planted his feet squarely on the dock.

"It doesn't have to be," he said with a stubborn set to his jaw. "I know it's hard to think about restarting the Lodge after Austin's betrayal, but please reconsider." When his parents looked unmoved, Levi continued with a pleading tone. "You were planning to fully hand over manager duties to me, anyway. I can do everything going forward. You can be owners in name only. Take this opportunity to retire early."

His parents glanced at each other with searching looks.

"We'll think about it," Seafoam said finally. "Let's not decide anything today."

After a final nod at Lune, they wandered away, Kane's arm around Seafoam's shoulder. Levi sighed deeply and ran a hand through his hair. It stood on end in an endearing way, and I wanted to smooth the silky locks down with gentle fingers.

"I haven't said thank you yet," he said suddenly. "You came back and saved me from burning to death." He shuddered. "I can't thank you enough."

"I couldn't leave you to take all the credit for solving the mystery," I said with a grin that faded when I remembered who had done the deed. "I'm sorry about your brother. That must be a tough shell to crack."

His mouth quirked. "You say the same expressions my mother always said growing up. Do you know what kind of teasing I got at school for some of those?" His smile faded, and he sighed. "Yeah, Austin was a shock. I didn't want to believe it of him—of anyone at the Lodge, really—but looking back, it shouldn't have been such a surprise. I'm worried for him, though. What did he get himself into? What do the pale folk want with him?"

Privately, I felt Austin could haul in the line he'd baited for himself. To Levi, I said, "I hope you reopen the Lodge. It's a decent enough place, despite the infestation of pale folk."

I chuckled to invite him into the joke. Levi eyed me strangely.

"What really happened when you left the Seamount? Why did you—" He paused. When I opened my mouth to deny the truth that I'd already blurted out to him the night of the party, he put up his hand. "You don't need to tell me anything more than you already have. But if we do reopen, you're welcome back anytime. Consider the Lodge your second home."

Levi gave me a ride back to my clothes and backpack, and then to the ferry. Despite our chatter on lighter topics, his words stuck with me. I didn't know if I was quite ready to consider the Lodge a second home, but it was a good place, and I was happy to count Levi in my short list of friends.

A few days later, after reconnecting with Squirter in Vancouver waters, doing laundry, and stashing my money behind my bed, I found myself at work once more. My rag wiped at greasy fingerprints on aquarium glass. A small child cooed at the black-eyed goby fish within, and I smiled at her.

"Cute, isn't he?" I said. The goby was tucked into a crack in the artificial rock, as snug as a feather duster worm in its casing. "He really likes his home."

The little girl gave me a gap-toothed smile and wiggled her fingers at the goby. I chuckled and stood straight. The glass was clean enough. New fingerprints already smeared the tank from the child's hands, but the point of the aquarium was to showcase the ocean world to dry folk children like this. I could deal with a few marks on the glass.

It was the end of my shift, so I sauntered toward the staff room. At the lockers, Mireille was lacing up her outdoor shoes.

"Hi, Mireille," I said brightly. "Long shift?"

"Not too bad," she said with a surprised look in my direction. "You?"

"Pretty good. Hey, are you around tomorrow night? I'd love to try out that tapas place on Granville and Robson."

"Yeah," she said, her shock clear but a smile growing on her face. "Yeah, that'd be great. Meet you at eight?"

"I'll be there."

It was time to embrace my new life on land, and if making friends with dry folk was the way, then that was an easy kelp bed to swim through.

A text from Branc brought down my spirits the next

evening. I had time before meeting Mireille, so I answered Branc's summons by walking to his club with a heavy heart. I hadn't yet given him any of the money I'd earned from the Lodge. I was too afraid of retaliation, and I was looking forward to the day when I could hand over the entire sum with a flourish and never look back.

I was still as determined as ever to be free of his influence but was resigned to a slightly longer timeline. I might have used up the Grace earmarked for Branc, but I'd gained the promise of community in exchange for my sacrifice. It was tenuous but more valuable than salvaged coins to me. I could bow to Branc's will for a little longer. A real life full of potential awaited me, not just the absence of debt. Life wouldn't always be like this, but it had to be for now. Patience wasn't a virtue I was comfortable exerting, but I was starting to recognize that I could build my life now instead of waiting for the magical day of my emancipation.

The oversized bouncer with a pearl stud in one ear nodded and opened the velvet barricade for me to a chorus of groans from those waiting in slinky dresses and artfully unbuttoned shirts. I walked down the narrow hallway lit with flashing lights, but I turned into a half-hidden entrance before reaching the main club area. Tonight, the theme was Night of the Vampire, and servers wore black with pale makeup and high-quality fang prosthetics. Caesars were tonight's drink special, and most customers had a tall glass of thick red liquid before them. Branc liked to switch up the themes to avoid suspicion over the authenticity of siren night.

Branc's office was the first door on the left. I took a

deep breath before knocking.

"Come in," Branc's voice called out through the door.

I walked in and assessed the situation. Branc was alone and looked self-satisfied as usual.

"How was the Lodge?" he said. "Did you make any money or Grace for me?"

I tried to look sheepish, and I hung my head. "I took most of the Grace. I couldn't help it. It'd been so long since…"

I let my voice trail off and peeked at Branc's face. He wore a satisfied expression that he quickly wiped off and replaced with a look of grave concern. I'd been right to withhold what I'd earned from him. He wouldn't let me go without a fight, so I didn't want to give him one.

"That's your choice," he said. "You can take as long or as little time as you need."

And earn you more interest, I said to myself, but I'd accepted that reality when I'd eaten my Grace on the shore before swimming to the Lodge to help Levi. I completed my charade with a penitent nod.

"I have another chance for you to pay off your debt," Branc said, leaning back in his chair. "One of my contacts is back, and I'm sure he knows something about the latest dockside rumors I've been hearing through my other sources. Your info from Tyrell was good, but I need more. My contact will be at the club this evening."

I considered Branc's face, filled with confidence that I would immediately grovel and say yes to anything he offered. A few weeks ago, I might have. Now? I was learning about balancing my desires to be free of Branc with building a new life for myself.

"Sorry," I said without regret. "I already have plans tonight. Keep me in mind for your next assignment, though."

I gave his confused face a cheery wave and left the room. I had a dinner date with Mireille, and I didn't want the taint of questionable actions in my mouth to pollute my outing. Branc never ran out of opportunities to use my abilities, and there would be more in the future. For today, I wanted a modicum of control. Branc and my debt could wait.

A week later, I slid into a booth at the Crispy Prawn across from Hades, whose smug grin made me stare.

"Why do you look like the shark that swallowed the eel?" I said.

"Rachel agreed to a date tonight." Hades admired his reflection on the screen of his phone. "I'm not surprised, obviously."

"She couldn't resist your charms for long," I teased. "Who isn't attracted to skunks?"

"Zebrafish," he said indignantly. "Honestly."

"Lune." Byssa placed a platter of sushi on the table and sat next to her brother. Her eyes raked over my head. "You're not wearing a wig."

I touched my hair, feeling naked without my wig in the human world. "I know, it looks weird. I found this temporary dye, just to play with, but I didn't do a great job and it's kind of uneven…"

"It looks amazing." Byssa reached out and ran her hand over the subtle green highlights in my pale hair. "So fun."

"I can't believe you have the gall to criticize my dye job," Hades grumbled.

"Your makeup looks good, too." Byssa narrowed her eyes at me with suppressed mirth. "Trying to impress someone?"

Hades raised his voice. "Levi, you made it."

Byssa's grin widened as my cheeks flushed. I kicked her under the table then turned to look at the newcomer.

Levi looked as good as ever. Even the strange discoloration on his neck glinted with an attractive silver tint, and his flat blue contacts were almost endearing. His wounds from the incident at the Lodge must have healed quickly, because I saw no sign of bruising or cuts on his face.

"Line-ups at the hardware store were crazy, but I pulled through." Levi's words answered Hades, but his eyes were on me.

I swallowed my sudden nerves and patted the bench. "Sit down. The sushi rolls won't eat themselves."

"I don't know." Levi slid in beside me, and the scent of salt and stormy seas enveloped me with pleasant warmth. "They look fresh enough to eat themselves."

Byssa giggled and pushed the platter toward Levi.

"Dig in," she said. "First dibs always goes to the one who compliments the chef."

"I didn't know that was a rule," Hades complained.

Byssa raised an eyebrow at her brother. "Maybe if you complimented me more often, you would have found out."

We chatted about light topics, and I quickly eased into the conversation. Levi was more relaxed than I'd ever seen him—barring that night at the afterparty—and he practically glowed with contentment. I had to endure Byssa's meaningful glances when I laughed at Levi's jokes, but it was worth it to feel this odd mixture of connection and freedom. He didn't mention the secret I'd shared with him that reckless night, and I was grateful for his discretion.

"What brings you to the big city today?" Hades asked as his chopsticks hovered over the platter. "I didn't think anyone ever wanted to leave the Lodge."

Levi glanced at me, and my traitorous cheeks warmed.

"Supplies," he said to Hades. "We're rebuilding the Grace-house, bigger and better than ever. Out of metal, obviously. And not just one Grace-house—a few of them in secret locations—so our supply isn't centralized. I need some specialized materials that our local lumberyard doesn't carry." He turned to me. "That reminds me. I'm planning a grand reopening of the Lodge in a few weeks, and you three are invited as guests. It's the least I can do after all your help investigating the arson."

Byssa looked flabbergasted, and my eyes widened.

"No cleaning toilets?" I said.

Levi chuckled. "Only if that's your hobby. I'm not judging."

I laughed with the others, but inside a bright swell of happiness threatened to burst out of me. I hadn't looked forward to something for ages. It was easier now that I

270

wasn't dreading the future.

"I'd love to come," I said.

Levi's mouth twitched, and Byssa kicked me under the table and waggled her eyebrows.

Subjects definitely needed to be changed.

"Any word from Austin?" I said. Byssa sighed at my mood-killer words.

Levi looked thoughtful. "Not a word, not even at Otto's wake." His lips tightened. "But I did get a message of sorts. Someone left a piece of Grace on the dock, stabbed through with a bone knife. What else can I conclude except that whoever Austin is working with isn't finished with me yet? But letting threats loom over me is no way to live my life. Until I know more, I have to carry on like nothing is wrong."

I pushed the new flicker of worry deep into my chest. The future would bring what it would. At least now I wasn't alone to greet it.

ALSO BY EMMA SHELFORD

Depths of Magic
Sea Fire
Sea Song
Sea Dragon

Nautilus Legends
Free Dive
Caught
Surfacing
Hooked
Riptide

Magical Morgan
Daughters of Dusk
Mothers of Mist
Elders of Ether

Immortal Merlin
Ignition
Winded
Floodgates
Buried
Possessed
Unleashed
Worshiped
Unraveled

Forest Fae
Mark of the Breenan
Garden of Last Hope
Realm of the Forgotten

ACKNOWLEDGEMENTS

First and foremost, thank you to my Kickstarter backers **Angie Bowles**, **Anne Lynch**, and **Cornelia Papiorek**. You earned this spot in *Sea Fire*, and I'm so happy to honor you here.

A special thanks to Fiona McLaren, my editor who helped me polish this manuscript, as well as to beta readers Fianna McKnight, Bettina, Nadene, and Steven Shelford. Vincentas Saladis created the enchanting interior illustrations.

Sea Fire launched early on the platform Kickstarter, and I owe gratitude to Anna McCluskey, Russell Nohelty, and Dean Wesley Smith for their guidance.